LEANING IN THE WIND

By the same author

Fiction
FEELINGS HAVE CHANGED
KITH

Biography
SALADIN IN HIS TIME

History
WARRIOR PHARAOHS

ff

LEANING IN
THE WIND

P. H. Newby

faber and faber

LONDON · BOSTON

First published in 1986 by
Faber and Faber Limited
3 Queen Square London WC1N 3AU

Phototypeset by Wilmaset Birkenhead Wirral
Printed in Great Britain by
Mackays of Chatham Ltd Kent
All rights reserved

British Library Cataloguing in Publication Data

Newby, P. H.
Leaning in the wind.
I. Title
823'.914 [F]   PR6027.E855
ISBN 0–571–14572–4

1

The first time he met Lisa she was just a kid and a great show-off. Pretty and knew it, with big, bold, blue-green eyes that outstared everyone and a lot of loose, coppery hair tied with a ribbon, so it stood up and out like wings. Later the eyes darkened, the hair darkened, thickened and was cut elegantly, but her face never lost that early look of being able to glow as the light faded.

In those days Parsler made trips to the States by sea (it was the late 1950s, the steamers were still running) and one fall he booked not on the usual Cunarder but on the SS *America*. Its European terminal was the German port of Bremerhaven, where Lisa and her family embarked. He joined at Southampton and, being alone, was directed to take up the spare place at the table in the restaurant already occupied by this German-American family, the Mullers, and was told by the steward he would eat there for the rest of the trip. The steward would see to it that any unfinished bottle of wine was brought back at the next meal.

In addition to Lisa and her parents, Herr and Frau Muller, there were Lisa's brother Hans who was 17 or 18 and another couple, friends of the Mullers. When they and the Mullers laughed, which was often, the noise was stunning. And when they weren't laughing they shouted at each other. Lisa and her brother had been born in the States but their parents were immigrants (their parents' friends too) from Westphalia who went over to Cincinnati, where they had relations, to carry on their business of making musical instruments. Percussion instruments, naturally, timpani, drums, cymbals, gongs, xylophones and the like. They just loved to deafen people. This move was made in the 1930s but the Mullers were not, as you might suppose, Jews. They were Lutherans who saw a business opportunity in the States and took it; they were good American citizens now but they never forgot they were Germans. They spoke German at home, as they spoke it now at the table until they realized the Englishman could not understand and switched to English. They prided themselves on speaking British English and not American English but it sounded like German English.

They made this trip back to Germany every summer as soon as it became possible after the end of the war. They were really impressed by the way people were picking themselves up off the floor there. Germany might have lost the war but, by God! the Fatherland was going to win the peace! Such commitment! Such determination. Look at Frankfurt. A phoenix rising from the ashes and Goethe's house surviving from the old city, a marvellous symbol of the new Germany's continuity with its cultural past. The Mullers were even thinking of going back there permanently, taking their business with them; or maybe just starting a subsidiary in Cologne. But anyway, going back to Germany to live. Now that there were not so many Jews around there was no limit to what the country could achieve.

'Hey,' said Muller. 'I know what you're thinking. You're not Jewish, are you? Of course not. The English are the same basic stock as ourselves. The Führer never wanted to fight England. I can tell you the Jews were a real problem. Still are. Their commitment is some place else. Not to the country they live in. How could they? All this talk of gas chambers is exaggerated. A lot have gone to Israel. A lot have gone to the States. And when I walk the German streets I feel the difference.'

The upshot of this was a row. Parsler took himself off to another table which, as luck would have it, was for two only and the other place was occupied by a Jew, an American publisher, who was on his way home after his annual visit to London. Parsler told him about the Mullers.

'There are still some around. There really are.' This was one Jewish American who refused to get worked up. 'Why don't you sit at this table for the rest of the trip? I'd like that.'

After dinner Parsler was taking a turn on the deck when young Hans Muller came up, his face twitching with nervous embarrassment, and said, 'I was very upset this evening. It is all a terrible misunderstanding.'

'*You* were upset!'

'My father had been drinking some wine. He was excited.'

Hans really did speak British English or what, to an American ear would sound British English. But it wasn't Germanic and neither was Lisa's English as Parsler later discovered. 'It's just that everything good to him is German. He can't stop thinking that way.'

'You don't have to explain your father to me.'

'He'd like you to have a drink with him in the bar.'

'Thanks, but I couldn't do that.'

Hans looked at him mournfully and then trailed off to report.

At this time the McCarthy witch-hunt was still going strong. According to him, cryptos were everywhere – in the universities, in the media, in government – and unless the traitors were flushed out there could be a communist takeover. Trial was by accusation and guilt proved by association. In that atmosphere it was a lot safer for Nazi sympathizers like the Mullers and their friends to shoot their mouths off in public than it would have been for some lefty to score General Motors, say, for their labour relations. It would be too much to say Parsler was all the angrier over the Muller incident because of this political background. The reaction was more complicated. What made him want to spit was the way he had caught himself out in the assumption that Marxist-Leninism was a paler shade of black than Fascism, was more intellectually respectable and therefore more legitimate. He thought he'd lived that one out.

Any foreigner with a communist background found it difficult to get a visa for the States and his own interrogation in Grosvenor Square was fresh in his mind. The visa clerk went through the application with care. There was a question about membership of political parties. He had left this unanswered, not wishing to perjure himself, in the vain hope the blank would not be noticed. The clerk tapped it with her pencil. 'Sir, I know this isn't appreciated, particularly by somebody who's been to the States before, like you. But we've got to know. Are you now, or have you ever been, a member of any political party?'

'Yes.'

'I know you resent being asked this. I understand that, but it's got to be asked. Don't get mad at us bureaucrats.'

'I'm not angry.'

As a matter of fact he thought the question not unreasonable. The McCarthy hysteria was contagious but you couldn't be sure he was entirely wrong. Parsler knew enough to realize, certainly more than this clerk in the rimless glasses did, the dangers were not entirely imaginary.

'You'd better fill me in, sir,' she said.

'I was a member of the Communist Party at university but I gave it up at the time of the Soviet–German pact in 1939.'

'We'll have to send your papers to Washington,' she said and proceeded to ask a lot more questions and take notes. Maybe it was not logical to give up being a Marxist because of the ruthlessness of the Soviet regime, but that's the way he saw it and nothing that happened since had caused him to change his mind. Just the opposite. He got the visa because the company pulled a few strings, the Foreign Office intervened with some information about Parsler's war record. He had purged his errors. But he remembered the old idealism: from each according to his what's-its, to each according to his you-know, or whatever it was. Idealism like that paved the road to hell. But who were the goddam Mullers to set him thinking about it all again?

He was not allowed to escape from them as easily as all that because the following day he was lying in a deckchair under a blanket (it was a cold, grey morning with white waves as far as the eye could see) drinking some hot bouillon the stewards were bringing round when Muller came up with his hand stretched out, his face beaming, as though nothing untoward had happened; or, rather, as though Parsler and not he had been the one who had said something disgraceful and he was now prepared to overlook it, to be friends. 'My little daughter wants to speak with you. No, she wants to hear you speak. She says your English is so cute and she wants to know how you do it.'

'Aw! I didn't say that, Pa.' It came out as a squeal.

'You know what the English do? They pronounce their Ts. That's classic. You know what that word means? Classic means *as it should be*. Proper.'

He couldn't get away from the Mullers after that. He played Horseracing in the Promenade Lounge – that's a game in which you throw dice and move toy horses along a numbered course – and there they were in the next lane. Three days out and Hans started going round with his autograph book. Relations had been so poor that although Parsler knew the Mullers' name they didn't know his and when he scribbled his signature Hans said, 'What's that?'

'Edwin Parsler.'

Hans looked at the scribble for a while and then said, 'Not *the* Edwin Parsler?'

Parsler was surprised because his stuff hadn't been published in the States at this time. And, in any case, who reads poetry? Hans must be rather special. He read English literary magazines. Parsler was so taken aback he pretended not to know what the kid was talking about.

'I thought *Lemon Cream* was just about *it*.' Hans was pink and sweating. How the hell had he got hold of *Lemon Cream*? He bought books published in England.

'I'm going to be a writer,' Hans said. 'I'm going to be great. Not poetry. That's a dead end. Sorry, but that's all played out, sir. I don't mean to upset you but it's just a game. I'm going to be great in dramatic ideas you can exploit in the movies, or TV, or radio. Little black words on white paper. No, sir. I'm going to be into real impact. Success and profitability. But it's all rooted in poetry. I so admire your poems but you've got to confess, words don't communicate like they did.'

This sounded aggressive but he was too nervous, too unsure of himself, to draw any blood. He wanted to know how much money Parsler made out of poetry. 'Jeez! It's what I say, you can't live on poetry and if you can't live on it it's not wanted in any significant way except by nutters like me. How d'you get by? I mean, first class on this steamer, and all that.'

'I'm a lawyer working in insurance.'

'Like Wallace Stevens? I find him kinda difficult. I put it down to treating poetry on the side, the way he does, and not wanting to sell himself too hard because of the guys he mixes with and what they might think. But you're not like that. You're not difficult, sir. You're too easy if anything.'

This was the beginning of Parsler's relationship with the Muller kids because Hans insisted on keeping in touch. Over the years that put Lisa in touch too. They never gave any evidence of sharing their parents' Nazi sympathies. (Oh, yes. Frau Muller

11

was in it. She had nodded vigorously while her husband spoke. The other couple had patted the table when he mentioned Jews.) Hans and Lisa seemed quite untainted but they were not the outgoing, confident and sometimes insufferable kind of young American. They had their fun, particularly Lisa who could actually spurt tears of laughter (like only one other person Parsler knew) but they could be earnest too. And how! Prig is the word that comes to mind.

They were the opposite of drop-outs. They were drop-ins. A lot of their earnestness came from not knowing which lot to drop into. No minority cult, no Californian Buddhism, no beads, no drug cult, not the New Ecology, not, even Trotskyite Marxism, but something much bigger. Something with a purpose they could identify with. Something that would give them a sense of belonging. It was a tall order and not one being placed by any young people in England, where (even more so in Europe) their elders were still numb from the war and they themselves looking more and more like a generation on the scrounge. Hans's talk about literature being played out had been intended as bitter irony. He had spoken to be contradicted and been disappointed. The world was out of joint. Somewhere there must be some band of like-minded brothers who would set it right. Lisa wanted to belong to something too. If they had been Jews they would have found the answer in Zionism but not being Jews and having no religious instincts they looked around for substitutes. One thing for sure. They had money to spend and that's the way they always wanted it to be.

Hans went to drama school. Then to Vienna for a year and on his way back to the States dropped in on the Parslers, unexpectedly; he had had an unhappy love affair and thought England would be as good a place to write poems about it as anywhere. He said he would not embarrass anybody by killing himself. It would be a nasty thing to do to friends, involving them in too much; fixing the inquest and answering questions. He had grown a moustache – a lighter shade than his dark chestnut hair but a bit too big and heavy for his rather thin face to carry off. He wore American fancy dress (that is how it struck the Parslers), a tie with a lightweight suit with waistcoat and watch chain and wide-brimmed hat. So as he drove round the countryside in his hired Austin Somerset he looked out of place, a professional gambler far from the nearest casino.

Harriet and Ed were still putting down roots in the country. They had decided to move out of town when Jessica, at the age of 6, showed symptoms of what became an obsession with ponies and horses. Harriet was pregnant again and she, too, felt the need for green fields. They established that Bicester was a reasonable place to commute from and then cast round until they found Troy Corner which was a modernized farmhouse on a south-facing slope. Ed worked like mad in the garden, hacking down thistles, burning brushwood, planting lilac, cotoneaster, witch hazel (flowering shrubs that would save labour later on) really punishing himself because for the first time he had a block. He couldn't write poetry. The explanation lay in the poetry Hans had been writing and regularly sending, first of all from Cincinnati and then from Vienna. It read like a horrid parody of his own work and although Hans did not intend it that way (he regarded himself as a disciple, he was absorbing an influence he would eventually outgrow) the effect was destructive.

Hans came back from one of his jaunts to ask what Mau Mau was. He made it sound edible. Ed asked why he wanted to know. His answer might be a pointer where to start. He might not know where East Africa was, still less Kenya. Hans said he had stopped to photograph an old house not very far away and was walking up the drive to get a better shot when a man had appeared and asked what his business was. Hans explained. The man said, Oh yes, it was a fine old house, it was his but he never wanted to have anything to do with it and he wouldn't be there now but for the Mau Mau. Hans had been too shy to ask any questions. After he had taken his photographs the man walked back to the gate with him, saying 'I suppose you're from the US Air Force base. They're not interested in hiring civilian guards, are they? I'm trained. I need a job.' When Hans said he was a poet, not a soldier, the man said he was interested in any sort of opening in the States, anything to get out of this godforsaken country. With which they had parted. So what, Hans asked, was Mau Mau?

This man and Ed had met. He had a clipped auburn beard and wore breeches and leggings. Ed had been working in the garden

13

that spring when he poked his head over the hedge and asked how much Ed was paid an hour; whatever it was he'd give him five quid a week extra to come and work for him. His name was Hart and he lived in a house called Wood End, an old place half-timbered in parts with eighteenth century and Victorian additions; it had some vague Shakespeare association like the house at Grendon Underwood not far away which was a one-time inn. There is a story that Shakespeare stayed there en route from Stratford to London, met a member of the local watch and made use of him for the character of Dogberry. Wood End was supposed to have been owned at some time by a Shakespeare relative but that was probably an estate agent's invention. A recent owner had been Hart's bachelor uncle, a geologist who made money as a mining engineer and finished up as a director of Rio Tinto Zinc. He collected Japanese bronzes, Coptic tapestries and (rather a comedown, this) George V Coronation mugs of which no less than 500 were found ranged round his shelves when eventually he died. He left his collection and money to the Anti-Vivisection League and Wood End to his nephew in Kenya. This nephew was the father of the man who had tried to hire Ed as gardener, Aston Hart. The family were white settlers who grew coffee and, when Aston's parents were murdered by Mau Mau, he inherited Wood End and decided the best way to make money out of the place was to put it out to rent. His tenants were US Air Force staff but there were gaps in the tenancy from time to time when he came home with his wife Shirley. Hans had struck one of these interim periods. That is why Ed had to tell him about Mau Mau.

It was the name given to the guerrillas, mainly Kikuyu tribesmen, who attacked the white settlers. Gangs came out of the forest to raid, loot and kill. The Emergency did not win a lot of column inches in the States where it was seen as the kind of bloody mess the still imperialist Brits could expect until they realized that colonialism in the second half of the twentieth century was strictly out. But the Brits themselves and a lot of the black (and all the Asian) population of Kenya did not think the issue was that clear-cut. British troops were sent out and a friend of Ed's, Archie Wavell, was killed serving with the Green Howards.

'I don't see what the Mau Mau have to do with Mr Hart needing to live in this country.'

'Wood End wouldn't be his if his parents were still alive. It's a responsibility.'

'Funny way to put it. I mean, he said he wouldn't be here but for the Mau Mau and, hell, d'you know what he's talking about? His pa and ma being chopped up. It's almost as though being here is the worst part of it for him. See what I mean?'

Hans was so intrigued by his encounter that he wrote a poem in which Hart was represented as a man who had been through such an unhappy love affair he wanted to kill himself but was stiffened by the knowledge his parents had an even worse time, being murdered by savages. He would live on, defiantly. Ed told him the last thing a poet should do is take himself as evidence about the rest of the universe. Hart wasn't like that at all, as Hans would have realized if he knew more about him. Particularly if he had met Hart's wife, Shirley.

Hans was upset. 'That's not the point. What Mr Hart is really like isn't the point at all. But you know that.' After a while he said, 'I'm sorry, sir. I suppose your ma and pa being chopped up isn't the end of the world. I guess it's an experience I'd survive if it happened to me but it'd be tough on Lisa.' The next day he spoke about his parents again. 'We get on okay. But they're strict and I take notice of what they say. Now other kids, they don't take notice, not what their ma and pa say. That's real American I guess. Free. But I love my ma and pa. What they say is right anyway. You don't like them though and that's embarrassing, sir. It embarrasses me a lot.'

Embarrass was a word that came up often. It merely indicated a state of uncompromising disagreement.

To get back to that occasion when Aston Hart tried to hire Ed as a gardener. He was flattered in a perverse sort of way. Leaving the obvious example aside, some quite unusual people have been mistaken for gardeners, including His Late Majesty King George VI who, wearing a Guard's bearskin (because of the cold he needed something to keep his head warm) was chanced upon slashing away in the shrubbery. Though the bearskin must have been a giveaway. Many a visitor to a stately home has reported seeing an old man in a torn tweed jacket and

15

wellingtons pruning the roses who turned out to be the earl or marquis. Hart's offer went up to an extra six pounds a week and when Ed said no to that too he became insistent in an amazed sort of way. It was a fair enough offer, wasn't it? Why the hell should he say no? One of those old stories came into Ed's mind. He said he didn't job around. He was happy where he was. He ate well, he had a couple every evening and when it suited him he slept with the lady of the house.

Hart didn't laugh as expected. He said, more to himself than to Ed, 'Well, I'm buggered!' and made off.

A couple of days later his wife phoned, said she was Shirley Hart of Wood End and hoped they would not take it amiss if she asked whether they employed a gardener. The Parslers did as it happened and when Ed said so there was silence. To ease her difficulty Ed explained that the gardener was a pensioner and came in two days a week. He hoped the Harts were not going to steal him. She said that was exactly what her husband had been trying to do and she had rung up to apologize. When Ed explained that the man her husband had spoken to was actually himself she said, 'Oh, I was *sure* it was you, Mr Parsler', and began laughing so that he had to hold the receiver away from his ear. It was as though two people were laughing, the one setting the other off, peal upon peal.

The upshot was that the Parslers were invited round for a drink and Aston said it was easy to make a sucker out of him because he didn't understand England. He had been coming down from London in the train and in the same compartment was a girl with her leg in plaster that was covered with signatures. She had wanted him to sign too, which he did. Everybody looked at him. What he had done meant something, but he didn't know what. It was a secret. Then this girl got up and tried to open the door, not the one to the corridor but the one that gave on to the track, and nobody moved. Hart grabbed her. She said, 'Christ!' and went out into the corridor. Hart asked the man by the door why he hadn't stopped her and got the reply, 'Well, I thought she might want to commit suicide.' Nobody batted an eyelid. They went on reading. This fellow might have been joking or covering up but how was Hart to know? He was an African in a foreign land and he didn't understand it. Out of his thirty odd years he had spent no more than eighteen months all told in England. Shirley was the same. They had been born and brought up in Kenya but now they were no longer at home even there. White settlers were on their way out. They had made the country, made it prosperous, but now their land would be expropriated under black rule. Not that he had anything against blacks. He was at home with blacks, when they knew who was master.

So he was disorientated. 'I apologize for taking you for the gardener, Mr Parsler, but when you came back to me with that claim you wouldn't leave your present job, you ate well and drank well and what's more you slept with the lady of the house, well, know what? If I'd been an Englishman I'd have known I was being ribbed. But I'm a bloody colonial so what do I think? We can't compete with that in our household. That's the thought that went through my head. For all I knew about this country sleeping with the boss's wife was a perk negotiated by the Agricultural Workers' Union. Almost anything can be believed. Nobody seems to care. The top people, like the chaps I meet in the ministry, the really top chaps who handle Commonwealth and Foreign Affairs, do you know what they advise? They say Shirley and I will never settle. Get out! Wish I was your age! That's what the old sods say, as they sit on their pensions. Get out of this country. But where to? Not back to Africa. There's no future in Africa.'

The Harts were like the Mullers, throwbacks to an earlier time. Ed was a throwback too and young Hans had put his finger on it; civilization, so called, was in flight from the word. Pictures and action were taking over. Ed sitting in his room at night making black marks on white paper was just a relic, a survival from a time when people took words seriously. When Harriet refused to buy some pegs from a gipsy the gipsy put a curse on her. Harriet was upset by this but Ed thought it was great. Somebody believes words count. The pagan gods be praised.

No point in telling Hans much about the Harts but Ed did tell him about the gipsy.

'Yeah? That's a point,' said Hans. 'You sure need words for some things.'

Hans may have loved his ma and pa but they could not

persuade him to go into the family business. He worked as stage manager in an experimental theatre group who had a Foundation grant and toured westerns written in the style of Japanese Noh plays. He was hired to make a Noh-style TV ad for Japanese autos (the launch of an American campaign), was sucked into the world of TV commercials, married a graduate student whose parents lived in Sweden, helped pioneer a TV news-gathering agency and went to Vietnam where he tripped over some cable in a helicopter, fell backwards through the open port and died a few hours later in hospital. Lisa was now in the top grade of her expensive private school and she wrote to Ed on the school notepaper.

Unless I write you nobody else will and poor Hans just admired you so much, and appreciated your interest, he would have wanted me to write now that he is dead, just to let you know. I wouldn't know how else you'd get to hear of this dreadful accident. It was so silly and trivial and undignified actually to fall out of a helicopter in Vietnam of all places. If he had to go there are better ways. But Pa says it was as good as being a soldier. There are more ways of fighting a war than with weapons. Communication is very important too. Hans just believed in communication of all kinds, poetry, drama, movies, ads, news reporting. It is very important that everybody understands the significance of this domino war. If one domino country goes down before the reds the other domino countries will follow. Hans was in this business of explaining what all have to understand. He was flown home. We had a moving service in the Lutheran church here and although Pa tried to get him interred in the military cemetery at Arlington he was not finally laid to rest there, but in our own sweetly pretty graveyard among flowering cherries.

And so on. She realized now she ought to have cabled. There would have been time for him to fly over for the funeral but the family had been so shattered, they had not thought. A later letter asked Ed if he would edit Hans's poems for publication, and for a fee. This he declined. Since the meeting on the *America* he had not laid eyes on Herr and Frau Muller but he sent them formal condolences and received a formal reply. That year Lisa sent a Christmas card. Then silence for years. The Muller episode seemed over and done with though occasionally Ed dreamed of Hans, often in Japanese traditional dress and strangely metamorphosed into a Noh play baddie, a scowl on his face.

His death pushed Ed for a while into thinking about 1939 again. He could have been wrong about the reason for leaving the party. It wasn't the German–Soviet Pact, or it wasn't just that. His father died about then and when Ed saw him in the mortuary chapel the immobility weighed heavily. Stone he'd seen like this, but not flesh, and the absence of any flicker, any animation, any promise of a future glow that could possibly be called human, made the chill of that vault more penetrating. Ed loved his father. The cold settled in the gut. He wanted to say something silly. 'I don't agree.' Or, 'I can't accept it. This is impossible.'

So, because of love, Ed was against death. He could not tolerate the materialism that would have summed up his father's life in the marmoreal form that lay before him. Anybody with wispy reservations about the reality of physical death is not a natural for Marxist-Leninism. Chucking communism was not just a political protest on Ed's part but it took the death of Hans to bring 1939 more fully back and recover something that had been buried.

2

'You haven't seen Sam by any chance?'

It was characteristic of Aston Hart that after an absence of about eighteen months he should ring up and, with no preliminaries, put this question. Ed didn't even know he was in the country. After his last tenant Wood End had been shut up for months. Who was Sam? Hart knew who Sam was so he took it for granted everybody else knew too. But Ed didn't even realize it was Hart at the other end of the line, the call was that unexpected. Hart was amazed when asked who was calling.

Sam turned out to be a lieutenant in the King's African Rifles who was staying as a guest at Wood End. He was a black Ugandan, one of only two commissioned blacks in this otherwise white-officered regiment. Hart had a lot of time for Sam. They first met during the Mau Mau troubles. Hart was a sergeant in the Kenya Regiment (European Territorials) while Sam was an NCO with the KARs and Sam, he said, undoubtedly saved his life. Hart was attached as a kind of intelligence officer to the KARs and was with a platoon when, with police, they located a Mau Mau gang in a swamp. Unexpectedly one of the gang glistening with mud from top to toe had run out of the reeds with a spear. He would have stuck the spear into Hart's back if Sam hadn't shouted and then managed to gun the man down. Very unusual, said Hart, for Mau Mau to use the spear. Must have run out of ammunition. Their usual weapon was the home-made gun, almost as lethal to the shooter as to the shot at.

What Aston did not like about that incident was the gangster's behaviour after Sam had killed him. He stood up with blood guggling out of his throat and belly, crusting with the mud and smearing it away, threatening Aston with outstretched arms and clawed hands. Aston remembered too the enormous erection. This Mau Mau warrior was the demonic rapist of a woman's nightmare. He spat, into Aston's face, and spoke in an unusually deep, restrained voice. But there was no mistaking the hate behind it. With the back of his hand Aston wiped away the blood and spittle that was sliding down his face, aware that Sam was just standing there, making no move. Aston had a hand gun at the ready but before he could use it the spearman pitched forward on to his face, stiff as a log.

'What was all that, Sam?'

'Strong curse on you and your family.'

'And you just watched?'

'You can't kill a man twice. When a dead man stands up to curse you just listen.'

Hart made Sam a present of a wristwatch and they kept in touch, even after Sam's battalion had been posted back to Uganda. His great ambition was to visit England. No doubt if Hart had gone about the matter in the orthodox way he could have arranged for Sam to come on an ordinary civilian flight, and with the right travel documents, but it amused him to wangle a passage on one of the RAF transports that regularly made the trip between East Africa and the UK. The consequence was that Sam, still in his khaki cotton slacks and KAR hat with the broad brim pinned vertically over his left ear, had to be smuggled out of the Wiltshire airfield with no other document but his Army pay book. Then, after being escorted by Hart to Wood End and spending the night there he just cleared off. Hart said Sam had no English money. He'd been gone for about twelve hours.

Shirley had not made the trip with Hart. She stayed with her new baby on the farm about fifteen miles out of Nairobi. As soon as Harriet realized the situation she said, 'The poor man. He won't even have any aired sheets, the house shut up all that time.' The real set-up was different. Hart treated the expedition as a safari and camped out in the house, not bothering with sheets or any cooking more ambitious than opening a can. The Parslers were on the point of leaving for a holiday, the first foreign holiday since Mark was born. They were, in fact, driving past Wood End on the way to Dover when there Hart and the black soldier were, coming out of the front gate obviously bound for the village to do some shopping, Hart with a BOAC bag and Sam, very smart and upright and smiling under his big hat with an empty army-issue kitbag. Hart actually stepped in front of the car and Ed had to brake.

21

'I thought it might be you. Nice of you to come over but there's no need to worry.' He introduced Sam. 'Doesn't speak much English, I'm afraid, but he's making progress. Do you know where he went? London. Without a ticket. Bluffed his way through. Went to the Tower, saw the BBC where the Swahili broadcasts come from. But the first place he made for was Buck House. Imagine that. Saw the Changing of the Guard. Wanted to do it all off his own bat. Wanted to show initiative. Ran into an Arab from Dar es Salaam and borrowed ten quid from him. Independent but respectful. Paying his respects. Sam is the very best kind of native colonial soldier. The British could be proud of him. But do you think they are? They're ashamed. D'you know why they're ashamed? They're afraid of responsibility and what they're really afraid of is that fear. Africa will be a poorer place when the Empire's gone. There won't be many men like Sam around.'

He was black and pulpy like a fine hothouse grape. He stood to attention, creasing his opulent features and showing white even teeth in a reassuring smile. He was big and he was going to be bigger. The dark pupils of his eyes were set in little beery pools. 'Rule Britannia,' he said, saluting. 'God save the Queen. For the sake of auld lang syne.' Hart laughed as the Parslers drove away as though he had performed some marvellous trick and now he would do something even more surprising, such as releasing the valve between Sam's shoulder blades and letting the air out, so that the inflated black figure could be collapsed and packed away once more in Hart's suitcase.

Odd to think he had left Shirley and the baby behind in that haunted house near Nairobi. Shirley said they had actually called in a witch doctor to tell them why there were strange noises, puffs of cold air and sometimes unidentifiable but very nasty smells. The witch doctor was quite young. He wore large white-rimmed sunglasses, was dressed in shorts, sandals and an old mac. He carried a bag of sticks with which he made a fire, inhaled the smoke and after a long period of grumbling and muttering pronounced the place free of the Kikuyu ghosts – the house was built on land the Kikuyu had farmed for themselves – but he had sent them away. He charged them five pounds and after he had left matters were as bad as before. But now they knew what the trouble was, the Harts put up with it. They both took it for granted that witch doctors had supernatural powers. On this occasion either the ghosts were too strong, or they had hired the wrong witch doctor, but they did not doubt the trouble was caused by dead Kikuyu. Hart used to shout at the ghosts. They never actually saw anything; but they heard boards creak as though someone was walking along the verandah, pictures fell off the walls, smells, whistles, laughter. Wood End was a place you might expect to have a reputation for ghosts but Shirley thought it was clean as a whistle. If there had been anything odd she would have known immediately.

But when eventually she did come with the baby she was not happy at Wood End. She was used to servants and now there weren't any. Cooking she just wasn't equal to and Hart himself did a lot of it. Her main interest seemed to be clothes (she was always off to London shopping). Her taste was good but expensive; she was always wearing something different. She was an attractive, fair-haired, fresh-faced girl who had bouts of boyish high spirits when she pranced about, laughing helplessly over things that didn't seem very funny in themselves. They went to see *The Boy Friend*. It was a world she would have fitted into rather well; she was a 1920s figure, a flapper, and Hart quite plainly worshipped her. He would sit with a smile on his face, just watching her as she skipped about, shrieking because he had cream on the end of his nose (he had been sniffing it to see if it had gone sour) or some other such triviality. Then she could switch to a moan about missing Kenya.

The baby was in England for the first time. She was always called Jo (her real name was Joanna) which was the Harts' way of confessing they had hoped for a boy. Jo was difficult, she cried a lot and fed reluctantly. On the whole Shirley did not cope at all well and Harriet used to go over, taking young Mark, to provide support. Giving Jo a bath terrified Shirley and Harriet actually found it easier to teach Hart how to do it rather than Shirley herself.

One morning Ed was driving to Bicester when he saw Sam standing on the grass verge with his back to a huge elderberry bush – it was August and the fruit was ripe, as black and shiny and plump as Sam himself. Or was it Sam? There was no one

23

there, just this bush loaded with black bunches of elderberries. When next Ed saw the Harts he said he thought he had seen Sam but they said no, that was impossible, he was in Kenya. At least, that is where he was so far as they knew. What's more, he was in disgrace.

'What's he been up to?'

Hart said the King's African Rifles spent a lot of time dealing with cattle thieves. There was a tribe, the Turkana, who operated in north-west Kenya and were particularly notorious because they used guns. There was a story going round in Nairobi that a certain platoon of the KARs had been particularly rough in one of their sweeps to disarm the Turkana who complained to the police and were able to lead them to where a number of bodies were buried in shallow graves. The officer in charge of this sweep had been none other than Sam.

'Anyway, he's not with us,' said Hart. 'That's for sure. He's probably being court-martialled. Then they'll sack him. But I hope not. His mother was a witch. Did I tell you that? You can't expect the son of a witch to become an officer and a gentleman overnight.'

Shirley remarked, quite seriously, that the figure in front of the elderberry bush had been some kind of phantasmal projection of Sam made possible by his mother's witchcraft; not only dead people could be ghosts, live people could be too. She had heard of such apparitions. They were intended as warnings, sometimes appeals for help. 'But in that case it's odd *you* shouldn't have seen him, Aston.'

'Nothing I could do to help,' Hart said in a matter-of-fact sort of way. 'Sorry!' Almost as though he was speaking to Sam direct. Ed said he'd never see elderberries again without thinking of Sam.

Hart was about 32 or 33 at this time and preoccupied with getting a job in England so that he could turn his back on Kenya. The country was on the verge of independence and he couldn't see the blacks running it. So he would sell out. There was talk of government money being available to compensate farmers who had to give up their land and he wanted to be one of these; there wouldn't be much money forthcoming from Kikuyu farmers themselves. Not that the official compensation would amount to much. It was bloody robbery. Did you realize his father had actually created this farm? He grew coffee and asparagus and maize where there had never been any cultivation before. The way people talk nowadays you'd think that was some sort of crime.

Hart went to Covent Garden to talk to the firm that imported his asparagus; he saw coffee importers, shipping firms, the BBC African service, Securicor, merchant banks with an interest in East Africa, but no one wanted to know. He had no qualifications or the wrong sort of qualifications. When asked why, if living under a black government was so intolerable, he didn't think of going to one of the white dominions, Australia say, and grow maize and asparagus there, he shook his head.

'No,' he said. 'England is home. I want Jo to grow up here. Another thing, if I went to Australia that's where I reckon I'd stay. But if there was some way back into Africa I could always slip out of England. Do you see that?'

'I don't really.' Ed was really puzzled.

'You ought to go to East Africa some time. The country itself is okay. It can be high and cold and wet. Then the sun comes out and it's hot and dry and clear. You might be right and all.' He said nothing for a while. 'Some way of staying on. It's been my life, I suppose. And I can't just throw it over. But I just don't know and that's the truth.'

'I'd have thought black Kenya would need people like you.'

'The blacks don't see it that way.'

On his way back from one of his job hunting expeditions to London Hart just missed his train out of Marylebone and Ed found him sitting at a table in the station forecourt, outside the bar, drinking beer. London had been a stewpot, up to 90° F on the Air Ministry roof, and Hart was wearing a crumpled white cotton suit and, incongruously, brown riding boots. No doubt it was Kenyan working kit. Because of his beard and untidy hair – his wide-brimmed straw hat was on the table in front of him – he looked like an actor got up as a Victorian explorer; Baker, say, with his Fortnum and Mason hampers and champagne setting off up the Nile. He caught sight of Ed and after some hesitation, waved. He hadn't seen him in his working gear before and was not sure he knew him.

'I didn't know bowlers were still worn.'

Ed was proud of his. It had a curled brim on either side of the head and he wore it with a tightly knotted dark tie, the collar being secured under it with a gold pin.

'You look like a trendy undertaker,' Hart said.

So they had typed each other, explorer and undertaker. Actually, Ed felt a bit of a fool, in this Edwardian get-up, with Hart's eyes upon him.

'Do you remember Hans Muller?'

Hart concentrated. A vertical furrow opened between his eyebrows. 'That young Yank? The one who got himself killed in Vietnam?'

'I had a letter from his sister. He kept a journal. We're all written up in it, you and me and the conversations we had. What interested Lisa was the information about you. Hans said you were a descendant of Shakespeare's sister, Joan Hart. Is that right?'

Ancestry was clearly not the matter uppermost in Hart's mind. No doubt he was still smarting from a brush-off in the City but he wanted to be agreeable and he gathered himself for a discussion of what, to him, was a boring subject. He raised his eyebrows in a bleary sort of way and stuck out his lips. 'Yes. I told him that. I thought he'd help to get me a job at Brize Norton if I shot this Shakespeare line. The Yanks are just crazy about Shakespeare. Cousin Will, we call him. Why cousin I don't know. He's been dead a thousand years and more.'

'But is it true? Lisa wanted me to check.'

'You mean, was I telling the truth? Yeah! I was telling the truth. It's why we're living at Wood End.'

'Then she'd be keen to come and see you.'

'I'd have nothing for her.'

'She's majoring in literature at Wellesley. There's an ad. the British Tourist Board run in the States. "Come to Stratford-upon-Avon and feel your spirit lift at the touch of an immortal." From what she says she's in that sort of mood. Very intense about it all.'

'I've bugger all to do with Shakespeare really. After all, the Harts were just poor relations. Nothing remarkable on our side of the family. Not a flicker. Don't even take to the plays, you know. I mean, I didn't. I could always have another go at them. There's one called *The Tempest*. That's about a storm. Well, is it?'

'To begin with.'

'It's the first in the book so I suppose it's the first he wrote and the easiest. What's this girl's name?'

'Lisa.'

'She'd waste her time coming to see me.'

Apparently Hans had taken much the same view because in the extract from his diary Lisa quoted in her letter he had written.

Aston said it (Wood End) was not the right house for him and his family and he was going to sell it and get out. He had an eccentric uncle who bought the place because he believed a seventeenth-century ancestor, George Hart, lived there having had it gifted to him by Lady Barnard who was Shakespeare's granddaughter. There's a mighty big question mark over all that, but apparently the Hart lineage is okay. What does it matter? This East African cowboy has a Shakespeare link but it's so stretched it must have snapped long ago. Let's face it. It doesn't really exist. And yet!

Lisa went on, 'And yet! it's more than that. It's terrific. I'm sure Mr Hart has vibrations he doesn't know about and if I could only touch his flesh I would detect them.'

Ed hadn't seen Lisa for ten years, but he'd been sent photographs and could imagine that strong little face, wide cheekbones, and rounded eyes being raised from her brother's journal and taking on an expression of excited, soulful intensity that might have been appropriate for the really big occasion (what? the sight of her firstborn, say; or to be expected in a nun seeing visions) but not for anything Aston Hart could spark off. In her letter Lisa continued at some length about Shakespeare. God knows what he was a substitute for but that he was a substitute there seemed little doubt. A flesh-and-blood boy-friend, perhaps. Or, being Lisa, some great cause she could commit herself to. She sounded irrational. The thought that, through Hart, there might be some physical link with this life-enhancing Shakespeare had really caught her.

'Anyway, I don't like Americans,' said Hart. 'They think we're living in the past. Imperialists ruling the roost. I mean, after

India! We gave it all away! But the Yanks still think we've got this boss psychology. What's wrong with that anyway? Without white bosses what do you get? Blood baths. Look at the way the Muslims and Hindus slaughtered each other the moment we turned our backs. It'll be the same in Africa. Vietnam means the Americans are learning the hard way. Even now, they still think we're toffee-nosed aristocrats grinding every black, brown and yellow face in sight. Did I tell you about that American professor I met on the plane? He told me white settlers like me were the commies' best friend. We were so offensive to the blacks they'll just have to turn to the Russians and the Chinese to get rid of us. So we ought to get out. Then the blacks could set up what he called viable democracies with free institutions. Have you ever heard such cock?' Hart had worked himself into a fury and after this they said nothing for some time.

'Did you talk politics with Hans?'

'With who?'

'Lisa's brother, Hans Muller.'

'That kid? He was a bit stiff. No jokes. He wanted to do something but he didn't know what. Wait a bit though! I gave him a piece of my mind about Suez.'

The Anglo-French invasion of Port Said and part of the Canal Zone at the time the Israelis attacked in Sinai was nine years before but it was plainly still fresh in Hart's mind. 'I told him I'd never forgive the Yanks for the way Dulles came out against us.'

'What did he say about that?'

'Seemed pretty confused about it all. Got it mixed up with the Gallipoli landings in 1915, which was a different sort of show altogether.'

'But you'd take a job with Americans?'

'I'm flexible. No choice, no money, nothing. What I need is a good burglary. Then Shirley and I could live on the insurance. I shouldn't have said that, should I, you being in the racket?' He rubbed his beard vigorously and grinned, his eyes widening with astonishment at the pretended indiscretion.

'I wouldn't advise a bogus burglary. Bound to get caught. Never take on an insurance company. Banks are different. Robbing banks is child's play in comparison. Going to be a lot more of it, I'm sure.'

Hart's grin went out like a light. 'Funny you should say that. A nice well-planned bank robbery's often been in my mind.' He stabbed a finger at Ed's city suit. 'There's more to you than meets the eye. That gear is overdone. Not the real thing. Fancy dress. You're dolled up to hide something.'

He seemed on the point of proposing they took this bank robbery idea seriously and got down to planning the detail but instead, he stretched, yawned and looked at his watch. 'They're going through the barrier. We'd better get moving.'

As they joined the queue he went on talking in a loud voice. 'What you say about robbing a bank interests me. But I'm kidding myself. Too much of a drifter to go in for that kind of action. You don't mind me calling you Ed?'

The other commuters were listening with great interest to all this but, ignoring them, Hart went on to make one of those remarks which seem colourless at the time but nevertheless stick in the mind and regularly surface for years. 'If a door opens I go through. If it shuts I go away.'

'So bank robbery is out?'

'Sure. I believe in keeping my head down. But it doesn't stop me thinking about a nice hold-up in a theoretical kind of way. You've got your kind of poetry and that kind of thinking is mine.'

Ed kept thinking of what Hart said about a door shutting and another one opening.

'If Lisa writes don't just give her a brush off,' he said. 'She's a bit special.'

Not so long after that Marylebone conversation the Harts dropped in on the Parslers unexpectedly to say they'd decided to go back to Kenya. They were putting Wood End in the hands of an agent to rent out furnished, with a clause in the contract providing for repossession on three months warning. Soon they would be off.

Perhaps the coming of winter had something to do with their decision. Certainly they were out of the country by Boxing Day because it was a bright, frosty day with snow powdering the hard ground. Jessica and her father rode over there and watched the sun yellow the western windows of the empty house as it sank. The first news came in a letter to Harriet (written by

Shirley from Nairobi) saying they had given their names to the agent. Would they mind vetting any prospective tenants?

It was Shirley who kept in touch. Aston had gone into partnership with an Asian businessman and was flying a plane in and out of Ethiopia ferrying rich refugees from the new Marxist regime there. Shirley had a flip way of writing and they could never be sure when she was serious. She spoke of a bit of smuggling on the side: rhinoceros horn which could still be procured in Ethiopia, ground down and marketed as an aphrodisiac in East Africa and Saudi Arabia. The picture given was of Aston in the cockpit, a couple of pistols and a rifle to hand with a family of almond-eyed, big-nosed Ethiopians squatting on the floor of the cabin behind him and sacks of rhino horn in the hold. But it was also clear he was still farming because Shirley spoke of dealers driving out of Nairobi to inspect the coffee and asparagus. There was a recurrence of the hauntings. Shirley seemed more concerned about these than the independence negotiations that were going on in Nairobi and Westminster. There were times, she said, when the house just stank of ghosts. Literally, a bad smell as from a latrine.

Then, though Harriet wrote back, silence for some considerable time. Wood End was taken on a three-year lease by a pleasant American major called Ritter and his wife who joined the local hunt where the Parslers met them. Only the agent in Bicester dealt directly with the Harts. Sometime in the following winter he rang up to ask whether he could come over. He'd had a letter from Nairobi and would like a word with somebody who knew Aston Hart better than he did before writing back.

His name was Suttle, but everyone called him Kim, a hesitant, slow-speaking man with a beard trimmed close and a way of throwing his head back to get a better view. It could not have been because of his height. He was over six foot. The trick added to his air of sometimes baffled self-consciousness. Why were people so critical? Couldn't they see he was doing his best? Questions like this seemed to be going through his mind all the time. A cautious, level-headed reliable type.

'What Mr Hart wants to know is whether there is anything – well, unusual going on at Wood End. And by that I don't think he means some sort of activity with lots of people turning up.

Or, say, sporting events. In fact, I know he doesn't mean that because Major Ritter would obviously know all about it. But Mr Hart seemed to be wondering whether anything unusual was going on in the house which Major Ritter might not have noticed. Now, what can I say? Particularly as Mr Hart said I wasn't to question Major Ritter directly.'

'Could I see the letter?'

'No, sorry.' Kim was embarrassed. 'After all it's a letter to my firm and professional confidences you know.' Maybe there was a reference or two to the Parslers in the letter which Kim thought it better to keep to himself. 'You see why I wanted to sound you,' he went on. 'Mr Hart writes in a strange way. He didn't seem odd to deal with. Then he writes this letter.'

'Does he write often?'

'No. Major Ritter pays quarterly in advance. We've got instructions to send it, less our commission of course, to his bank in Nairobi. Mr Hart doesn't acknowledge. There's no need, of course. This is the first letter we've had for over a year. Does he write to you?'

'His wife used to write, to my wife, that is. But that's stopped.'

Kim was looking at Ed with his chin up, defying him even fleetingly to think he was incompetent or not doing his best. 'I even wondered whether he was serious. It might be a game or a joke. But is he the sort of man to write out of the blue a jokey query like this? Might be his idea of fun. Why didn't he write to Major Ritter himself?' Kim thought about this. 'His letter raises other matters, of course. But make no mistake. That letter rings like a cracked bell. How could I possibly find out if anything unusual was going on in the house, particularly if Major Ritter had noticed nothing? And I'm not even to put a question to him.'

Kim had not given much to go on but it did seem he was off balance for no substantial reason.

'You've got to remember some people are bad at writing letters. They give a wrong impression. All you've got to do is drop in on the Ritters, or give them a ring, and ask them if everything is all right. When they say it is, as I'm sure they will, then write to Hart and say nothing odd is going on. And ask him what he had in mind.'

Harriet's view, on hearing about the visit, was that Aston Hart

31

must have written a much more dotty letter than Kim had conveyed. Must have been outrageous. Otherwise why should Kim come over from Bicester? The kind of question Aston was asking might be a bit eccentric but it didn't require a consultation. Aston was probably drunk when he wrote whatever he did write and by now had forgotten all about it.

After a spell of exceptionally hard frost when riding a horse across a ploughed field would have been like riding over furrows and ridges of metal the arctic grip slackened, the clear sky quilted over and the little river and flooded gravel pits disappeared under mist. Ed was hunting regularly now. The hunt gathered in the recreation ground and moved off after the almost hysterically excited hounds in the direction of Curtain Wood which he knew they wouldn't enter. They'd cross the rough pasture below the wood and hope the huntsman, Jack Price, would raise something in the tangle of poor grass and dead bracken this side of the moor. Guy Budgen, the MFH, had been in the job for twenty years and was becoming dithery. He turned back from a hedge and ditch and trotted his horse through a gateway. Major Ritter was unmistakable. He rode a fine chestnut gelding (and must have ridden it hard from Wood End because the animal was steaming and sweating) but his coat was the colour of tomato sauce and he wore the kind of steel hat, a yellow one, seen on building sites. Most MFHs would have ticked him off.

'Hiya!' he shouted, catching sight of Ed and then galloping off, straight in the stirrups, his behind well clear of the saddle. As it happened Wood End, on its hill, was visible from this point. One of its roofs was unmistakable, with an exceptionally high pitch, like the upturned keel of a boat. Hart said it had once been thatched but come a gale and the thatch would blow off. After three hundred years they gave up and tiled it. Now it could be seen in the morning grey with a point of light in one of the upper windows. In the sun of Africa Hart must think of it as a remote, impossible and alien habitation; but if he had written as peculiar a letter about it as Kim suggested then the house must have its hold on him. Ed saw quite a lot of Ritter that morning. He enjoyed himself hugely. They chatted while waiting for the hounds to draw a covert but Ritter didn't mention Wood End once, so if Kim had put a question to him it had made little impression. Otherwise, knowing Ed had some standing as a vetter of tenants, he would surely have said something.

3

That winter Ed seemed to be flying the Atlantic every fortnight or so. Since the early 1950s the company had been expanding, because of the reinsurance business they were taking on. This was not quite the Lloyd's monopoly it once had been. The rigid currency exchange controls of the time made international insurance all the more attractive; premiums were free of these controls because of International Monetary Fund rules, so the Lloyd's syndicates and companies like Ed's were free to transfer sterling abroad in a way closed to the private investor. He spent a lot of time in the States where the company had been picking up the tab for a series of big fires, office blocks curiously enough, in places as far apart as Washington, Buffalo and Denver. Their American insurers saw nothing odd about this but Ed's company wanted to know the answer to a few questions. For example, were the people claiming the insurance the real owners or were they nominees. They'd had a bad experience in Britain where apparently unrelated fires had turned out to be in property ultimately owned by the same obscure company though the ostensible owners were quite different, apparently independent, companies. Here they were able to prove arson. They wanted to be sure this could be ruled out in the States.

It was always understood that on one of these trips he would contact Lisa. But she was usually at college or away on holiday; and the truth was he'd never been keen on renewing old acquaintance. She was out of college now and had a job in Washington with the State Department, looking after distinguished foreign visitors (Leaders, she called them) who had been given a free ticket and all expenses paid by the US Government in order to let them see something of the country for themselves.

Lisa had this mixture of German earnestness and American confidence that made her sensitive to any accusation she was any kind of a propagandist. She really wanted these visiting dignitaries to see as much of the States as possible – the achievements, yes, like Chicago architecture; but the failures too, like the slums of black Chicago because she was quite sure they had only to see the country as it really was and they would just love it. Ed felt he knew her pretty well but the fact was that when she turned up, by appointment, at his hotel he did not recognize her. He could not believe this was Lisa. He couldn't think what the hell to say. He could only stare.

What caught his attention were the bright red boots and the white raincoat with a hood (outside it was raining hard). But when she threw back this hood and looked around she revealed a face of such radiance and yet such nunlike stillness it imposed quiet. In reality it would have done nothing of the sort. The usual hotel clamour went on but the reception clerks, the porters, the laughter of a group near the entrance to the bar, it really was as though they all fell silent. The hush was holy. It had that kind of awesomeness. He hadn't realized she was now a grown-up woman. Then she came up and said, 'Hello there, Edwin. You've not changed a bit.'

If, at that moment, she had been snatched away, borne up on a cloud or riding away on a swan, never to be seen again, he would nevertheless feel changed. She was a vision of calm and saintlike assurance putting out a statement of immense importance. Precisely what he didn't know. All is well and fair, perhaps not in this transitory world but at some profounder level. Nothing to worry about. At the centre of our being was an unquenchable good. This was the plane she lifted him to. Can numinous statements of that order be made without words, simply by a woman's bearing, colouring, complexion, eyes, nose, mouth and hair? And the expression on her face? He must have been in a state of abnormal receptivity. Her eyes were a darker blue than he had remembered in the child and now set in stainless white; large eyes that could lift him into a soaring thermal of such happiness. No exaggeration, he sobbed and was on the edge of tears.

'Say, what's the matter, Edwin? You had a shock or something? Am I that disappointing?' The tears actually spurted, tears of laughter. She just thought he was that funny. And he was still unable to say anything. 'You could do with a drink. Then why don't you buy me one, man? Where's your manners?'

'Sure. But, Lisa – '

'C'mon.' She slipped an arm through his and pushed him gently towards the bar. 'I've got George coming along at half after seven and he's going to take us *all* out to dinner in a *great* little eating place. But I thought we'd have time for a chat first, before he comes, because y'know, he does tend to talk a lot.'

'Who's George?'

'Well, Ed, he's a nice guy and even if he does talk a lot what he says is interesting.'

'I thought I was to be the host.'

'Difficult with George. It isn't his style. You'll see what I mean. Don't keep staring at me like that, Ed. You sure you're okay?' She gave his arm a shake. 'Look, Ed. He's rich. Why don't we soak him? But he's nice too. You can be rich and cute too. Did you know that?'

Lisa wanted to know about Harriet and the kids. And then, just before George arrived she said, 'Isn't it terrible about Shirley?'

'Shirley?'

'Yes. Shirley Hart in Kenya. You know. It's just too awful.'

'What is?'

'Haven't you heard from Aston? Well, how about that? You mean you didn't know Shirley had died?'

'No. That's terrible.'

He thought of Suttle coming over from Bicester saying he'd had a letter from Hart that rang like a cracked bell but plainly it had not reported Shirley's death. He would have said so. Even Kim would not think professional etiquette required him to keep that sort of information under his hat.

Lisa had written a number of letters to Hart, first of all to Wood End and then, after he had acknowledged them briefly from Kenya she had written to him there. They were mainly to ask questions about his family background and about Wood End itself – clearly she was still suffering from this Shakespeare bug – and, she said, Hart must have been bored by it all because there was a long silence. Then this long letter with its stunning news. Had Hart ever met Lisa he would have known she was a good person to communicate with. But Hart had not met her. How, without seeing her, could he have guessed she had this aura?

36

'Ed, do you mean Aston and you never corresponded? Didn't Shirley write?'

'She and Harriet wrote to each other.'

'But not Aston?'

The oddest thing touched on in Shirley's letter had been the haunting of the house they lived in, something Harriet and Ed even thought might be a joke, but when he said so to Lisa she gave a great cry that turned faces in their direction. 'Say, that's it! The hauntings! She died of a haunting.'

'What happened?'

They were now joined by a tall young man with a crew cut who turned out to be George arriving inconveniently early. He kissed Lisa on the cheek and turned to Ed, stretching out a hand, saying, 'Nice to meet you. Say, can I get you another drink?' Behind his gold-rimmed glasses his eyes were grey, almost colourless and because he had so little hair on his round head and eyebrows just two yellow, almost invisible lines, he looked inhuman, sinister, almost robotlike. Yet he was also snakey and sensual. And his lips had touched Lisa's cheek! 'What's the matter with you two, anyway? You fighting already?'

'I just gave him some bad news.'

'How do you mean, she died of a haunting?' Ed ignored George.

Lisa took a deep breath, looking around. All the public rooms were too noisy for confidential talk so Ed took them up to his room where there was an armchair for Lisa, a chair at the writing table for George. And he sat on the bed.

Lisa then began talking about the events in the Harts' house in Kenya almost as though she had been there and witnessed them for herself. Yet it all came out of two long letters Hart had written her. Oh! and she phoned him. Why not? Sure she had phoned him and they had quite a talk. The line was good and clear. He sounded okay in the circumstances. She'd like Ed to see these letters. She had them by heart. She knew the layout of the Hart home and, in her mind, she seemed to be walking about there as she spoke. Oddly enough, smiling now and again at some detail in the story.

'The home is isolated, that's for sure, right away from the main road, down a dirt track but from what Aston tells me it's big for that country. Just the one storey with a sort of marble-floored hall running the whole length at the front. And leading off this were the rooms. The drawing room was pretty big and that's where the hauntings were.'

George broke in. 'Say, what's all this? I thought we were all going out to eat. Well, okay, if you've got some message to give but I'd better ring up Toni's and ask them to keep that table. And what about some room service, Ed?'

'Go ahead.' Ed was amazed that Hart had written Lisa two long letters. She had clearly not spoken of him to George before and the guy resented what he was now hearing. He put on quite a performance at the phone. He took the opportunity to tell someone at Toni's exactly what to do in order that the duck, which was being cooked in some special Chinese way, would not go dry even though we might be – what? So he was a food freak and maybe did the cooking himself once in a while. He raised his marmalade eyebrows at Lisa – not there for half an hour or so. Then we all had to have a special kind of bourbon from room service.

'You don't believe in ghosts, do you, Ed?' he asked.

'No.'

'Neither do I,' commented Lisa. 'I'm just telling you what Aston said.'

George wanted to know who Aston was and, what with the supplementary questions he put, filling him in on the subject took some time. They were still at it when the waiter appeared with the drinks. George's comment was that family background, lineage, that sort of thing, counted for nothing these days. What if Shakespeare himself was way back up the family tree? More important was what a man did with his own life. 'You reading me, Ed?'

Lisa went straight on. The Hart home was 6000 feet up in the mountains. It was cold at night so they always had this big log fire. 'In spite of the fire, there were times when there was a sudden enormous drop in temperature. This bitter cold came night after night and their dog took fright. He was real scared. He whined and moved slowly backwards as though something nasty was coming for him.'

Lisa was quite unemotional about all this. She might have been telling a fairy story to a child. The Harts had a guest who, just before he went home, asked them quite casually who the tribesman in a white cape and holding a spear as he sat in the kitchen could be. This meant nothing to the Harts because they had seen no such figure. Then there was poltergeist activity. As Aston reached out to pour water into a glass it exploded. Another guest made an excuse to leave early. Later he said he'd found the atmosphere in the house so frightening, so oppressive and the temperature so cold he'd just invented this excuse to leave. There were the foul smells Shirley had written about in her letters to Harriet.

'Aston said the little girl – what's her name?'

'Joanna,' Ed said. 'They always call her Jo.'

'Well, the kid complained about being given a good shake in the night to wake her up. She said it happened every night and she was very cold and frightened. She wanted more bedclothes. So Aston and Shirley sent the kid down to the coast to stay with friends, just to be on the safe side. And then they didn't know what to do, because all these bad things were still happening. It was Shirley's idea to call in a priest. Did you know she was a Roman Catholic? Well, she was and she went and asked some priest to exorcize the place.'

Lisa was so still and silent she seemed almost to be not breathing and she stayed like that far too long, looking straight ahead with the mysterious smile about her lips. George sat awkwardly in his chair, watching her fixedly, his glass tilted at such an angle there was danger he might spill his drink.

'What happened?' Ed asked.

'This Catholic priest refused. He just did not want to do it. In any event such a procedure would need the approval of his bishop and he was not prepared to ask for this. So Aston went back with Shirley to plead with him. Eventually he agreed to come to the house the following Sunday after Mass, not to conduct an exorcism ceremony but to bless each room in the house in the hope it would help with their problem. Whatever it was. So that's what he did.'

'And – ' Because she had paused.

'He came and put on a chasuble and produced a bucket of holy water and a sprinkler. He went round every room in the house, sprinkled holy water and said a prayer and eventually they got to the drawing room, you know this really big room where the fire burned at night, and you could look down over the valley to a small river. I know this because Aston said on the phone just as the priest began sprinkling the water Shirley went to this window to look out and Aston could see her against the light. Now, this is the terrifying bit. Just as the priest said the prayer he saw Shirley give a kind of convulsive jerk, the sort of thing if she'd been electrocuted, and then she just collapsed. I guess it was some kind of fit. She was jerking and she couldn't speak. Nairobi was ten miles away. By the time they got to the hospital with her she was dead. That's what Aston said.'

'And that's it?' said George, after he had digested this information. 'Did the spook stuff go on? That's what it would be very interesting to know. But Lisa, you never told me this story before. You don't believe it, do you?'

'I don't want to talk about it any more, George. Why don't we go and eat that duck? I'm hungry.'

They went out into the rain now sheeting down, and took a taxi to Toni's in Georgetown, where George had secured a special table in an alcove with champagne cooling in a bucket on a side table. Inappropriately festive but then George couldn't have known Lisa was going to talk about the Harts. Come to that, champagne was not right for a meal when your girlfriend got together with a man she had last seen in childhood. Was Lisa George's girlfriend? Did American girls allow a man to buy her a dinner to honour some other (admittedly much older and presumably harmless) man if she wasn't his special date? Ed didn't even know whether he was entitled to be annoyed to find himself the guest of a stranger when he'd expected to play host to Lisa, just the two of them, eating and talking together instead of which there was George trying to pick over the bones of Lisa's story. Ed tried to intercept the bill from the waiter but George roared and grabbed it. When the time came for them to drop Ed off at his hotel Lisa said, 'You've been quiet.'

'Do you think it would be all right for me to write to Hart about all this?'

'Why not? Why don't you do just that?' And she kissed him, astonishingly, on the lips.

'Sometime,' he said, 'I'd like to see those letters from Hart.'

'Sure. I'll drop them into your hotel first thing.'

But she did not drop the letters in and it was not until sometime later he saw them, bearing out very much of what Lisa had said. He left for New York and a couple of days later flew back to Heathrow where Harriet picked him up. He'd taken a night flight, and now it was early morning, and there was snow, thin enough to have melted off the road which wound after they left the built-up area, black and shiny between white hills and dark woods. That bleak morning the vistas and valleys rode past looking as though they belonged to a more spacious country. The hard little sun was so low it seemed to wander from one hill to the next as the road twisted and turned, the sun now behind them, now just tagging along at one side, now ahead, like some orange on the loose. By the time they reached Aylesbury he'd told Harriet pretty well what Lisa had told him.

Harriet was driving. At the next lay-by she stopped and said, 'It's no good. It's one of the most awful things I've ever heard. Poor Shirley. You take over.'

They sat there in silence for some time, the car sprayed with slush from time to time as some truck thundered past.

'Tell you what, though,' said Harriet. 'That girl seems to have fascinated you, all right.' Almost as though Harriet wanted to cheer herself up.

'Lisa?'

'Yes. You seemed all caught up with her.'

'I didn't get much sleep on the flight. I'm tired.'

'Darling, I'm not reproaching you. She sounds absolutely cute.'

'No, she's not cute.' He thought about this. 'That isn't the way she is at all.'

Harriet began laughing, not what you'd expect in the circumstances but she laughed easily. It was one of her ways of invoking common sense. 'No, what I should have said was I think *you're* sweet. This girl has done something to you. I know from the way you talk and I think it's just sweet. There comes a time in a man's life when he needs something like that. A shot in the arm.'

'And in a woman's?'

'Oh, sure. We like shots too.'

Then, in an abrupt change from the teasing, she said, 'Oh, that poor little girl. Poor Jo without a mother. Are you going to write to him?'

After hesitation. 'Yes.'

'You may find the story is a fake. Lisa might be a fantasist. All part of the act to enthral you.'

'No chance. She had her boyfriend with her. He paid for the meal.' So *that* still rankled.

Harriet had a much closer relationship with Shirley than Ed had with Hart and, in her impatience, she did not wait for any reply he might send. She got on to her brother Tom who had a job in the Foreign and Commonwealth Office to ask whether he had a chum in the Nairobi High Commissioner's who could unofficially brief them on what had happened. She imagined that the British community in Kenya wasn't all that great and the circumstances of the sudden death of a woman who was still young would be widely known. This, quite apart from the fact that her death would be registered at the Consulate.

Tom's wife, Meg, rang up (Harriet had written to her brother's home address) saying he was away in Singapore, attending the Commonwealth Prime Ministers' Conference and as she had recognized Harriet's writing on the envelope she had taken the liberty of opening it. He would not be home for a couple of weeks, perhaps longer if he came via East Africa. Could the query wait? She did not feel she knew any of Tom's colleagues well enough to approach one of them. She would not be surprised, though, if Tom made contact from East Africa and he'd be right on the spot, wouldn't he, to find things out for himself. Meg had a way of chattering on, long after the main point had been made. 'What with the ruckus out there I don't think he'll have too much time for incidentals. I say, Hattie. You do make it sound very mysterious. What happened?'

'That's just what we're trying to find out. What do you mean, ruckus?'

'This takeover in Uganda. Tom's supposed to be an East Europe specialist but he gets more and more caught up in African affairs, I don't know why. And do you know what I think? The UK should cut its losses in Africa or the place will drain us. I know what'll happen. It'll end up with Tom being posted to one of these bloody places for years. And how am I going to like sweating it out in Zaire?'

The takeover in Uganda had been headline news for days. The President of Uganda, Milton Obote, had gone off to the Singapore conference leaving word that on his return he would be investigating a financial scandal that had been brought to his attention. The occasion of his absence was seized by a certain General Amin, a prime suspect in the financial scandal, to organize a *coup d'état*. The army had taken over in Kampala but fighting was still going on elsewhere in the country.

Amin was firmly in control some weeks later when Hart wrote, confirming that Shirley had died unexpectedly. He thanked them very much for their condolences. He was quite devastated but now that his friend Amin was running Uganda he saw a way out of his financial difficulties by taking a job with him. Amin was all right at heart but simple and he would need all the white expertise he could get. They were old comrades-in-arms. Hart would throw himself into the job and bury his miseries. Amin had once saved his life when they'd both been in the KARs fighting the Mau Mau and now was the chance to show his gratitude. If blacks had to run East Africa there were worse types who'd been to college and got above themselves. Amin had a modest background and would always know his place *vis-à-vis* Europeans. The first thing he'd advise Amin to do was visit the UK and show himself to be the brave, reasonable, moderate and rather jolly man Hart knew him to be from personal experience. Not like Obote, who was a bloody socialist. Hart's imagination ran wildly ahead. If Amin did come to England he would come with him. He would be Amin's political adviser. In all this there was no mention of Jo, nor for that matter of the hauntings and the blessing of the house.

Harriet's brother arrived home some time in February, pulled the appropriate strings and in due course was able to produce two cuttings from the *Nairobi Messenger*.

FATAL COLLAPSE AT ISOLATED FARM

A woman suddenly collapsed at the family home near Limuru yesterday and was found to be dead on arrival at the hospital in Nairobi. She was Mrs Shirley Hart, wife of Aston Hart, a member of the well-known settler family. Father Curtis, the

43

Roman Catholic priest-in-charge at Limuru who was visiting the isolated Hart residence, administered the last rites to Mrs Hart in the ambulance. It was in this same house that Mr Hart's parents, Major Rodney Hart and his wife Rachel, were murdered during the Mau Mau emergency eighteen years ago. Mrs Hart leaves a daughter, Joanna.

STRANGE HAPPENINGS OFF THE LIMURU ROAD

At the inquest on Mrs Shirley Hart, who collapsed and died last Wednesday, it was revealed that her home near Limuru was being ceremoniously blessed at the time. Father James Curtis said that, at the request of Mrs Hart's husband, Mr Aston Hart, he had blessed each room. He emphasized that he was in no way carrying out an exorcism but agreed that the family had complained of strange happenings in the house. Mr Hart said there had been certain manifestations. On an earlier occasion he had employed a witch doctor to 'clean the place up. But his spells didn't work'. After medical evidence had been given a verdict of death from natural causes was returned.

And that, apparently, was the extent of the press interest. Either there were more important stories claiming the space or hauntings that led to the calling in of witch doctors and priests were such a commonplace in Kenya no one would think there was cause for further investigation.

No reply came from Hart to the letter Ed wrote him, prompted by Harriet, to ask about Jo.

The Parslers threw a party one summer evening with lots of chairs out on the grass and under the trees. The Ritters came, so did the Cornishes (Hugh Cornish all those years ago had been Ed's tutor before Ed switched to law and, now retired, was living locally), Jerry Clutsam and his wife (he was a paediatrician at the Otmoor General Hospital who'd been called in to advise on Mark's ailments) and the Budgens. Guy Budgen was Master of the local hunt and Ed had been cultivating him for some time. Harriet's brother Tom and his wife drove over from Great Missenden.

Hugh Cornish pushed the conversation along with all the vigour of the newly retired. Being lazy he hadn't published anything for years. This irked. He had to prove he was as lively as ever, by no means finished, even though he was officially retired. He was ready for an argument, a row even, if that became necessary. Clutsam was a South African, he found out, and this made Hugh wonder why so many professional people of British stock took the easier line of leaving that country rather than staying to try and change the appalling apartheid system.

'Mind you,' Hugh said, 'I'm in no position to speak. I've had invitations to go and lecture in South Africa but I said no, I didn't want any truck with the country. I can see that's wrong now. I ought to have gone and spoken my mind.'

Clutsam was a tall, genial man with fuzzed red hair, not only in the usual place but on his cheek bones. For some reason he had decided against a moustache or beard, so his face appeared unclothed from his cheeks down. He looked a bit of a clown but was not.

'Yes, you ought to have gone, Mr Cornish, I reckon. But you'd find you weren't the only one speaking his mind.'

'I hear they've started extracting oil from coal now.'

'Yes, oil is where the Union's vulnerable. But there are still a lot of countries ready to sell. A lot of oil slopping about.'

'It will all end in some kind of mayhem.'

'I hope not, naturally.'

Tom came over and put on some Foreign Office protective camouflage. His manner implied that he had no idea what was going on in the world but was eager to learn.

'Coal from oil? That's cunning. Have to squeeze it hard, I should think. Talk about blood from a stone!'

Hugh Cornish broke in to address Jerry. 'When you say I'd find I wasn't the only one speaking his mind what do you mean, exactly? Do you mean I'd find myself locked in debate with members of the Brudersbund? Or whatever Boer fascists are called.'

'Could happen.' Jerry looked at Hugh as though for symptoms of some malady over the tops of spectacles that he was not, in fact, wearing. 'The kind of people you'd meet, though, they'd be much more likely to take the other point of view. It's still a remarkably free country, you know, in spite of everything. For the whites, that is. Not the others. Could be worse, remembering the circumstances. Anyone who believes there's a problem that could be cleared up by votes for all, banning discrimination, that sort of thing, he isn't really measuring up to it. But yes, it's hell.'

'You accept hell?'

Jerry began to laugh. 'I can't remember who said, "The universe!" All right, I accept it.'

'A woman,' said Hugh. 'A silly woman. "I accept the universe." Who she was, God knows. "She'd better!" somebody said. Carlyle, I think. That's different. You don't really mean accept South Africa as it is at present?'

'That woman may have been silly.' Jerry paused and looked at his glass of white wine. 'But I know what she meant. Accepting the bad because you can't do anything about it.'

'To hell with that,' said Hugh, 'I don't buy that sort of talk.'

'Any news of your Kenyan friend,' Tom asked Ed, obviously trying to break up a possible row with what he thought was a reasonably relevant sidetrack.

'Aston Hart? No. Major Ritter over there is his tenant. Maybe he's got news.'

No, Ritter had no news at all and then Tom, rather remarkably, launched into some calculated indiscretions. He said that East Africa was a headache and he was beginning to regret he had ignored his father's advice not to go into the Foreign Office but take up plumbing or cabinet making. That was where in the later part of the twentieth century prestige and money really lay. Particularly money. Possibly prestige.

Ed revealed that Aston Hart had gone into Uganda to take a job under his old friend Amin.

'Amin? You don't mean that?'

'What's wrong then?'

Tom hesitated. 'What sort of a chap is he? Hart, I mean.'

'Scarcely know him, really. Amiable in a sort of way. Bit of a throwback. I don't think he could ever come to terms with African nationalism.'

'Then what's he doing taking a job under Amin?'

'They were in the army together.'

'Must have been Mau Mau time.' Tom was muttering to himself rather than talking to the rest of us. 'How old is he?'

'Getting on for forty.'

'So he's had military training. I can see Amin using a man like that. What for? You may well ask. It's pretty common knowledge Amin wants to slice off the top of Tanzania and get access to the sea. He wants the port of Tanga. He wants a Tanga corridor. I mean,' Tom began to laugh. 'You've got to hand it to him. An adventure like that might be a way of uniting the country behind him. Bloody dangerous, though.'

'You think Hart might be in on this?'

'Is he the sort?'

The answer was yes, Hart might want to lose himself in a military strike no matter how unprincipled it was. After the death of Shirley he might well look for a violent and irrational way of hitting back at life.

That summer the ground was baked hard by week after week of hot sun and it was possible to dance on the lawn as you might dance on hard boards. From the record-player in the sitting room Mark was feeding rock music into a loudspeaker he and Jessica had lodged in a tree and soon they and some other kids, the Lowther twins from Brill, were prancing about. Guy Budgen was out there too, Rocking Round the Clock on his own, like a dervish. Hugh declared that if only there had been dancing like this in his youth he would have been among the wildest. Why had he been born so early? Life was something he'd missed out on. He used Americanisms like this under the impression they would annoy. Other couples were joining in, with Jessica's Jack Russell terrier dashing about and barking at them in great excitement.

Jerry Clutsam had caught Harriet by the hand and drawn her out of her chair in an elegant movement more appropriate as introduction to an old-fashioned waltz than the almost gymnastic abandon of the free-for-all they began to work up. Jerry was wearing fairly tight white trousers. He looked almost insectlike, waving his immensely long legs about in a predatory, voluptuous and oddly threatening manner. Harriet was enjoying herself no end. She loved dancing. She was never more herself, she used to say, than when she was dancing. Her legs were so beautiful one of her friends in advertising had once talked her into using them to sell stockings; for months photographs of Harriet's legs were in the colour supplements. She was showing a great deal of them now. Jerry had his arm round her and

47

when she spun away, still holding hands, to the extent of their two arms, her loose cotton dress rose thigh-high.

Jerry's wife, Olwen, came out of the house where presumably she'd been to the loo to ask Ed, 'You seen Jerry, then?' She was Welsh, on the plump side and with black hair cut close. At last seeing what was going on she gasped, 'Oh, he's with your *wife!*' as though her worst fears had been realized. '*Again!*' was the unspoken word. 'Oh, look at them dancing! I've never seen anything like it!'

Ed thought he'd better ask her to dance but she said no, she wasn't going to make an exhibition of herself, so he danced with Tom's wife, Meg, both bad dancers who could think of nothing more inventive than placing their hands on the other's shoulders and doing a kind of Charleston. Harriet's laughter – shrieks rather – let everyone know she was having one hell of a good time. Olwen was certainly hearing her and having a bad time.

The courtship display by Jerry and Harriet was disturbing but for some, Ed included, it was exciting. She was enjoying herself and he enjoyed himself too. Times like this old words take on a new life. Ed was thinking of the marriage service where a man and his wife are declared one flesh. That is how they were dancing, as one flesh, with different partners, that hot summer evening with the sweat shining on them in the almost African sun.

4

Whether as a result of Hart's suggestion or not, Amin, having first visited Israel, arrived in London to see the Prime Minister, then Ted Heath, and lunch in Buckingham Palace where (according to the press) he greeted the Duke of Edinburgh as Mr Philip. Aston Hart did not accompany him, so either he had not got the job he had hoped for or had been left behind in Kampala to do something more important. Harriet suggested it might be to make sure nobody pulled the rug from under Amin as Amin had done for Milton Obote. Ed began to wonder whether this really was Amin's first visit to England. He could have been Sam, Hart's African guest at Wood End all those years ago, who made such an impression on Ed that long after he had left the country the black clusters of the plump and shiny fruit of the elder bush conjured up his presence. Tom thought Amin was too comical to be worried about. He was a big, chubby, very black and shiny figure of fun, who was photographed looking jolly in his Scottish glengarry. He wore splendid bemedalled military uniforms and sported Israeli Air Force wings. Even when he took against Israel he still sported those wings which shows how clueless he was. He was out of his depth in international politics, but what could you expect? Perhaps, too, he was not particularly bright but the whites who knew him best (Tom said), the British officers of the old King's African Rifles, thought he was a splendid chap. Our friend, Aston Hart, was one of these. Otherwise why would he go and work for him? The great thing was Amin had this marvellous sense of humour. You could ask Big Daddy if he ate people and he'd be delighted with the question. He'd wobble with laughter.

All that worried Tom was whether too many of these ex-KAR officers would be masterminding Amin's invasion of Tanzania, if it ever came off. Not good for Commonwealth relations.

Oddly enough, the first person the Parslers ever heard attacking Amin was Lisa when in due course, the late spring in

1973 it must have been, she came over on her honeymoon. Yes, she married her George and they decided to take a short trip to England, short because she was not giving up her job in the State Department and the honeymoon had to be fitted into her annual holiday. George could please himself. He was big in the chemical industry and could take what holidays he liked. They were lent a car by one of George's business associates in London. Being George, it was not even a Mercedes or a Jaguar but a Rolls which, he thought, was the only possible automobile in which to negotiate the bumpy British roads, no doubt unpaved in some areas. You needed an automobile with good springs and enough power to climb out of a ditch if it slid into one, as it would, the terrain being what it is. He kept on saying he was in England – in which he located Scotland – for the first time. The Pomeroys, as they now had to be thought of, Lisa and George Pomeroy, made straight for the Highlands and then they made their way south, through the Yorkshire Dales and the Dukeries to Stratford-upon-Avon where they stayed at the Welcombe for a few days so that Lisa could project herself into the Shakespearian past; the birthplace, Anne Hathaway's Cottage, the stile with the falling bar where the Bard was caught poaching deer, and, of course, the tomb. Then, since they were only just down the road they dropped in on the Parslers.

She was still the same Lisa, very happy, but a bit dimmed by marriage, slightly coarsened, no doubt a natural consequence of marrying George. She had two sherries and looked flushed when they all went into the garden to look at the daffodils and lilacs.

Out of politeness Ed asked after her parents. 'You know Pop died? Oh, yes. Cancer. Too bad for Mommie. First Hans then Pop.'

'I'm very sorry.'

Lisa brushed this aside.

'Isn't that just incredible,' she said, waving a hand at the house. 'It doesn't look as though it was built. It just grew up out of the stone. It's living. Is Wood End far from here?'

'Over there! Not far. If you went up to the top of the field you could see it from the stile, just about. You can't see it later on when the trees are fully out.'

'Do you think we could drive over?'

'The Ritters would love to show you round, I'm sure.'

Over lunch they talked for a while about Aston Hart, Lisa saying she'd heard nothing from him since he had told her about Shirley's death and she would not have known he was working in Uganda if Ed hadn't passed the news on. 'That can't last, surely, that job.'

George broke in and began talking about East Africa in a way that showed he had been reading the subject up, perhaps out of pique at the way Lisa took an interest in this Englishman who lived out there. George had to show he was well informed on a wide range of important matters. If Kenya or Uganda came up in conversation, as they did now, he wanted to be in a position to correct Lisa on some point. And not only of fact.

'Lisa and I don't see eye to eye on this but I can understand Amin wanting to get rid of the Asians. Shit, they run the country! And they don't belong there. Well, perhaps they don't run the country but they run the commercial side. Four out of five businesses are Asian. So Amin wanting them out and getting the economy back in the hands of black Ugandans, that isn't unreasonable.' He turned to Ed. 'You British have a responsibility there. These Asians are British.'

'They've no other home, George.' Lisa had heard all this.

'They're the Jews of East Africa.'

At this Lisa tore into him. George could not possibly have made this remark in her presence before or he would have hesitated to repeat it. She said it was anti-Semitic.

'Oh, come off it, Lisa. These Asians are good operators. It's a compliment to say they are the Jews of East Africa. An Asian wouldn't score what I said. Neither would a Jew. So why should you?'

A honeymoon row is not all that uncommon but it was embarrassing for the Parslers to be in on one. Lisa sat upright and stiff, looking straight at George who was sitting opposite and had eyes only for his lamb chop. 'I think it's terrible, and too god-awful to make generalizations about people, particularly the Jews. You know what Amin said in that cable to the UN last fall. Hitler was right about the Jews. Can you imagine anything more obscene?'

That is what it was all about. She was at odds with her parents. Lisa probably would not have remembered her father making that very same remark all those years ago but she would have known what her father's views were, her mother's too. They were the sort who talked about Germany and the past. Through her family Lisa felt implicated in what the Nazis had done.

'Sure, Lisa, that's real awful but don't get at me. I like Jews. My own grandmother was one.'

'It isn't enough just to like them you've got to be *for* them. I'm a Zionist. There was a time I seriously thought of going to Israel to live if they'd have me. I want Israel to flourish and get bigger. Things don't stand still. Either Israel gets bigger and stronger or it goes under, so Eretz Israel is all right by me. I'm cheering for it. They're entitled to Samaria and wherever else they once were, the Jews, *Yes, sir!*'

If George had been sensible he would have kept his mouth shut but he had picked every scrap of meat off his lamb chop, left the bone, a cog with three big teeth, and was now able to lift his head and see the expression on Lisa's face. 'Aw, now! The Arabs wouldn't swallow that. The Arabs have rights too, honey, don't you think?' He called them ay-rabs. 'The way you talk anyone couldn't even mention Jews. It wouldn't be okay at all, Eretz Israel.'

George clearly did not know who this girl was he had married. There were other defects too, as emerged later, but this set-to over the lunch at Troy Corner was when the marriage really began to crumble. Lisa was not eating. 'Okay I can see what Amin's got his mind on when he says Hitler was right and you say the Asians are the Jews of East Africa. If you say it other people must say it too and, for sure, it must have occurred to Amin.'

Harriet was so concerned that she put out a hand and rested it on one of Lisa's. Lisa looked at her. A smile flashed and then was gone. 'It makes one's stomach turn, just to think of Aston Hart working for a man like Amin.'

George crumpled his napkin. 'Another thing! That man's name gives me a pain in the arse. Sorry, Harriet! Sorry Ed! We must give the impression we're screwing it all up. But no, sir!

Everything's okay. We're on our honeymoon and naturally things get hyped. Let's change the subject. Lisa tells me you write poetry, Ed. How's it going then?'

Since meeting Lisa again in Washington Ed had started writing again. The Hans block just melted away. It was something to do with not only electing Lisa to be his latest muse but with Shirley's death. He had a volume coming out in the autumn and said so, as a way of getting out of this god-awful row. They were in a wax not just about Amin and Aston Hart. The marriage was moving into that phase when they were just looking for something to snarl about. Or Lisa was, anyway.

George wanted to know what the book was called.

'*Signals*.'

'Sweetie,' said George to Lisa, 'this solves our Christmas present problem. We'll buy a hundred copies and get Ed to sign them. What do you think of that? Ed, it's your year. 1973 is the year of Ed – ' He paused, having forgotten the name.

'Parsler.' Harriet was ready to help him out. Nobody else was.

George raised his glass. '1973, the year of *Signals* and Ed Parsler. May God bless him and all who sail in him!' He had drunk a few sherries and a couple of glasses of Santerre. He behaved as though he had taken much more than that on board and he put his hand on Ed's knee. 'You're cute. And you write poetry too. It isn't fair. The guys I've known who were cute and just nothing at all, not beyond that.'

Harriet was enjoying herself. Inwardly she was purring. The entire conversation, every nuance, every detail of behaviour – the way George held his fork in the right hand, for example – was stacked into her memory and would, at appropriate moments in the future, be retrieved. Ed's response to Lisa, the way he looked at her, what he said to her, was what Harriet would regard as particularly sensitive information. She could not see in Lisa what Ed did but this did not mean she didn't want to try.

Harriet took to George, though. She thought he was a beast and quite understood why Lisa had married him. There were some women, she said, who if sufficiently repelled by a man found him irresistible.

'No, I mean it.' The Parslers were talking after the Pomeroys

53

had left. 'George really has something, and I don't mean money. He looks menacing and he is, too. Didn't you feel those vibrations? He's a bit scary.'

'Lisa didn't sound scared of him.'

'Don't you believe it. She's scared to hell. She was just ratcheting him up to make him even more scary and sexy. I'm starry-eyed about him. He's a queer too, you know that?'

They had tried ringing Wood End but there was no reply. That night Ed worked late and the phone rang just before midnight. It was George to say how much Lisa and he had enjoyed visiting with them. They'd been to the theatre and seen a performance of *Taming of the Shrew*. 'Ed, you've no idea. It was like Lisa and me all over again. Say, did we laugh! Anyway, what I phoned for was to say I contacted Drew Ritter. I just rang him, they'd been in town, and I fixed it we'd go over tomorrow. It's Sunday. So they'll be around. That okay?'

'Sure.'

'It's our only chance. We're flying back on Tuesday.'

Lisa took the phone from him and said 'Ed, it's been a great day and I *love* Harriet', before she cradled it.

Sunday morning was bright, windless, cold. As usual Ed had been to eight o'clock communion. But not Harriet. She did not like the Rector. The loose gravel of the drive was frozen so it crunched the more loudly when the Pomeroy Rolls glided in and Lisa wearing what looked like a fur balaclava helmet and an expensive fur coat stepped out. George smoking a cigar, waved but stayed where he was behind the wheel. He began shouting, the cigar still in his mouth.

'Let's make a day of it. We thought we'd collect the Parslers, then stop off at Wood End to pick up the Ritters and all go off to the Waterside Inn at Bray for lunch. You know that place has two stars and two crowns in Egon Ronay? Now this is *our* treat. You've got to let it be that way because, hell, it's our honeymoon, ain't it, and folk are allowed to do what they like on a honeymoon.' George assumed he could drive round shovelling up lunch guests.

'Ed,' said Lisa, 'know what? You're the most romantic-looking sort of Englishman. You know that? Dark and tall and sort of emaciated with brown eyes.'

'Like John the Baptist,' George removed his cigar and called out, just to show he had heard.

'George is just crazy about Rodin,' said Lisa. 'We've got a full size replica of his John the Baptist in resin, and George is right, you know. Say, you ought to be in loin cloth and sandals.'

Ed was wearing wellingtons, a blue turtleneck jersey and hadn't shaved that morning. Harriet, who had changed into dungarees and gardening boots, came out and said they just planned to muck out the stables. It had not occurred to the Parslers they were even in on the Wood End visit. Lisa went on enthusing, though. It was hot in that Rolls (George was in his shirt sleeves) and in her furs she was just sweating. This bubbling fun at Ed's expense was brought on by the shock of the cold air.

'Ed – oh, excuse me, Harriet! – you're so fabulous you must have forgotten more romantic attachments than most men ever actually get involved in. As a special treat for the rest of us you can tell us about them at Bray. Well, not all of them. Just the first. That's always the most exciting.'

Harriet said it would be a treat not only for her but for the people at the next table too. 'But I'm sorry we can't come. It's sweet of you to ask us to Bray but you know how it is. We've put in some hard work getting in the mood to muck out and we can't waste it. Besides I've got to get the kids their lunch.'

'Bring them along too.'

'I'm not having them acquire a taste for expensive food.'

'C'mon, break the mould for once.'

Harriet would have none of it. When Ed tried to give instructions how to get to Wood End George said they sounded like complicated clues that had to be solved before the buried treasure could be found. He'd never find the place and would end up in some farm yard. So Ed agreed to be navigator, changed out of the wellingtons, and climbed into the back seat. As they crunched out he could see Harriet waving and shouting but it was too late to respond and George took the Rolls down the narrow lane as though it was a balloon and would go pop in any brush with the hedge. Then Ed realized Harriet was asking how he would get back.

It was well up in the eighties in that car and thick with cigar smoke. The sun added to the bemusement. They drove straight into it and the light bounced off the wet track and beamed into their eyes like a searchlight. The glare was painful. It switched off and on as they drifted round corners, up and down hills; George turned the car radio on and they might have been in a disco, the rock beating away and the lights flashing. Lisa turned and began questioning Ed again in the same mocking, laughing, way about his 'romantic attachment' (extraordinary to use this old-fashioned expression). She had to shout to make herself heard.

'When I was a kid,' Ed shouted back, 'I met a girl on holiday. After the holiday we wrote. I was besotted. Then she invited me to her home for a week and, do you know, when I was there she absolutely ignored me. Her parents took pity on me and we used to go off on walks. But Sally stayed at home. Or she went shopping. Or maybe she went out with some other guy. Anyway, not with me. At the end of the week I went home. Rigid. Angry. Humiliated.'

'Then what happened?'

'Nothing. I never saw her again. Who the hell did she think she was? Funny I never asked why she snubbed me. I never even made a pass.'

'That's why,' said George, with obvious pleasure and no sympathy.

'That's hilarious,' Lisa yelled. 'It's arousing. You know, it's terribly erotic.'

'For Chrissake!' George's cigar scattered ash as it waggled between his teeth. 'What's erotic about that? The guy was dumb, that's all. You know what, some guys have no sex drive. Now me, I was the sexiest teenager in town and everyone knew it. Played every ball pitched. And I did some pitching too, I tell ya.'

Lisa said she thought men with control were arousing and erotic so far as she was concerned.

'The guy had nothing to control. Let's face it, honey. One of nature's eunuchs.'

As if Ed was miles away. The shouting, the heat and the sun dazzle made the five-minute trip in that psychedelic capsule a whole odyssey.

'Look at that!' Lisa said as they drew up in front of Wood End. 'Just like a postcard.'

56

Stepping out into the cold air was rather like taking the first gin and tonic of the day. The front door opened immediately so Harriet had probably phoned ahead and there was Ritter in a Harris tweed jacket and a Russian fur hat. George did not need any introductions. He was there already with his hand stretched out, saying, 'Hi there, Drew!' and Drew was hi-ing back and they were giving those great laughs and slaps which American extroverts go in for.

Lisa stood there, taking the house in. 'Look at that chimney. All those bricks in all those shapes and patterns! And the moss on the tiles! Don't you just feel it's all just Time made Visible.' She used the language of the ad-man without embarrassment.

Mrs Ritter, a plump and severe lady in canary yellow jodhpurs, was waiting in the hall, saying that everyone was to call her Dawn which wasn't her real first name, that being Eleanor, but it was the one she felt most at home with.

'Dawn,' said George. 'That's a really lovely name.'

'About this house,' said Dawn. 'We have to dress like this because there's no central heating or double glazing. We've got these night storage heaters but they've pooped out. We've got this log fire going and another in the parlour. But I've told Drew I can't take it much longer. It's damp, it's falling down, there are rats in the barn, the wind whistles through everywhere like it was some sort of Walt Disney spooky castle. But it's not a castle, no way, it's a dump and I can't wait to get out. Have some coffee.'

While Dawn showed the Pomeroys over the house Drew Ritter and Ed stood in the hall, which was a kind of sitting room with chintz-covered furniture, antlers and a fox's mask on the wall, warming themselves at the logs burning on a bed of white ash in the great open fireplace. They talked about the latest hunt scandal. A young fallow deer had managed to escape from Barton Park, which had a wall round it and rails over a shallow pit at each gate, so how it got out was a mystery. As bad luck had it the hounds were searching, came across the fawn unexpectedly and pulled it down. Jack Price, the huntsman, was helpless. This meant the hounds were undisciplined and that was a bad mark against him. The Earl of Garsington, who lived at the Park, was furious when he heard of the mishap, said it had happened once before in his father's time, and twice was too much. He wanted the whole pack of hounds put down. Which was absurd. Garsington was anti-blood sports. That was the root of the matter, said Drew, and the bastard had deliberately let this fawn escape, just when he knew the hunt was out. How else did you explain what happened? He wanted us in court. That wasn't the worrying thing. Jack Price couldn't control the hounds, that reflected on Guy Budgen, the MFH himself, and maybe we wanted a few changes. The hunt needed bringing into the twentieth century.

Dawn came down and said 'God knows why but Lisa wants to get up into the roof and is there a ladder?'

'Up in the roof?'

'Yeah! There's a trapdoor and Lisa wants up and through it.'

'What the heck for?'

Lisa shouted down. 'This is the most thrilling place I've ever been in. *Please* get a ladder.'

They had a conference scattered around on the stairs and first landing.

'Dawn and Drew. Have you Ritters been up in that roof space? Tell me that,' Lisa was really bubbling.

'Why should we? There's only the cold water tank up there and that's about the one thing that hasn't given trouble so far.'

'Do you realize,' said Lisa, 'that when they got up into the roof of Shakespeare's birthplace in Stratford-upon-Avon they found the will of Shakespeare's father stuck between the rafters and the tiling? This, Wood End, was George Hart's house, gifted to him by Shakespeare's granddaughter, Lady Barnard, and I just know George would have stuffed odd books and papers up there. Just to be out of the way. Think what might be there! Manuscripts! Notebooks! Letters!' Lisa was shrieking with excitement. 'The holograph of Hamlet, all the alterations, speeches hatched out. And bits added. I've had a vision. I can just see it all. Can't you see there's a sort of light leaking out of that trapdoor? It's all holy up there.'

'I sometimes think that this girl married me', said George, 'because my name was George.'

The Ritters had not heard of the supposed Shakespeare connection with Wood End and Drew was so impressed he went off and found a stepladder. Lisa said she wanted an electric torch too and was up the ladder and pressing at the trapdoor with the heels of her hands before Dawn had pulled herself together and said if it was all so holy and so much light up there how come she wanted a torch?

'You can't do it, Lisa.' George began to plead with her. 'You'll have to walk about just on joists. If you put a foot wrong you'll come through the ceiling. Bound to be mice and birds and God knows what!'

'Sure there are mice,' said Dawn. 'And bats, I guess.'

Lisa lifted the trapdoor, shoved it to one side and hoisted herself up into the roof space, holding the torch, which Drew had provided in one hand, and saying, 'I don't care if there's a dragon.'

'Lisa! Come down, for God's sake.' George was so upset he might have had a phobia about roof spaces. A trauma he'd have called it. Perhaps he had a thing about bats.

'Gee! It's a forest!' Lisa was up in the roof space, flashing her torch around. 'Beams going up like a forest. Come on up here, why don't you?'

No one else made a move so Ed thought he'd go up and join Lisa. It was black. She used the torch to show him where he could put his feet and, as they stood there, among the beams and dust and what looked like piles of sacking, what chiefly struck was the cold. Lisa shivered. A bitter day like this a roof space would be cold, wouldn't it, but the same thought occurred to both of them.

'This is special cold. It's what Aston felt in that house in Kenya.'

Normally, a tiled roof like this is boarded or at least made weatherproof with felt or something, anyway more than just the tiles; but here there were just tiles with daylight between some of them. Planks were thrown here and there over the joists. A couple of cladded tanks stood on stilts but the pipes running to and from them were not insulated, so the Ritters had been lucky there had been no bursts. Lisa plonked about on her wedge shoes as though she was playing hunt the thimble. Occasionally the beam of her torch picked out a mummified bird. But there was no chest stuffed with papers, no roll of parchment tucked in the angle of two beams. She would not have given up but the cold defeated her and she might have fallen down the steps if Ed hadn't managed to grab her.

'It wasn't really a proper will they found at the birthplace.' Back in the hall Lisa lectured once she had warmed herself at the fire. 'It was a Roman Catholic spiritual testament. There were lots of them around, I guess, at one time. They all had the same form of words but this one was signed John Shakespeare. And now it's lost again. Don't you call that very annoying?'

'What's so hot about Shakespeare anyway?' Dawn thought about her own question. 'If you made a find you could sell it to some museum, yeah, or one of those rich collectors.'

'I just wouldn't give it up if I were you.' Lisa spoke as though the Ritters, not she, had suggested going up into the roof space and were now in need of encouragement.

George was trying to persuade the Ritters to join them for lunch at Bray but they had their excuses and while the argument raged Lisa and Ed went into the little sitting room to look at the view down the valley. It seemed incredible to him that if she wanted a Shakespeare relic the house had not produced one. She was a muse who fired the imagination and to the point joy seemed the natural state of mankind. 'If it would apprehend some joy, It comprehends some bringer of that joy.' Lisa was a bringer of joy and a muse like her was entitled to tribute. So Ed thought. No matter if the tradition that Lady Barnard gave Wood End to her cousin George Hart was quite bogus.

'It was wrong what I said about the cold in the roof. It isn't like the cold Aston felt at all. It was just ordinary cold. You feel that, don't you, Ed? This is a magic sort of house. A good house.'

'If you say so.' He hesitated. 'I mean, if you are saying a thing is that way I just accept it. You could brainwash me into anything.'

Those genuinely astonished, even startled, wide blue eyes now turned upon him. They became, ever afterwards, unforgettable, inescapable. They could flash upon him at any time, in any place.

'Your life could have been different if you'd said something like that to your teenager girl-friend, wouldn't it?' Then came her tears of laughter.

Eventually George drove her off to Bray and Dawn, finally abandoning all effort to restrain her amazement, burst out, 'You ever know anybody invite herself to look over your house and then climb up in your roof space? That's rape, sort of. Know what I think? It's lust after dead men and that's what the shrinks call necrophilia. I guess her analyst put her up to this climbing into people's roof spaces, it's so Freudian I can't bear it, like she can get this morbid fascination with the dead out of the system.' She looked at her husband. 'Just like Drew here. He had hang-ups. Did he have hang-ups? Yes, by Jeez! So his analyst put him on to fishing for sharks and now we're in this place, hunting. So he chases foxes instead of tarts.'

Drew drove Ed home. 'It just isn't true what Dawn said, but then she doesn't know what she does say half the time.' He sighed. 'I don't have any analyst but Dawn thinks I need one, just for the status. I'm okay. I just *like* hunting.'

To prove it, he was on to the subject of hunt discipline and whether anything could really be achieved without getting rid of the present set-up. 'But who would take over? I'd offer myself but I'll be posted to Vietnam, anyway, to some combat station.'

With the sun behind them they could see cow parsley floating its lace against the new green nettles and the pale spires of lords-and-ladies; yes, and violets. Drew drove slowly because of the narrow lane so the wildflowers came up slowly too. The violets were the very colour of those eyes, brimming and bright from the thawed out frost (the imagination took over now, because you couldn't see that amount of detail from the car), Lisa's eyes, overflowing with laughter.

5

Ed came home one summer evening to be told by Harriet that Kim Suttle, the estate agent in Bicester, had been on the telephone to ask how they'd like the money.

'What money?'

'You may well ask. He says he's had instructions from Aston Hart in Kampala to pay us £100 on the first day of each calendar month. It would be out of the rent from Wood End. I must say Kim sounded a bit incredulous. He wanted to know whether you'd like a cheque or whether he could arrange a transfer into our banking account. This is what he'd like, he said. Reduce the paperwork.'

If Hart was organizing a fiddle of some sort the Parslers wanted to know just what it was before joining in. So Harriet phoned Kim and told him to hold the money for the time being. No move to be made until they heard from Aston Hart themselves. Nothing happened for some considerable time. Not surprising when you remember Hart was in a country where, according to the *Guardian*, Amin's killer squads were out eliminating prominent people and tribesmen, supposedly hostile to his regime. And then a telex arrived in the office from Kampala addressed to Ed, saying, 'Parsler. Meet Jo Heathrow 12 July stop Hart rpt 12 rpt.' The telex had originated in the office of the firm's representatives in Kampala, James Freebond Associates. Clever of Hart to find the cheapest way to send a quick message. Another telex arrived two hours later giving the airline and flight number.

The 12th was a Saturday so the Parslers were able to drive over to Heathrow together. The flight was due in at three in the afternoon and, while waiting in the Arrival lounge, they tried to work out how old Jo would be. Astonishing to realize she must be 8 years old. Astonishing too that Hart should, without checking, have made the calm assumption that the Parslers would be on hand to meet her. For Hart to fire blind in this way implied he was either desperate to get Jo out of Uganda or without any imagination. He needed the Parslers, so they just *had* to be available.

The passengers from Jo's flight, when they emerged from Customs, were mainly Asians pushing baggage trolleys laden with bloated, soft-sided, suitcases, other possessions tied in bundles. The women steadied the luggage with one hand and held a great shopping basket, or a child, with the other, giving out a dry biscuit aroma as they passed by as though a hot iron had only just been briskly run over their brightly coloured saris.

'Must have been given an easy passage through Customs to get through this quick,' said Harriet. Blacks, in their westerns suits came out of Customs, looking this way and that for whoever was meeting them, then waving and laughing. An elderly white woman in tweeds came out wearing a rucksack and carrying a small suitcase. But nobody who looked like Jo.

Then, there she was, a serious-looking little girl in a white cotton hat in a neatly buttoned up blue coat, carrying a doll and an attaché case. The British Airways stewardess was pushing a trolley with the rest of her luggage on it and when Ed called out, 'Is that you, Joanna?' the stewardess came over, saying, 'Are you Mr and Mrs Parsler? I really am sorry to have been such a long time. But we're short-staffed and there were things I had to do on the plane. She's been *very* good.'

'Hello, Joanna,' said Harriet, going down into a crouch so that her face was on the same level as the child's. 'Had a good flight? It's lovely to see you. Welcome to England. What's your dolly called?'

'She's not a dolly,' said Jo in a clear, deliberate, unembarrassed, even bored sort of way. 'She's a real person and her name is Miss Jackson.' As though they ought to have known. She turned to the air hostess. She spoke slowly, to make sure they understood. 'Are they Mr and Mrs Parsler?'

Ed produced his driving licence and Harriet her credit card. The air hostess said, 'I never thought there'd be any problem. Do I get you to sign for her?'

Jo asked to see the documents too. She handed them back. 'I knew you were Mr Parsler all along because Daddy said you looked like Father Curtis, only worse. He said Mrs Parsler had big lips. I knew you straightaway.' She turned to the air hostess and held out her hand. 'Goodbye, Janet. Thank you. Miss Jackson would have seen to everything. I'll take my passport now, if you don't mind.'

This precocious style was maintained throughout the whole of her stay. Miss Jackson was in charge and it was almost as though Miss Jackson, a governess type in spite of her yellow silk hair and plump pink cheeks, (a disguise to allay suspicion) was speaking *through* Jo to put the Parslers in their place. Miss Jackson was the ventriloquist and Jo was her dummy.

On the way back to Troy Corner Harriet asked if there was any message from her father. She might even have brought a letter.

'No,' said Jo. 'Daddy said if the money isn't enough he'd pay more.'

By putting together bits and pieces from Jo's talk, during the days that followed, they were able to form some picture of the life she led with her father – always on the move, from one flat or house to another in Kampala. One black nanny or Asian amah followed each other in rapid succession. Jo had, however, been going to the same school, St Hilda's Convent, for a year or so but she did not like it because 'there were too many games'. She had an aunt and cousins in Dar es Salaam, Shirley's sister and family but 'they were beastly to us and daddy said he would be beastly to them too'. A German nun called Sister Elizabeth was a particular friend but every time she came she took a pot of Marmite away with her. Marmite was hard to get; only through the High Commissioner's. There were two children, Joan and Mary Stubbs, Jo was taken to play with but the Stubbs family had gone to Kenya earlier in the year. David Lubega worked in Radio Uganda and he used to take Jo and his own two children into the studios; but Jo did not like the Lubega children because they made fun of Miss Jackson. Hart was away for long periods at a time. When he came it was always unexpectedly but he always brought a present. He did not wear uniform, just ordinary clothes. He used to say that if ever they heard shooting they were to take no notice – the nanny or amah of the day, Jo and Miss Jackson, that is – because the shooting was nothing to do with them and they would be safe provided they stayed indoors. Miss Jackson was Jo's real guardian. She played a part no servant could. She and Jo had long talks in the evening, when they were not reading, playing patience or listening to the BBC World Service.

Jessica and Mark were instructed not to question Jo about her life in Kampala. If she wanted to talk, that was fine. But they were not to show too much curiosity. In spite of her composure and apparent independence Jo was brittle inside. She reserved her real confidences for Miss Jackson and took her wherever she went, even riding when she was held in front of Jo by a strap that went round both of them. In spite of her coolness about games she loved riding (it was something she missed from her life in Kenya) and she and the kids went out every day, Jo wearing a pair of Jessica's grown-out-of jeans and riding hat. She never mentioned her mother and although Ed had telexed her father soon after she arrived, c/o James Freebond Ass., and then wrote, c/o Barclay's Bank, Kampala, there was no word from Hart and Harriet got on to her brother, Tom, to see if the Foreign and Commonwealth Office would winkle out any information. The Parslers were glad to have Jo with them and would be pleased to let her stay indefinitely but they wanted to know what to do about schooling, after the summer holidays. Jo was sure that her father would arrive as unexpectedly as he did in Kampala and take her back to Uganda.

Tom reported that Hart was no longer at the address he had registered at the Consulate. He had often been seen, in civilian clothes, in Amin's company and was last sighted with three other white men carrying Amin in a litter, a form of transport Amin enjoyed because it showed who was master. The other three men had taken Ugandan citizenship in Obote's time and the Consulate could do nothing for them. But Hart was British and they were greatly exercised about the way he was, apparently willingly and cheerfully, lending himself to Amin's glorification. That had been quite a long time ago now. As Uganda was a country where people disappeared without trace this could be worrying but the buzz came that Hart was working (nobody knew what at) down near the Tanzanian border. There were no Hart relations in England, so far as Jo knew (at least, not near ones) and as the weeks passed the feeling grew that the Parslers were the only family Jo could belong to. Fortunately

65

they had planned no summer holiday that year. Mark went off with a school party to Austria and Jessica got herself invited to a family holiday in Corfu by one of her friends, which left Jo and Miss Jackson in occupation. When they were not riding they were in their room busy writing, on A4 ruled paper, what Jo said were their True Confessions, like some Hollywood film star's confessions which they had read in a newspaper. 'Actually,' said Jo, 'they were going to be made-up confessions, and they would be mainly Miss Jackson's.'

Then suddenly two letters arrived from Uganda, one for Jo and one for the Parslers. Jo was incredulous. Daddy never wrote letters and she carried hers off to read with Miss Jackson in private in case, she said, it contained anything upsetting. The letter to the Parslers was brief.

Entebbe, Uganda, 18 Aug. '74

Dear Erica and Ted (he wrote, getting both the names wrong)
  I'm terribly grateful for the way you've taken Jo in and I'm sorry for not replying before to your Telex and to your spiffing letter. Everything is absolutely fine here too. After the odd bit of turmoil and mayhem things are planing along pretty good. The active life suits me. I'm down to 12 stone 10. Not sure what happens about school in England. Can you fix Jo up with one? Isn't there one in Bicester? Tell them to send the bill to the agents. There must be a bus or something. I'll be in touch again. Money no problem. Jo can buy what clothes she needs. I'll settle. Is a hundred a month okay? In haste.

Yours sincerely, Aston Hart

There was no sign of the envelope having been opened but the inadequacy of Hart's letter must have been due to fear it might be. Why else be so uncommunicative? There wasn't even an address they or, more important, Jo could write to.

'Let's face it,' said Harriet. 'He's stupid.'

Because of the long spell of hot, dry weather their neighbour, Arthur Crick, thought he might be able to cut his barley a couple of weeks earlier than usual. He kept about a score of horses, for hacking mainly or hunting, but he also bred for racing and was the only local farmer who regularly got about on horseback. He rode over one evening, following the footpath now completely obscured by the silvery, bewhiskered barley, and he plucked a few ears to show them. It would be a good crop though not so good as the year when he'd sold it to the brewers at a top price. He chafed an ear between thumb and forefinger. 'Good grain but it's a bit moist. Brewers pick and choose. This lot'll go for biscuit flour.' He had the combine out next day and when, the following week, Ed arrived home from Bicester station he thought, seeing the smoke from a distance, that Troy Corner itself must be on fire. But it was only Arthur burning off his stubble.

He had ploughed a firebreak about ten yards wide all around the field. The lines of fire ran like slow red and yellow breakers roughly at a right angle to the top end of the paddock, sometimes sending up tongues twice the height of a man, and then changing to black smoke that moved off in towering clouds to the north-east.

Harriet was in a rage because she had called Arthur Crick to tick him off. Stubble burning was something she was not prepared to put up with, not in fields next to Troy Corner. But Crick was out with the fire, so Harriet spoke to his wife who was rude. Ed put up a defence of stubble burning which enraged Harriet all the more. He said it was good farming. Jo and the Parsler kids had been excited by the fire. They went up to Jo's bedroom window for a better view.

'One year the wind will change and then we'll cop it. That firebreak he ploughs isn't wide enough.'

That night they woke to screaming. But was it screaming? By the time Ed was properly awake the screaming had stopped. He could tell Harriet was awake because she wasn't breathing.

'What the hell was that?' Might be a vixen but foxes didn't scream in the late summer. Well, an owl then. But there were no screech owls locally. Then they heard the screaming again and Harriet was already out of bed. 'It's one of the children. A nightmare, I expect.'

Mark was already up and standing on the landing in his pyjamas.

'That's Jo. What's she making that row for?'

They found Jo, the bedclothes thrown off, lying on her side with Miss Jackson in her arms, moaning and turning her head from side to side. It was a hot, clammy night with the moonlight like mist on the other side of the uncurtained and open window; as though someone had gone through there taking flight.

Jo had terrible back pains and when Harriet tried to examine her the child said, 'No, no', and arched her body away. Mark and Jessica were sent back to bed. For the rest of the night Harriet and Ed sat up with Jo, feeling helpless, though blessedly the stabbing pains, which had made Jo jerk and scream, abated. Harriet was even able to examine her back. Jo said the pains had been low down and indicated a spot in the hollow of her back but there was nothing to see. By the time it was light Jo was lying on her side, clutching Miss Jackson, and occasionally whimpering.

Ed had to leave before Brownlow, the local GP, called, even though Harriet had managed to persuade him to come over before morning surgery. Ed's first act in the office was to put in a call to James Freebond Associates in Kampala but it was hours coming through. By the time it did Harriet had telephoned to say Brownlow was pretty sure it was renal trouble of some kind, possibly an infection, possibly a tiny crystal had formed; he had given an analgesic and now wanted her to go to hospital for observation. Harriet resisted this. She was quite ready to take Jo into hospital for tests but not to stay, and since by this time Jo had calmed down considerably, Brownlow agreed and telephoned the paediatric wing at the Otmoor General where he was able to talk to one of the doctors who, as it happened, was making his morning round.

'I've made an appointment for you with a specialist,' Brownlow told Harriet. 'If you can get – what's her name? Joanna – there by three that would be ideal. But if not any time before five. I think she's okay to travel. You can be there in, what? twenty minutes? and you can give her another of these tablets before you go.' He was in such a tearing hurry to get back to his surgery that he would have left without telling Harriet whom she was to ask for in the paediatric wing and she had to run after him.

'Dr Clutsam,' he said. 'Jerry Clutsam. Oh! you know him? So much the better. A South African. One of the best paediatricians in the country.'

The call to Kampala came through. It was a terrible line and Ed had difficulty in making it clear to Jack Wragg (who ran

Freebond Associates) just what he wanted. No, he didn't know Aston Hart personally but maybe there was someone around the office who did. Sure, they'd try and make contact. Communication was difficult. The old club life had quite gone. You just didn't run into people over a pink gin, like in the old days.

After this conversation Ed sent Wragg a telex. 'In confirmation please ask Aston Hart to telephone me at the office here urgently. Or at my home telephone number which is 086 71 420. Regards Parsler.' What Jo's back pains signified Ed didn't know but they brought home the realization that, although she was in their care, Harriet and he had no legal status to authorize – well, if the worst came to the worst, an operation. If Hart was to remain as elusive as he had been they just had to get a written authority from him that would put them *in loco parentis*.

'Jo and I saw Jerry,' Harriet said as soon as he got home that evening, 'and he was sweet. He took us in for x-ray and he x-rayed Miss Jackson first and said that in his opinion she would respond to ice-cream treatment. Strawberry or chocolate or vanilla, it didn't matter, they were all equally effective. Then he x-rayed Jo, took blood samples and said as soon as the results were known he'd come over. There was no need to take Jo there. Isn't that good of him?'

'Did he say what he thought it might be?'

'He said he was pretty sure it wasn't anything serious. Even mild kidney trouble can cause horrible pains. But there won't be more attacks, he thinks. He's given her some pain-killers.'

Ed was silent for so long that Harriet said, 'What's the matter?'

'That window being wide open and the curtains drawn. She doesn't normally sleep like that, does she?'

'It was a hot night. She'd have opened the window for some fresh air. Maybe she wanted to look at the field.'

'I wouldn't have thought anyone used to African weather would have found it hot.'

Jo was in bed, still looking pale, but sufficiently recovered to be busy with a watercolour book, full of line drawings of flowers and animals that came up in pinks and blues and yellows when a wet brush was passed over them. She announced she was feeling 'a lot better thank you, and *quite* relaxed'. No, she had never had any nasty pains in her back like that before and she hoped she never would again. It was like being stabbed. But she insisted that what woke her up was not the pain but her own screams, rather as though that version of events was more dignified. No, she remembered nothing else, but screaming and the pain and she did not know whether she had opened the window or not. Possibly Miss Jackson had, to look at the burnt field.

'You're not thinking there's any link between this and what happened to Shirley?' They were having supper alone.

'I don't understand about the window.'

'That story is rubbish about Shirley's seizure being brought on by that priest blessing the place.'

'Think so?'

'Anyway, Jo's trouble has been properly diagnosed. There's nothing supernatural about it.'

The conversation wandered off, as such conversations do, to quite a different subject, the lice Mark had found in the mane of one of the horses and whether or not they ought to call in the vet, but eventually they returned to the supernatural. If you've never had experience of ghostly happenings there seems no alternative to charitable scepticism towards people who claim they have. There was well-attested evidence for poltergeists. They were often active when a young girl was in the house but when Ed said so Harriet commented that Jo was too young. To be the focus of poltergeist activity the girl must have reached the age of puberty. 'I mean, that's what I've seen in reports but I doubt all this, you know. I'd need to see for myself.'

'Which Hart did.'

'You've only his word for it. Or Lisa Pomeroy's word.'

'I saw Hart's letter. And there were those newspaper reports.'

'It's all just the say-so of Hart and I wouldn't trust him an inch. Like as not he did for poor Shirley himself.'

'You don't mean that?'

'Well, not deliberately. He's so bloody stupid and clumsy he's capable of knocking somebody off by accident and of not even noticing.'

Jack Wragg telexed a few days later to say he had been unable to locate Hart but he would keep trying. Fortunately Jo's crisis seemed to have passed. Jerry Clutsam reported that the tests had revealed nothing alarming and, although he was keeping her on antibiotics there was no reason why Jo should not get up, provided she took things easily. He would pop in from time to time to see how she was getting on. Harriet said it was a relief to have a doctor you could feel was taking a personal interest, not like Brownlow. She even told Jerry of the strange circumstances in which Jo's mother had died; all he said was that when you lived in Africa there were times when you had to suspend judgement.

In early September Hart telephoned from Heathrow to say he had just flown in. Harriet took the call. Before asking if Jo was okay Hart announced that he was coming to Troy Corner by taxi; he planned to take Jo to London to see the Tower of London and Madame Tussaud's. After what he'd been through he needed a holiday. They would have fun. And then, when he learned that Jo had been ill he had the brass to say, 'Why didn't you let me know?' In a few moments he was actually talking to Jo who wanted to know whether he had come to take her back. She hoped so.

Jerry Clutsam happened to be in the house at the time on one of his visits so he was able to talk to Hart too and put his mind at rest about the state of Jo's health. However, when Ed reached home Jerry had gone and Aston Hart had already been there for some time. Harriet reported that at the sight of her father Jo burst into tears. It might have been because Hart had shaved his beard off and his face, now naked but for a moustache, gave Jo a shock but Harriet thought they were tears of joy.

Aston Hart reported that he had fallen out with Amin. Not, you understand, because Hart had done anything wrong in Amin's eyes, they had not had a row, Amin had not actually threatened him in person; if he had Hart's situation might have been easier because he was confident he could talk Amin out of any ill humour and get him laughing again. He just could not make contact with the President. There were always excuses and the situation became so jumpy, Hart said, that he took to moving about the country without telling anyone where he was going. But it was no life for an Englishman. He had made a great mistake going to Uganda. He ought to have known that Amin would take against him simply because he had been Hart's subordinate in the KARs and would not want to be reminded of it. Well, perhaps it was not entirely Amin's fault. He was surrounded by the most unscrupulous and bloodthirsty bastards. Naturally they would spread rumours about Hart, about his friendship with Archbishop Luwum, for example, a prelate who was his own man and therefore in disfavour. Well, he *was* friendly with the Archbishop, that was true enough. A great man. Hart thanked God he'd not taken Ugandan citizenship. He'd crossed the lake to Kenya in a coffee smuggler's canoe, landed at Kisumu and, Christ! was he glad to be back home! Kenya, he meant. He sat in the garden, drinking beer but still looking round sharply from time to time. He was nervy.

He was a handsome, healthy-looking man now in his very early forties with a fine head of sandy to chestnut hair. His beard gone he showed that for all his wide jaw he had a small, forward pointing chin. He had kept a full, square-ended cavalry officer moustache and in the lobe of his left ear he wore a gold ring which he'd put in, he said, on the advice of a witch to improve his sight. He had brown eyes with a hint of gold in them too. Under his bush jacket he wore no shirt, just a white vest, showing as a white crescent, lying on its back against the dark chest hairs. Between his eyebrows was a vertical line that never softened. His elegance was almost Edwardian.

After the children had gone to bed they stayed on in the garden, it was that warm, sitting there in the starlight with a couple of bats occasionally jittering overhead and making Harriet yell and put her hands on her head. She was sitting where she could pick at the thyme in the border and she had been rubbing the leaves between her fingers so the air was lemony.

'I wasn't too impressed by that doctor chap,' said Aston, 'but then I don't like the way South Africans talk and he was South African, wasn't he? He didn't know much about what happened. Jo seems all right but you never know, she might have another attack. Now, what I'd like to know – ' He paused. He might even have been going to change his mind and not say after all, what he wanted to know. He breathed out noisily. If it had been somebody else that would have been a sigh – 'Put it another way. Just how did it happen? You heard Jo yelling, you say.'

Harriet described how they'd heard Jo crying out and they had gone to her.

'That was all? Nothing unusual? I mean, there was nothing broken?'

There was the open window with the curtains drawn back but Ed decided not to mention it and hoped that Harriet would not mention it either.

'We got our own local GP. He thought it was something to do with the kidneys and then Jerry did those tests. He said the same.'

'I just don't trust South Africans.'

'That's hard on Jerry,' said Harriet. 'He's been marvellous, Jo likes him. He's really taken trouble.'

'Sure, I ought to keep my big mouth shut. I'm a white African too.'

He lit up and his face flushed out of the darkness, lips beneath the golden moustache pouted over the cigarette.

'I guess I'm African at bottom,' he went on. 'The doctors say what they do say. But I'm African. And I wonder *who* did it. Or *what* did it?'

Harriet screamed again because the bats had come back and she feared they would tangle in her hair. Aston pulled a floppy hat out of a pocket, handed it to Harriet who put it on with a great cry of relief. 'So if the pig dies it's because somebody has cursed it?'

'Sure. You can't say it's bred in me. My father and mother, no. They stayed European but not everybody is like that. Some breathe in the African air and dust and it changes them. For me, at bottom, things don't just happen. There are devils out there and ghosts, bad men, bad women.'

'That's witchcraft.'

'Don't turn up your nose at it. Cousin Will Shakespeare believed in witches all right. There was a touring company came out to Nairobi and I went to see *Macbeth*. There were two murderers. They said the world had dealt them such a bad hand they didn't give a sod what they did to spite it. One of them said he was ready to risk his life. "To mend it or be rid of it." I remember those words. They stuck. I received that message after Shirley died and they just triggered me. Because that's just how I felt.'

'Triggered into going and working for Amin?'

'I was crazy. Who was making me crazy? That's what I wanted to know. Who was my enemy?'

They sat in silence until Aston said Uganda was a mad house and he had been one of the inmates. He had found no enemy there. He had kept his nose clean. A lot of men, women and children were still living who would have been dead but for him.

'What were you doing exactly?' Harriet liked needling people.

'NCO training, mainly. Square bashing. Rifle drill. That and reconnaisance. That was the best. You could get right away. Went down into Toro. Never been there before. Herds of elephants and buffalo in the grassland and there were huge butterflies in the forest. And do you know what bait you use to catch butterflies? Fermented banana. They get high on it. Some hunters use leopard shit. I like looking at everything. Then out of the forest you can see snow away on the Ruwenzori. Snow in Africa. I did a lot of this sort of scouting. Intelligence work Amin called it, but that was all balls. He paid me and I was conning him. To be frank. After that I was set on to the coffee smugglers. They smuggled it across the lake into Kenya where they got two thousand shillings for a bag. And, of course, they eliminated anyone who got in the way. Sure! Cut their throats. Then they bought knives and shovels and crockery and God knows what to take back from Kisumu and that brought them another three thousand shillings when they smuggled the stuff into Uganda. It was good trading and it was my job to stop it. Sometimes we did.'

Aston was not telling everything he had done but it was as much as could be expected, enough to be going on with anyway. Reconnaisance for what?

Harriet was still curious. 'It was the coffee smugglers who got you out of Uganda?'

'They were murderous bastards but you got to know them, see, and you could make arrangements.'

74

'What are your plans for Jo?'

Aston plainly had not given that much thought. 'We're going to look around a bit. Sea air would do her good. Base ourselves at Brighton, hire a car, that sort of thing.'

'You know, she's welcome to stay here as long as she likes. Or you like.'

'Hell, no, that's good of you but when I've got my Pathfinder out of mothballs I'll get fixed up with something. In Nairobi. Then you can send Jo out to join me.'

'What's a Pathfinder?'

'That's my little plane. A pal looks after it. Ideal weather for flying in Kenya. A small operator can pick up a lot of freelance work.'

A long silence. Then Harriet asked Aston, 'Do I know you well enough to give some advice?'

'Go ahead.'

'You can't bring up Jo by yourself. You ought to marry again so that Jo can be under somebody's wing. She's a lonely child. You know that?'

'The situation isn't one of my making.'

'I'm telling you that for Jo's sake, and for your own too, you ought to marry again. Somebody not too young, somebody house-trained. A widow with a young child of her own.'

'Anybody in mind?' Aston was amused by the way she was trying to boss him.

'Nobody. Have you?'

Aston drank his whisky and water, all of it, in one go. He made mooing noises as though lost for the right words, but trying hard. 'I've got problems.'

'It's what Shirley would have wanted.'

'She wouldn't have wished a stepmother on Jo. I couldn't marry anyone after Shirley.' He began choking and grunting but even then Harriet did not let up.

'Shirley wasn't like that. She'd just have wanted what was best for you and Jo.'

'I know you mean well, Erica.'

'My name is Harriet.'

'Then who's Erica? There's *somebody* called Erica.'

'That widow, perhaps.'

75

Aston began to complain. 'You really do hand it out, girl. Perhaps I'll be able to do the same for you one day.'

'You are young enough to start another family.'

Not much more to be said after that, and Aston went off to bed in the attic. Next day he took Jo off to Brighton.

Before going back to Kenya Aston went over to Wood End to see the Ritters. He inspected the house, listened to Dawn's complaints, and gave instructions for Rentokil to come in and check up on the woodworm and dry rot. To Dawn's grudging satisfaction and Drew's annoyance he gave them a three month rent amnesty to compensate for the poor state the house was in. It was merely a gesture. As Dawn said, it didn't make the place any easier to live in. Aston could afford the gesture because soon after returning he wrote from Nairobi asking for Jo to be put on a plane. So he no longer had to pay out the money for her keep. Quite recovered from whatever she had been suffering from Jo went wild with excitement. It was uncharacteristic, refreshingly kidlike, and kept under control only because she knew Miss Jackson did not like airplanes and would probably be sick.

6

From October onwards there was rain, the scent was poor, the
hounds couldn't find and on two occasions Guy Budgen, the
Master, was reduced to arranging a drag hunt (laying an artificial
scent) so that they could all, man and beast, stretch their legs.
There were other meets spent trotting round dun, soaked woods
that had been fantasticated by mist. Horses and hounds ran,
splashed to the belly in mud. November, the weather hardened
and they started a dog fox but lost him because he dodged
through a wood where local sportsmen, farmers' sons mainly,
were blazing away with shotguns at a huge rookery high in the
tall trees. As late as February Guy Budgen was laying on a drag.

Drew Ritter had a new mount, a big roan mare it was unwise
to stand behind because she was a kicker and would lash out
with her hind legs like the war horses she was probably
descended from. Drew's dress was by this time more conven-
tional, brown breeches, a patched pink coat he had bought from
Oxfam and, instead of the hard hat, a jockey's helmet. It still said
a lot for the tolerance of the Master, Guy Budgen, who
sometimes studied Drew with his lower lip stuck out; but it has
to be remembered that Drew was generous with his hunt
subscription.

Harriet was anti-bloodsports and would never have ridden out
on a real hunt but she came on this February drag. She wore
some rather fetching tight lemon-coloured cord breeches, had
fished out her old faded pink coat and a riding hat and rode
Conrad, a four-year-old stallion who, in reality, was not big
enough for hunting. She said in advance she was not going to set
Conrad at any hedge so it was a subdued day for Ed, trotting
ahead and opening gates. At one point they seemed to have lost
the rest of the hunt altogether and rode up a woodland glade
where there were masses of snowdrops, china-white and fading
away into the blue recesses of the wood.

They came out of the wood just as another member of the

hunt, a swarthy man with a malevolent expression on his face, galloped past. He waved his crop. 'Never seen such a fiasco,' he shouted. 'This isn't a hunt. It's a townee free for all. I've had enough.' Away he went. They cantered down a long sloping field in the direction he had come from. On the other side of the hedge at the bottom there were a dozen hounds or so, part of the pack, streaming up the opposite hill with Jo Potter, the whipper-in, unmistakable in his yellow jacket, trying to head them off. Soon they found themselves in the middle of a very bad-tempered hunt indeed. Drew said the hounds had picked up the scent of hares and found it more interesting, some of them, than the drag.

Guy Budgen's face was the colour of one of those purplish house bricks and it seemed likely there'd be no more drags while he was Master. After what seemed an eternity of confusion Jack Price got the hounds pointing in the right direction and moving again, blowing a defiant blast on his little horn to foster the pretence a real fox lay ahead. Harriet said this was just the kind of hunt she liked, galloped ahead then, changing her mind remarkably, set Conrad at a tall quickthorn hedge and cleared it triumphantly. Drew Ritter and Ed jumped together, not giving it a second thought; Ed knew this bit of country well. The ground was the same height both sides of the six foot or so high hedge, there was no wire and his horse rose like a stag. Then something went wrong. Drew gave a yell, just why Ed couldn't make out because he was concentrating on staying in his own saddle but some way into the next field he was able to look back and see Drew on the ground and his big mare, four legs in the air, apparently rolling on him.

Talking about the accident later Drew said it was all his fault. He had set his mare too late at the hedge and it was as though the beast realized this, would have liked to refuse but was too far committed. As bad luck would have it the hedge, unlike so many these days, had been properly laid so, instead of the mare's front legs crashing through fairly loose growth, they struck against firmly interlocked wood. Drew was off and the beast came down almost vertically and toppled over. It must have been pretty spectacular, said Drew, and if it hadn't been that the ground was soft, almost marshy at that point, he would have come out of it

78

worse than he did. The mare was little worse for the tumble, she pressed Drew into the ground doing most of the damage with the pommel of the saddle, leaving him with a few broken ribs. He did not know this at the time. Drew lay there for a while, in pain and obviously shocked. Coats were draped over him to keep him warm but after a while he insisted on getting to his feet so that he could examine his mount, which had bolted, been caught and brought back. The creature was trembling and sweating, with cuts on the front legs where they had caught the hedge, but Ed was able to walk her up and down.

'Damn bad horsemanship,' somebody muttered.

Harriet said it was her fault. 'If I hadn't jumped you two wouldn't have followed.'

Drew would have none of it. 'I'd have gone anyway. The whole point of coming out is to jump.' He wanted to climb back into the saddle but at that stage no one knew what his injuries were and Ed was all for getting him to the nearest road where they could flag down a car. Drew was still wearing the racing jockey helmet and what with the plastering of mud he'd received, and the blood on his head from feeling the mare's legs he looked defiantly heroic.

'What we want is a telephone,' said Harriet. 'I'll ride over to the Mortons and ring up Jerry.'

This surprised Ed. 'Ring up who?'

'I'd get Jerry Clutsam to send an ambulance.'

'He's not the right person to phone at all. You want to get on to Casualty at the nearest hospital.'

'Of course. How silly of me,' said Harriet. 'I wasn't thinking,' and she set off at a spanking pace on Conrad while Drew sat on a stile and drank bourbon out of a flask while the rest of the hunt, satisfied Drew and his horse were okay, streamed away towards Packley Wood and whatever reward Guy Budgen had prepared for the hounds at the end of their run. Drew handed Ed the flask and he was glad enough to take a swig too. The air was sweet with the smell of bruised turf and horse droppings, and the sweat of horses steaming in the fresh spring air. They stayed silent for some time watching a couple of magpies fooling in and out of the hedge but looking smart in their crisp white and tuxedo black.

'My last tally-ho,' said Drew.

'What do you mean?'

'I'm real sad. This tumble means I'm out till the end of the season, I guess. Then as sure as little apples I'll be posted back to the States. One thing, Dawn'll be tickled pink to get out of this country. She's not been at all happy in England. That house is a lot to do with it. I'm used to roughing it but Dawn was brought up in Poughkeepsie and she goes for mod cons. Back home in Evanston she spent $20,000 just on the kitchen. You know the kitchen at Wood End. I don't know what our landlord's intentions are but he'll have to spend a heck of a lot of money if he's to find any takers after we're gone. But I expect he gets rich pickings out there in Africa.'

'Doubt it.'

'That infestation expert said the house needed thousands spent on it. He just couldn't wait. Wanted to start taking the place apart there and then.' Drew gasped with pain.

'Think we might try walking you over to that gate?'

'Sure if you'll look after the horses.' He walked with difficulty, gasping and swearing while Ed kept well clear, leading the two horses who made no trouble. 'It isn't just England I'll miss, and all this.' He made a gesture intended to encompass valley, hill, wood. 'It's the folk we'll miss. You and your wife to start with. Harriet's a real nice girl. Shall I tell you something? Seeing her go over that hedge in those tight breeches, well I just had to follow, she was right enough about that. She knows about herself. She's a smart girl, you know that? And intelligent. I wouldn't be saying this but there's this pain. You get high on pain, too. Jeez, there she is already.'

The white ambulance showed over the far hedge. Harriet was climbing over the gate, at that distance, the colour of her breeches being what it was, seemingly naked between the bottom of her coat and the top of her boots.

Drew clutched his chest. 'Something's gone in there. Jeez, it hurts. And not for real fox hunting. Just a drag hunt. Well, I'll just lie about it. When I tell the tale. I'll lie! and how!'

The news of Lisa's divorce came through by chance. Ed was in New York that summer and one evening found himself sitting next to an athletic-looking woman in her fifties who was tanned, had vermilion lips, wore dark glasses and seemed made of whipcord. Tough dieting, no doubt. She was the quintessential thin woman crying to get out of every fat woman. The price was heavy. She was the fashion editor of a woman's magazine called *Top Girls*. The dinner was given by Kurt White, a vice-president of an assurance group Ed's firm had an interest in. Too early to talk of buying up the equity but talk in the boardroom back in London had gone that way.

The conversation at this dinner turned to some tycoon in the news. He was a Washington businessman who had formed a consortium to take over a baseball club (the Baltimore Blackfeet? Anyway, some Indian tribe) and had run into a lot of resistance from the resident board. This businessman had been so frustrated by the resistance that he had taken to wearing baseball gear on all public occasions and letting his beard grow, saying that he had made a solemn vow not to discard this attire or cut his beard until the Baltimore Blackfeet were his. 'He looks curiously like a blond Fidel Castro,' said the fashion editor, whose name turned out to be Franky, 'particularly with that peaked cap and he gets lots of TV coverage, which is what he's after, of course.' She was drinking yoghurt givré with her chicken and took another sip of it. 'I think the beard is problematic. I just have to say that. All the rest is okay but not the beard.'

At this point the subject petered out, so far as Kurt White and his other guests were concerned. It was kept going just by Franky and Ed.

'What's so shocking about a beard?'

'Not in Europe. Here it's aggressive. Sexually aggressive, too. A man with a beard gets his fair share of bar violence. If it's a pointed one, specially.' She thought about this. 'I guess bushy beards are not so aggressive sexually. But they sure are politically. Makes it all the more surprising that dear old George should risk it.'

'Sounds as though you know him personally.'

'Sure I know him. I know everybody.'

'Fashion writing takes in this sort of thing?'

'I said everybody and I mean everybody. Because fashion is everything. It isn't sitting on your ass matching make-up to dress material or turning up at the Paris fashion circus. How people

81

look and what they wear – I mean to do it elegantly and with, you know, confidence – is a statement about the world they live in. What I say about fashion is conditioned by Watergate and Vietnam. So it's a real intellectual discipline, sonny boy. Edwin, isn't it? And with this philosophy – no, retake! – this way I'm programming things, I find it all the more surprising George has grown a great beard. Like I said. A Viking Fidel Castro. He's boobed, I reckon. *Panache* yes, but big, fluffy yellow beards, no! Not the right image at all.'

'George sounds fun.'

'He's a maverick and I adore him. Fun? Sure he's fun and, do you know what? He's an intellectual, as businessmen go. What I like about him is he's so unexpected. A Washington business-man, a baseball tycoon, or would-be, and he's an expert on Africa. I told him he ought to run for the Democratic nomina-tion. Nixon has so fouled it up for the Republicans it would be a good time for a Democratic intellectual like George. He'd be better than Adlai Stevenson who was my pin-up when I was a kid. But hell! It's out. George Pomeroy isn't even a senator.'

'Pomeroy?'

'Sure. Funny name. He says it's Irish.'

The whipcord woman had built up such a picture of a go-getting, up-market, even reasonably intelligent operator (why else should she bring Adlai Stevenson into it?) that Ed simply could not square it with the George Pomeroy that he knew. They had hit on some cultural divide that was wider than just the usual Anglo-American one. Pomeroy? There couldn't be two George Pomeroys in Washington.

'I think I know George too,' he said. 'Or, rather, I know his wife, Lisa.'

'You do? Well, isn't that interesting? Yes, Lisa *was* his wife. But they've divorced. I think there ought to be an entry in newspapers not only for births and deaths and marriages but for divorces too. I guess it would be too enormous. And who'd pay for the entry anyway? Yes, they're divorced and George has taken up with a boy-friend and that's not smart either. Not politically.'

'I'm sorry the marriage broke up.' A phantom shouted in his ear, 'Liar! Hypocrite!'

'The lawyers are still arguing about the alimony. George and Lisa've been married such a short time and there are no kids. From the legal angle Lisa is as good as new. George is generous though. He'll see Lisa is okay but only until she marries again or even (and this is where the lawyers are picking up their huge tab) unmatrimonially shacks up with another partner. How do you monitor that? Does it include one-night stands? Probably not, but what kind of a relationship are we talking about? Something more regular? Well, what do you mean regular? You can see what fun it all is lawyerwise. George wouldn't want to finance anything immoral, would he? But how would he get to know?'

While she had been talking Franky had been busy lighting a cigarette. Finally, she succeeded, blew out a lot of smoke with her laugh and dug him in the side with her elbow. 'You're very quiet.'

'Do you know where Lisa is? I'd like to get in touch.'

'Leave it to me. What's your hotel?'

A couple of days later there was a note waiting when he picked up the room key asking him to call Franky at *Top Girls* (number given), which he did.

Franky sounded puzzled. 'I took it Lisa was still in the State Department but when I got through to the office where she worked there was a guy who hesitated a bit, said she hadn't been there in months, and rang off. So I got on to George himself. When I mentioned your name he lit up like Hong Kong harbour and said you were the greatest poet since Robert Service (say, who's Robert Service? But that's George all over. He's just wise to everything). I thought you were in insurance. You didn't tell me you were a poet, too. I don't like that, holding back. We could use smart poetry in *Top Girls* and the pay's good. We'll talk about that. Anyway, George put me on to his lawyers and they put me on to Lisa's lawyers and their line was they didn't know where Lisa was either.

'They said Lisa had gotten herself a new analyst who said she was in such a trauma she just had to cut herself off. This shrink (a woman, by the way, and I spoke to her too) said she was in a safe cabin somewhere out in the woods. What's a safe cabin? It sounds spy thriller stuff. No way would this shrink give me

Lisa's address or a number where I could call her. But I made her take a note of your name and hotel in the hope she'd pass it on. But she won't, the bitch. She can't be a good shrink. If Lisa is depressed to all hell she shouldn't be isolated. That's the worst thing. You bet she's where this shrink wants her and for no good reason. I just hate analysts. They're a lot of bogus bastards.'

He could have phoned Harriet for Lisa's family address in Cincinnati, then rung her mother but the idea did not appeal. If the analyst passed on Franky's message Lisa would be in touch. How could she fail to? Now that she was purified of the George contamination ('as good as new') she had become alluring and imagination-stretching all over again. She was charged with an even more compelling power because of her breakdown. Previously she had been the great helper and inspirer but now it was Ed's turn (not to inspire) but to provide comfort and consolation. The idealized Lisa, the Muse, had merged with the real flesh-and-blood Lisa and it was inconceivable, such was the bond between them, she would not send out a signal.

Ed was sleeping late after a party when Franky phoned to say she had located Lisa and would he meet her, Franky, for lunch at The Top of the Park? Ed failed to recognize her. Franky had the same wiry, starved, sprinter's frame, but her hair was different, her face was different, and her dress was different. She had knocked ten years off her age. She wore a little black straw hat with a white ostrich feather half covering it, a green, clinging, shiny sort of dress under a loose white coat. Instead of the big vermilion lips there were small, dewy, pink lips. She no longer had a tan. She was all apple blossom and dancing sunlight. No dark glasses. Without them her eyes were disconcertingly, glassily, brilliant but that was only because she was wearing contact lenses. She smelt lemony and carried a zip-up leather portfolio instead of a handbag. All in the line of business, no doubt, for fashion editors.

'Hi, Ed! What are you goggling like that for?' She raised a gloved hand in mock despair at his failure to greet her adequately and kissed him on the cheek. 'Here I am, sweetie! Look at me.'

'Sorry. You just looked so different at Kurt White's party.'

'Better or worse?'

'Just different. I think you look smashing.'

'What funny things you Brits say. Never mind. It's the *way* you say it. What'll you have to drink?'

'Oh, but – '

'No, sweetie. Be my guest. It's on the account.'

Franky at once showed a couple of failings. She turned out to be a non-eater. They started with fruit salad (peaches, mango, melon, strawberries, lychees, and heaven knows what else) and Ed was well into his before he noticed Franky had not even started. She was busy talking about the poetry he could write for *Top Girls*. When the waiter came to clear away she waved a dismissive hand at her untouched fruit salad, went on talking about poetry, and said they'd like just a few tomatoes and peppers with the lobster. As for wine, a bottle of Montrachet would do. Ed was put off eating too. The other failing, so far as he was concerned, was this talk about poetry.

'What about Lisa?' he said.

'I was coming to that.' She actually took a fragment of white lobster flesh and transferred it to her mouth. 'That shrink lied to me.'

'So?'

'Ed!' She put her fork down and looked him in the eyes. 'No one has ever said "so" to me before. We really are having an intelligent conversation. So!' And it turned out Franky had had the same idea as Ed, extracted Lisa's family address and phone number from George, and spoken to Lisa's mother. 'I said I was – well, who am I? A journalist interested in stories and what interested me this moment was I had this English poet, Ed Parsler, making enquiries about her. And, do you know, Ed, she had you all taped. She'd met you. She remembered you. And Lisa wasn't in any safe cabin. She was staying with an old school friend outside Chicago and no, she wasn't letting on any more than that, Lisa wanted to be left alone, but she was basically okay and pulling out of whatever. Isn't that great?'

'Is it just depression? I can't imagine Lisa feeling low somehow.'

'The first divorce is always the worst. I've divorced three times and the first time I *flopped*. You just feel guilty as all hell. Mind you I *was* guilty and I had No. 2 all lined up, but it didn't help somehow and did I *flop*! Lisa has no No. 2 lined up, I did establish that much, and she's had this feeling. You know, rejected. Though *she* did the rejecting all right.'

Before they went their separate ways Franky said she planned to take a trip to England in the fall. She wrote down Ed's office and home telephone numbers with the object of getting in touch and then presented him with a copy of *Top Girls* which she produced out of her portfolio. Her name, together with all the other editors, associate editors and advisers, was printed on the contents page and she made a cross against it: Franky Lutfaya, so that he would know who to send the poetry to. If he failed to produce something printable they'd really rib her in the office.

Back from New York Ed wrote to Lisa's address in Cincinnati to be forwarded but that was a couple of months ago. Silence. This nagged. A couple of poems had gone off to *Top Girls* but they had been received with silence too so he didn't want to enlist the help of Franky. No doubt, it being August, the editors in *Top Girls* were all on holiday but it could also mean they didn't like the poems and were embarrassed. If you can imagine New York journalists being embarrassed.

No more than three days before the Parslers were due to go on holiday Ed's secretary said there was a woman on the line who wanted a private word.

'What's her name?'

'Mrs Clutsam. She's in a call box by the sound of it.'

Mrs Clutsam as a name meant nothing and it was not until she had been speaking for some time Ed realized it was Olwen, Jerry's wife. She was incoherent and emotional. She was not only in London but quite near the office and wanted to come and see him. A quarter of an hour later she was shown in, a bit fatter, if anything, since he last saw her but still with her black fringe. She was wearing a smart-looking, grey trouser suit in light material and a floppy beret to match. Plainly she had second thoughts about being there and looked round the office, almost as though for a way of escape. Eventually she sat down, crossed one plump leg over the other and refused coffee.

'I've had it right up to here.' She levelled a hand in front of her mouth. 'I suppose it's no news to you your wife and Jerry are having an affair?'

86

Ed said he didn't know what she was talking about.

'You didn't know your wife was two-timing you?'

Ed flipped a switch and said to Fiona in the outer office, 'If Mr Parsons shows up tell him I'll not keep him more than a few minutes.' A moment of incomprehension before the hidden message got through. Then Fiona said 'okay' and he knew that in a few minutes time she would report the non-existent Mr Parsons had arrived and was in a hurry.

'You've got to excuse me,' Ed said to Mrs Clutsam.

'This is incredible. And you with those two lovely children. At least I've got no kids, so there's only me. It all falls on me.'

'You're upset and I think you've been imagining things.'

'Imagining? Hell, if you'd seen what I've seen. There's a cubicle at the hospital Jerry's got the key of. That's where they have it off. And in my own house, when they think my back's turned.'

A thought occurred to Ed. 'Does Jerry know you've got these suspicions?'

'Suspicions? What are you talking about. Jerry's the only thing I've got and that bitch of a woman, your wife, is taking him away. What's going to happen to me?' She mopped at her eyes.

'So far as you know Jerry's quite unaware you might have contacted me?'

'He wouldn't care.'

'But does he know?'

She raised her voice and Fiona, his secretary, could scarcely not have heard. 'I came here to discuss what we could do to break it up.'

'I don't think there's any "it" to break up. My wife and I get on just fine. We are happily married.' A pause. 'Why don't you get Jerry to take you on a long holiday in South Africa so you can get yourselves sorted out.'

'Mr Parsons is here,' Fiona called through.

'Jerry has become a stranger to me. He's always making excuses not to be there. He hates me.'

'That can't be right, Mrs Clutsam.'

'You hate me too. You don't even call me Olwen.'

'I'm sorry, Olwen, but you see I've got this client in the waiting room.'

Before leaving she said, 'You're just ignoring it in the hope it will go away. A lot of other weak-minded cuckolds have thought that. That's what you are, weak. You're as bad as one another, all three of you. If my father was still alive he'd have set about Jerry, I can tell you. And your wife. And you. He was a real man, a soldier. He was in the Welsh Guards.' She was screaming with rage and, Fiona appearing in the doorway, just pushed her on one side.

Every night Harriet had her routine. No matter how late it was she would take a bath and then go down to the kitchen for a cup of Earl Grey tea. That night she found Ed waiting for her with a pot of Earl Grey almost ready for pouring. They sat drinking in silence – and it really was silence. The house did not creak as it sometimes did. Outside, the night was windless.

'What goes on? I thought you didn't like this sort of tea.'

'Right.'

'So?'

'Olwen Clutsam came to see me in the office this afternoon.'

'How nice for you.'

'No it wasn't.' He spoke slowly and with silences that Harriet found unsettling. 'She is a morbidly unhappy and jealous woman and she's been letting her imagination run riot. She said you were having an affair with Jerry, and she'd come to discuss what could be done to stop it. She trotted out a lot of stuff. I told her straightaway what I thought. I didn't buy it. Not at all. You can imagine. She's a bit of a worry.'

It was so quiet they could hear the other's breathing and a click every second as the hand on the wall clock jerked on. Harriet was looking hard at Ed but he kept his eyes on the tea he was gently swilling round his cup.

'Just what precisely did she say?'

'She said Jerry had a cubicle at the hospital. He could lock it and make love to you there. And at his own home too when you thought Olwen's back was turned.'

'Go on.'

'Well, that's about it, really. I had her turned out. What chiefly worries her is the thought of losing Jerry. She says she's got nothing but Jerry. She wouldn't want to divorce him or get a legal separation. But she's not going to keep this misery bottled up. She mentioned Mark and Jessica.'

'Why?'

'Children are what we have and she hasn't.'

'So, what do you want me to say?'

'Nothing. I know it must be a bit horrid. Sorry to raise it this time of night but for all I know you might run into Jerry tomorrow. By now he must know Olwen came to see me. It would have been unfair if you didn't know. You don't have to say anything at all, not to me that is. You might have to say something to Jerry. Make no mistake, Olwen is crazy. He'll know all about that. She leads him a hell of a life, I can see that. She's the obsessive type. Once the devil gets inside her she never lets him out. So we've all got to be careful.'

'We?'

'Yes, you and Jerry and me. My anxiety is that she might get hold of Mark or Jessica in some way. I won't have them exposed to this. They depend a lot on the way our marriage is okay.'

'But if the devil has entered into this woman there's nothing I can do to cast him out and if she means to get hold of the kids, she will. But I doubt it. And if she did, so what? They are sensible. Kids are tougher than you think. They could be made to understand what is going on. Even see the funny side.'

'It is important not to do anything that could stoke her up.'

Harriet finished her Earl Grey. 'You can't stop living and having friends just because there are Olwens in the world.'

'I don't know what you mean by the funny side.'

'Well, Jerry and I make a comical pair. He's all nose, ears, knees and elbows. And me?' She sighed. 'Why can't we all be loving and affectionate to one another? And just have fun. I'd even like to be friendly with Olwen.'

'Keep things simple, Hatty. That's what we've got to do. So the kids keep things simple too.' At last he lifted his eyes from the swilling tea and looked at her. Her face was innocent of make-up. It had a flushed transparent quality, as though a light were behind and glowing, as it might through alabaster. Much, much brighter, even glittering, through the eyes. He half-coughed, half-laughed. 'You were going to say something about yourself.'

'Okay,' she said, 'come on.'

They went up to bed in silence. Harriet took off her dressing gown, then slipped off her nightdress before climbing into the twin bed that was Ed's. He stripped slowly while Harriet lay on her back with her eyes closed until he switched the bedside lamp off and slipped in beside her. She put out a foot and engaged one of his, lifting it, pressing hard. Some time later, after she had shown how passionate she could be and Ed had anchored deep to ride out the storm, they lay arms clasped about each other.

'That's what I wanted to say.' Harriet had an afterthought, mumbled because she was on the edge of sleep, 'Keeping things simple can get boring.'

7

Franky Lutfaya was as good as her word. She arrived in the fall and called Ed at the office to say the literary editor liked the poems a lot and they would be printing 'Fever Ambulance' in the January issue. But for some reason they proposed calling it 'The Wrong End of the Telescope'.

'Was that okay, Ed? Don't hesitate to say you don't want that title and we'll dream up something. "Fever Ambulance" is, you know, a bit dated, I mean it makes you think of Florence Nightingale.'

He rang Harriet to see if it would be all right to invite Franky to Troy Corner. When she saw no objection Ed put the proposition to Franky who said she really had a full schedule but if they could fit her in for just one night (no longer) that would be fabulous. As matters turned out it was just as well Franky did not have a longer stay in mind because she and Harriet took an instant dislike to one another and even that one evening was a minefield.

He picked Franky up at her hotel soon after six and once again did not recognize her; or, at least, was not sure she was the real person. Presumably fashion editors regarded their appearance as some kind of traveller's sample. They were all the time demonstrating different styles. Now she looked all set for a yachting holiday in her dark blue toque, white blouse and enormous blue cravat. She saw herself at the wheel in a light breeze, standing at an angle to the deck, with the puckered sea scudding by.

Very nearly the first thing Harriet said to her on arriving at Troy Corner was, 'You really shouldn't have bothered to dress. We're terribly informal.'

'Dress?' Franky was surprised. 'I'm not dressed.'

'Sorry. I thought that was a long dress. It looks charming.'

'It's just a divided skirt. I designed it myself.' Harriet took Franky off to her room and they needled each other as they went up the stairs.

Franky made no comment on the house or garden. She did not even seem to notice them, she was much too taken up with some arrangements she was trying to make with a Paris fashion house to feature them in the March issue of *Top Girls* and how hellish the French were. They just wouldn't let her know details of their spring collection.

'I know how these fashion houses work but they've really got to get into the twentieth century. They don't want leaks. Okay, I'd respect their confidentiality.' She was going over to Paris tomorrow to beat some sense into them.

'Do you speak French?' Harriet asked.

'I can get by.'

Harriet spoke passable French (she had been to school in Switzerland) and she began using it now with the idea, she said, of giving Franky some practice. 'Ça doit, être trés difficile de s'adapter. A New York vous n'avez pas l'occasion de parler le français, tandis qu'ici on est tout le temps à Paris. Sans blague.' It was quite untrue. The Parslers hadn't been to Paris for years.

'Le moment que j'arrive à Paris,' said Franky, 'Je deviens parisienne. Mais c'est vrai. Tu parles le français beaucoup mieux que moi. Je propose que tu m'accompagnes comme interprète! *Top Girls* paiera tes frais.'

Harriet was furious to be offered hired employment as Franky's interpreter and Ed had to introduce a different subject. He asked Franky if she had any news of Lisa.

'Lisa Pomeroy?'

'I wrote her a couple of letters to Cincinnati but there was never any reply.'

They were dining off warmed up cold chicken with curry sauce and broccoli spears, a dish Harriet often prepared when in a hurry and for guests she didn't approve of. Franky was playing her old game of talking but not eating.

'It is called Chicken Divan,' said Harriet. 'But perhaps you don't like the curry sauce. Though it is very mild. Can I get you something else?' There was not much else to be got without raiding the deep freeze, as everyone present realized.

The danger was that Franky would ask for something simple, like crackers and cheese with a glass of Perrier water, but fortunately she said Chicken Divan was a favourite with her, especially with asparagus. Which, of course, she was not provided with, only the more plebeian broccoli. Harriet shuddered at the thought of polluting asparagus with a curry-flavoured sauce.

'Lisa Pomeroy got married again,' said Franky, 'so I guess she isn't Pomeroy any more though don't ask me what.' She clapped a well-beringed hand to her brow. 'Now how should I know she gotten herself a new husband?'

Of late whenever Lisa's name had cropped up in conversation, which was rarely, Harriet had taken to calling her 'the Muse'.

'She doesn't mess about, does she,' said Harriet. 'The Muse. Married again. How tiresome for you, Edwin.'

Franky gave quite a yell. 'I've got it. I don't see George these days but Cy Chaseman's a good friend and he does business with George. And Cy and I got talking. It came out that George was spitting blood. One thing about George, he may be a fat cat but he watches the stuff. Small tips to the waiter, that sort of thing, a real tightwad, so one part of him's cheering he doesn't have to pay alimony any more but the main part of him is real upset. He can't bear the thought of another man getting his hands on Lisa. Even after the break. I call that small.'

'Who's she married?'

'No idea. The way Cy told it the whole point of the story was George's reaction. Can you imagine that? A marriage breaks up and the man is all calm about it inside, he doesn't care if he never sees her again, but when the lawyer tells him there's another man in his ex's life, seriously and contractually in her life, you know, he just runs beserk. Cy claimed George actually said he'd fix this new guy, but I don't credit that. George may be bouncy but he's not homicidal, not so far. He's sweet really. A softy. And all that think-tank stuff behind him too. I call that impressive. Cy said he was sure George didn't expect Lisa to take the veil. After the divorce that is. No way. He just thought she'd have a man now and again for medical reasons, like my mother used to drink a glass of Irish Guinness every day, but to go to bed regularly and respectable with the same man night after night! George climbs up the wall thinking of it. How immature can you get? Particularly when you remember the way George plays around and always has done.'

'I suppose he still loves her,' said Harriet. Ed detected the irony but Franky did not.

'I don't call that love. That's male chauvinism. One rule for the guys, another for the girls. George is a throwback. Tell you what, whoever this new husband is George feels he's been raped by him. This isn't what Cy told me, but I know my George. He feels buggered. Something intimately *him* has been invaded and penetrated and violated. Sure, I know my George. He seems outgoing but he's the anal neurotic type and in my book that's unAmerican.'

Harriet was getting tense because Franky was not eating. 'You sure I can't make you an omelette?'

'No, I love these dishes made up from leftovers. It's the way I want to live. I come from peasant stock, too, way back.' She forked up a fragment of chicken and took a sip of wine. 'It's so wonderful to be here, in a real English home.'

'You are pretty hard on George,' said Harriet. 'I wonder why.'

'Sure, I used to think he was great but he never made me, I can tell you, if that's what you're thinking. George got me disillusioned. I don't go for this feminist crap. I don't believe society would be okay with just women in it and a sperm bank in deep freeze but it's men like George who give Women's Lib a good name.'

Ed really wanted to know about Lisa. 'I still don't understand why she doesn't reply to my letters. Anyway, I hope she's struck lucky the second time. Found somebody a bit different from George, I mean.'

Harriet began to clear away the dishes, including Franky's which still had most of her meal on it. She almost spilled some of it into Franky's lap but changed her mind. 'George wasn't so bad. I'm surprised he's mean with money. He seemed to like splashing it around. What I liked about him was he was so thick-skinned. You didn't have to worry what you said.'

'Nothing else for me,' said Franky. 'No sweet, just coffee. You can be sure Lisa's new husband is just like George. That's the way it goes. I've had three husbands. I didn't know it at the time but now I look back they were the same guy in only slightly different incarnations. They all had moustaches so I guess I've a thing about hair on the upper lip. A bit of a con because what really got them going was taking a chance; gambling, lending money to the Argentines, starting up crazy businesses, and I caught that kind of man three times, says something about me. And he'll be like George, choked with dollars, and he'll be like George and be a yacht with the wind in his sails. That kid likes somebody who's confident. Maybe because she isn't.'

The following morning Franky and Ed travelled up to town together on the commuter train and they were scarcely out of Bicester station before she said, 'Why does Harriet never call Lisa Lisa but always the Muse?'

'For a time I couldn't write. It happens. I had a block. I first knew Lisa when she was a kid and then I met her years later. She had a kind of aura. It made a terrific impression. Just the way she looked gave me a thermal.'

'Sounds indecent.'

'I used to go gliding. It all turned on finding an upwelling of warm air. A thermal. So I could soar again. And write.'

'Eddie, I don't get this. You mean you fell for a kid so young she could almost be your daughter?'

'Franky, it isn't on that level.'

'You could have fooled me. Did she set up "Fever Ambulance" for you?'

'No.'

'She must be a great fan of yours.'

'No, Lisa was no fan.' So far as Ed knew she'd never read a line. 'I guess you're right. Middle-aged poet gee-upped by pretty young girl.'

'You don't look middle-aged to me, Edwin, and I like the smell of your aftershave.' She herself smelt of stephanotis. She put out a hand, in a lavender glove, and patted his thigh. 'If I get any news of Lisa I'll let you know.'

The Ritters came back from a vacation in the States to say Drew was being sent to Texas in October for reassignment, which he was pretty sure meant a posting to somewhere in the Pacific. He was still (unlike Dawn) sad about going. His tumble in the hunting field had cracked only a few ribs. He was in sick bay for a few days and returned to duty with a strapped-up torso. They threw a farewell party to which the Parslers were invited. Dawn

95

seized the opportunity to show them once more, what a bad state Wood End was in. Drew had, at her insistence, stopped paying the rent in protest way back in the summer. Now they were getting out. Dawn really believed it was only some effort of will on her part – not the stone and the beams – that kept the house from falling about their ears. She could answer for nothing when the magic of her presence was removed. Another guest was Kim Suttle, the agent, and Ed asked him whether he had anybody lined up to take over from the Ritters.

'No, it's turned out providentially, really. I heard from Mr Hart only the other day. You know his wife died? Well, he's married again and says he's giving up Africa for good and coming to live here with his new wife. And the daughter, of course.'

So Aston had taken Harriet's advice. Thinking she would be pleased Ed went across and told her.

'I hope Jo was properly consulted,' she said. 'And Miss Jackson. Those two could put paid to any stepmother they didn't like.'

'But it's good, isn't it? And that they're all coming back from Kenya to live here.'

'You didn't tell me that.'

'Oh yes. Kim says it's all fixed.'

Harriet looked around. 'All I can say is I hope she's rich. He'll need all the money he can get his hands on. Let's hope she is the widow of an American oil millionaire he's met on one of these safaris he conducts' – for that, until today, was the latest news they'd had of Aston. 'This place needs it.'

'I'll drop him a note of congratulation.'

With the result that a few weeks later the Parslers received a letter to say who the new Mrs Hart was. She was an American all right, but Aston had not met her on safari and she was not the widow of an oil millionaire. She was Lisa, the ex-Mrs Pomeroy, née Muller, and she wrote them a letter that was exultant to the point of frenzy.

It turned out the real reason Lisa went into hiding after divorcing George had nothing to do with the state of her nerves and needing time to sort herself out. True, she had been consulting an analyst (who doesn't?) but the real reason was to avoid being pestered by George. Apparently he called her regularly, often in the small hours. What for, she didn't quite know because he seemed to accept there was no way the marriage could be patched up. His language was often brutal, sometimes threatening. He was acting crazy and Lisa, still working in the State Department, put in for a foreign posting. She asked for Nairobi, thinking there'd be no chance. But if not Nairobi, anywhere in Africa. Failing that, London. Lisa had her friends in the State Department. They rallied round and, within a week of her application, she was on a plane, first stop Rome, then on to Nairobi. Her job in the Visa Section of the American Embassy there was a secret kept by her mother, her analyst, her lawyers and her colleagues in the Washington office where she had worked. They covered for her because if George learned where she was he'd be calling her in Kenya.

Nairobi because Aston Hart was there. What fascinated Lisa, idiotic though it might be, was that he was descended from Shakespeare's sister. In the emotional crisis brought on by her divorce, this fascination developed into an obsession. She just had to meet this man she corresponded with. It was a bonus that he lived a long way away from George. Only when she saw him did she decide to marry Aston. And the decision was taken immediately.

Lisa had called Aston a few times from the States so she knew his number but when she phoned, soon after her arrival in Nairobi (she had not cabled ahead she was coming) a woman, with an accent that indicated she was Asian of some kind, said, 'Mr Hart was on safari.' This must be Jo's *amah*. It was not difficult to discover when Aston's party would return, to which hotel, and at (roughly) what time. Lisa was there in the reception hall when the troops of Americans, the men in floppy hats and shorts, the women in brightly-coloured trousers and enormous dark glasses, arrived boisterously, waving hands and shouting greetings to their compatriots who, sitting over their drinks, wanted to establish they'd had a hard time too. Out of this world! Fabulous, etc. They had seen game from a helicopter; giraffe, antelope, zebra. If confirmed them in their original belief that God had given man dominion over all beasts. That is just

97

how it seemed from a helicopter. There was talk of covering the game parks by balloon and that would be even better. Being silent, in a basket suspended from a balloon you could see the wild life real close. The tourists did not actually say so but it was clear their belief that man was the greatest of God's creations had been confirmed. A shower and a stiff bourbon was double confirmation.

Lisa did not know what Aston looked like. She had not seen so much as a photograph. She had a vague expectation he must look like Shakespeare but there was no candidate in sight. A clean-shaven man with white hair was answering questions from one of the party in a way that showed he had been professionally involved in the trip. Much too old. All the tourists were in fun clothes and looked as though the outdoor life did not come naturally, bleached by the central heating back home. So that one man, standing at the bar with a tankard of beer in his hand, stood out. He was dressed for work in a dun-coloured shirt and slacks with enormous brown boots (to stamp on snakes, she thought). He had a moustache of a kind only Englishmen wore these days, a gold earring, and a complexion that looked purple in the artificial light.

'Mr Hart?' she said. The tankard of beer was between them and the malty tang brought back low-ceilinged English pubs. Out of Nairobi, out of Kenya, into a green land with black and white cottages in apple orchards. 'You must be Mr Hart.'

She thought he was not going to answer. He took a great swig of beer and she could see his adam's apple move up and down. When he put the tankard on the bar counter it was half empty.

'I needed that,' he said, turning towards her. 'You're not in my group.' For the first time he really focussed, taking in the bright, shining eyes and the glimpse of white teeth between the slightly parted lips. 'Yes, my name's Hart. What's yours?'

'I'm your pen friend. I'm Lisa, Hans's sister.'

'You are.' Again a silence. 'Lisa, eh? Bloody hell! That's amazing! What are you doing here? A facer. What'll you have to drink? Look, let's get out of here. Let's go and sit outside. You on a trip? You're Lisa? I wouldn't have known. Well, how could I?'

It needed a week or so for them to take stock of each other and then they were having supper together every other night. Lisa met Jo and Jo said Miss Jackson liked the American lady. What all this might signify he wasn't sure. Maybe Lisa was trying to compromise him so that he could be enrolled for intelligence work by the CIA. She worked for the American government, didn't she? They could very well have given her this Nairobi assignment to meet him. The Russians did it. Why not the Americans? What other explanation could there be for the obvious interest she took? She touched him a lot, seizing his hand and laughing when he made some feeble joke; asking him to tease grit out of her eye, kissing him good night and on the lips. She walked so close he had to grab her now and again to avoid tripping over her (he was a good nine inches taller than she was) and then she just hung on to his arm. He touched curves that were firm but pliable and responsive. She told him about George and her divorce. That, too, aroused him erotically. He knew that she knew he was aware of what she was up to and he couldn't think why he was worth the trouble unless he was being recruited. He even wondered whether he'd take everything on offer and to hell with the consequences. What consequences? He hadn't a wife or any kind of official position so he couldn't be blackmailed. Perhaps he was to be the victim of one of those brainwashing operations and then sent out to assassinate somebody, Castro, say, or Gaddafi, and Lisa was just softening him up before he was turned over to some other agent. Living in Uganda under Amin put that kind of thought into his mind with no trouble at all.

One afternoon they drove out to the haunted house where he had lived with Shirley. It was Thanksgiving so Lisa had time off.

Ten miles out of town they left the metalled road and drove west along a dirt track trailing red dust like a comet. They were on a ridge with miles of coffee bushes fanning away to right and left. Huts with corrugated iron roofs were set in islands of banana fronds and flowering beans. The going was rough but became rougher when Aston found a murram track lined with thorn trees and set the old Mercedes up it at the gallop. Aston was all right. He had the steering wheel to hold on to but Lisa had to brace herself, pushing hard at the floor with her feet and forcing herself against the back of her seat, at the same time clutching a handle over the door.

'The only way to take these tracks,' said Aston. 'You've just got to jump the wheels from one ridge to the next. If you slow down you get stuck in a hole.'

A couple of women with babies on their backs and suitcases balanced on their heads stepped off the track and turned away to reduce the amount of dust they swallowed. On the other side of the thorn trees was a maize field in full tassel. Then a long pinky-grey single-storey house appeared at the end of a short drive lined with dusty oleanders.

'The Gadds both work and the kids are away at school in England so the place will be locked up this time of day. The servants live in those huts under the flame trees. But they won't come out till it's time to cook dinner. We can't get in the house but I'm sure the Gadds won't mind us just walking round.'

To prove him wrong a tall black man with hollow cheeks and protruding eyes appeared. He was wearing a neatly laundered white shirt and slacks and obviously wanted to know what they were up to. Then he recognized Aston and the two were soon laughing together. Aston did not introduce the man who looked at Lisa with a mischievous kind of grin on his face. The veins on his high forehead stood out as though he was suppressing laughter. He raised his hand in salute, returned to his hut and left the house and grounds to the visitors.

Through the windows they could see a marble-floored hall running the whole length of the front of the house, with rooms opening off it.

'That's the drawing room through there. Let's go round to the other side of the house.' A terrace, on the other side of the house, overlooked a neglected garden of flowering shrubs down to a brown river some two hundred yards away with a great patch of reed and rush beyond that looked like swamp.

'The Gadds bought the garden furniture. That's the chair Shirley was sitting in.'

'So that room behind is the big drawing room?' From what Aston had told her in letters and on the phone she had a good idea of the layout. 'That's where the priest was doing his blessing.'

'I was right in there with him.'

'But you're not Catholic yourself?'

'I'm not anything really. Even Shirley was a wobbly Catholic. Me, I'm C of E. Lapsed. Jo's technically a Papist and she goes and talks to the nuns now and again. But it's all pretty relaxed out here.'

He led the way to quite a hillock with a spiral path to the top. It was an artificial mound. Nobody knew why it had been raised; possibly as a lookout in tribal days. Here they stood in the shade of a thorn tree looking away to a white kite remotely floating in the blue air, the peaks of Mount Kenya eighty miles away. Behind the brown tiles of the house looked ready to slither, come the next storm.

'The Gadds have no trouble. Houses can be haunted. Then whatever it is causing the trouble clears off. A lot of things have got to come together for a real haunting. The people in the house, for one thing. How old they are, how screwed up, neurotic, I mean. And the background's got to be right. What happened in a place years and years ago, not necessarily that house. But the place. The site.'

'But you weren't screwed up?'

'That's what makes it all the more surprising. When your nerves are all to hell the ghosts flock in like bloody vultures. In our case they flocked in anyway.'

Aston seemed fascinated by the place. They went back to the house and walked all round again, peering in at the windows, Aston exclaiming on the changes the Gadds had made. In his time they had a long padded bench in front of the fireplace where they could sit and talk on the cold evenings. The Gadds had a settee and armchairs. That sort of thing.

'The colobus skin was just there.' Aston pointed through the window at the polished boarded floor of the drawing room. 'Just there. This side of the carpet.'

'The what?'

'Colobus. Prettiest monkeys in Africa. So they get hunted for their skins. There are different kinds but this was the black and white. He has long silky black hair hanging over him like a cape. And he's snowy white underneath. Now, I won't have a colobus skin in the house. Dead against that sort of traffic. So, it was a sort of mystery, how this skin got where it was.'

'You asked around? I mean, the woman who did the cleaning.'

'No chance. None of the servants had seen it before. Everybody knew I was against the colobus trade. In my book they're people. Shoot a monkey and the whole family mourns. You know that? But the colobus is the only big monkey trade so they're the ones who get shot.'

'You don't see any connection between this skin and what happened to Shirley?'

'It was the only time a colobus skin entered my house.'

'What did you do with it?'

'Nothing. It disappeared. When I went back to pick it up some time later it wasn't there. One of the servants could have picked it up and flogged it. Worth a packet in Nairobi.'

'It stuck in your mind, that's for sure.'

'Everything that happened that day sticks in my mind.'

'You don't *really* believe Shirley died because of some evil spirit?'

He looked at her sharply. 'I believe just that.'

'But you *can't*. If you believe such things there's no end to it. There must be a natural explanation. I mean, if you don't hang on to the idea there are natural explanations for everything you're back in the dark ages.'

'What went on in that house was real.'

'I know there's research into these things. You can graduate in parapsychology. There are laboratories and controlled experiments but that's just the way it is in this crazy world. I guess I'm old-fashioned. I just can't swallow these stories.'

'So you think I'm a liar.'

'Oh no, no, no! What am I saying? I don't mean that at all. I just think you were so bugged by Shirley dying you just couldn't accept it, not as natural, or fair. So the only way you could see it was in this spooky way. I don't blame you. But it's all too *weird*.'

Aston said nothing for a long time, he was so furious. He reached the Mercedes minutes before she did. Her shoes were wrong, with high, spiky heels to make her look taller, so that Aston did not have to look down on her so much. But they were not good for trotting in. There was a moment when she thought he'd drive off and leave her stranded but he did not wish to punish her that much; he just drove down the murram track faster and hanging on so desperately and, being bumped about so violently, Lisa just screamed. He said nothing at all on the way back to Nairobi until he pointed out the RC cemetery where he said Shirley was buried and where he had an annual subscription for the maintenance of the grave.

'I'd like to see it,' she said.

'Some other time. I'm off on another safari the end of the week. Then I've business in the Aberdares so I'll be out of Nairobi for months, maybe. By which time you Americans being what you are you may have hopped it. So perhaps I ought to say it's been nice meeting you and goodbye.'

'Oh, I'm a fixture in Nairobi. For some time. I'll be here at least two years.'

When he dropped her outside the house in Muthaiga where she had a flat he just grunted, waved and shot off down the flowery avenue, like a man desperate for a drink, or to relieve nature, or to smash something up, himself possibly.

A few weeks later Aston called Lisa at the office to say Jo was in a great state and asking for her.

'I thought you were out of town.'

'No, I'm back. Things didn't work out. Just as well. Jo says Miss Jackson is dead and she wants to have a proper funeral. How do you deal with that, eh? How can you explain to the kid the doll is no more dead – nor any more live, for that matter – than it's ever been. It's all in the kid's mind. It's real enough for her but it's just not healthy. She wants to talk to you about something but she won't tell me what.'

Lisa had seen and talked with Jo several times and knew all about Miss Jackson. They were looked after, and Aston when he was there, by a Goan couple, Tonia and Luiz, Tonia being the *amah* and Luiz doing the cooking and cleaning. Jo was sufficiently grown up now to have a brace on her front teeth and her auburn hair styled so that it just flopped about and didn't need a slide or ribbon. When she was older she would grow her hair long and braided on top of her head like her grandma who had been murdered by the Mau Mau and whose photograph stood in a silver frame on the TV set. But in the meantime she could shake her head vigorously at Tonia and Luiz. The hair bobbed about by way of emphasizing a point. It was one of the tricks she used to keep the rather simple couple under control, no doubt all on Miss Jackson's advice. And now Miss Jackson was dead. When Lisa heard the news she was appalled and said, sure, she would come round as soon as the office shut down for the day.

'I'll pick you up at your place if you don't mind. I'd like to have a word or two before you actually see Jo.'

Lisa had time to take a shower and put on something a bit more seductive than her office gear – a stunning lightweight trouser suit in moss green to set off her fair hair – and when she came down to the hall and found Aston waiting there she experienced a real throb in the plexus, a squiggling of the nerves, that made her give an involuntary cry which she managed to transform into an ordinarily happy greeting. 'Aaaw! Aston. It's great to see you. I thought you'd cut me off your list.' In his great white hunter style outfit of cream bush jacket and slacks, with those hard blue eyes and big rectangular moustache he was the most arousing man. George had been heavy and thick running to paunch. Flab. But this man was bone and muscle. He had such wide shoulders he could wrap his arms around her and still have enough stretch left over to slip a hand under her armpits and further. So it wasn't just the Shakespeare connection. She kissed him unhesitatingly on the lips and he kissed her back, passionately, open-mouthed, then tongues caressing.

They both forgot they were on their way to see Jo.

'I'm sorry what I blurted out when we were at your old house.'

Aston was in a daze. He could not collect himself for a while and then the words tumbled out. 'You may have something. I might be fantasizing but it wasn't just the way Shirley died. It was what led up to it. I was sick in bed one day and the boy brought me a glass of water but it exploded before I could touch it. Oh, there were a hell of a lot of things.' They were still holding on to each other. 'Are you working for the CIA?'

Lisa laughed. He could smell her breath, sweet as though she had been eating *loucoum*, and see beyond her white teeth and curved red tongue to darkness. An irresistibly erotic darkness. 'I'm just a clerk in the visa section.'

'A coincidence you being sent here?'

'I asked for the posting but I didn't think I'd get it.'

'So there's nobody planning to set me up?'

'What for?'

'Quite a lot of people you Americans would like bumped off. I'm no candidate for that game.'

'I'm just me and you are you.'

When they arrived at the apartment Jo said that she would like to speak to Lisa alone if he had no objection. She was pale, bright eyed and wearing pink and white striped pyjamas like seaside rock. She looked slightly crazy.

Aston went off to the kitchen to mix drinks and Jo, sitting cross-legged and erect on a divan so low it was only about a foot above the floor, said, 'Sister Sweeney says it is wrong to mourn for the dead. But it is natural. So why should we not be natural?'

'How old are you, Jo?'

'Ten.'

'What happened? Why did Miss Jackson die? I mean, was she sick?'

'She was very old. She had had a hard life. She had lots of lovers but she never married because her mother stopped her. Her mother wanted her just for herself. She died because she was old. My mother died. You will die. I shall die. We shall all die. But I shall go to heaven and what worries me about Miss Jackson is she'd given up being a Christian. She had friends from Bombay and became a person who believed in fire. We've got to burn her. That is what I wanted to talk to you about. My father doesn't understand.'

Lisa inspected Miss Jackson in her box. 'I don't think you need burn her. If you look at her carefully you will see there is no reason she shouldn't go on for ever.'

'She's got to be burned.'

Aston came back in time to hear this and said they did not have to burn Miss Jackson that very evening, there was no hurry and in the meantime he wanted to make an announcement.

'We can burn her first thing tomorrow morning,' said Jo.

'No hurry,' said Aston. 'She won't run away. Jo, do you like Lisa?'

'Miss Jackson did but I don't care much one way or the other.'

'She's going to be your new mother.'

Lisa coloured and stood up. 'Aston, what are you saying?'

'She's all right,' said Jo.

'We're going to be married and you'll be looked after.'

'Miss Jackson – ' but Jo could not go on and she began to cry.

That is how it seemed. Indeed, was. Just as Aston never actually asked Lisa to marry him so he never, in so many words, said that he was taking her and Jo back to England to live. At first Lisa thought they were just going on a visit. Only when he sold a couple of guns to pay for the airline tickets did the truth click home; he would have needed those guns (they were expensive) for any future safari and when she asked him about the sale he said, 'No big game in England.'

'But aren't we coming back?'

'No. Everything's being Africanized. Five years ago I could have been a game warden. Today, no chance. Skin wrong colour. All the jobs in the national parks have been taken over by black Kenyans. Jobs of any consequence, that is. Next it'll be the safaris. Anyway I don't like nannying. Some of these tourists treat you like servants, particularly the women when they're not treating you like a bloody gigolo.'

Lisa was furious he could take decisions like this without consulting her. When she told him she was not going to be treated like a squaw he was amazed. But I thought we discussed this, was always his line. If he knew something he took it for granted other people did and Lisa had to say, 'Look, I don't read you, Aston. You've got to communicate.' She thought this extraordinary blind spot had something to do with solitary hunting where thoughts went unspoken for weeks on end; but when she suggested this he said, 'No, Africa's a place where you can't be alone. Pitch a tent in the desert and half a dozen tribesmen turn up immediately. No privacy. But I get your drift.'

Fixing the date of the wedding took some time because the British Consul, who eventually took them through the formalities, wanted proof of Lisa's divorce and the documents were weeks arriving from the States. The US Embassy seemed uncertain what job could be legitimately carried out by one of their staff married to a foreign national and since Lisa, to begin with, assumed she would be staying on in Kenya and still be working, questions had to be asked in Washington. To make up for the red tape some of the Embassy staff clubbed together to give Lisa a noisy party. Champagne was drunk, everybody became high-spirited and Aston found himself being told by a white-faced redhead that Lisa was one helluva fast mover, it wasn't fair, she'd only been in the country a month or so and if she, the redhead, had seen Aston first he'd be marrying *her*.

'What sort of brought you together?' the redhead asked.

'I knew her brother. He was killed in Vietnam.'

'She's so *happy*. She'll be good for you. Keep you young. Mind you I don't think a girl should *always* marry a man older than herself. Ask any, well, mature lady. Old men get tired.' The redhead was nearer forty than thirty and Aston thought she spoke from the heart.

Lisa would have been quite ready to go to bed with him before they were married but Aston would have none of this. He wasn't an angel. He'd had affairs with a couple of women since Shirley's death but he'd never had any intention of marrying them, so that was all right. But when you had a marriage in prospect you respected the conventions. He did not want to look back and realize that his wife had been to bed with a man she was not married to, even if that man had been himself. Lisa was amazed and put it down to his being English. Now she came to think of it she did not know a lot about the English. She always thought she knew a lot about them but that was because she just *loved* English literature, Shakespeare in particular. She began to wonder, when it had finally been established they were going to England, whether the reality (living there, not just on honeymoons or vacations) would turn out to be different.

8

Round about then, Harriet was telling Jerry Clutsam yet again that though she was delighted, no, excited, they could be lovers now and again she had no intention of leaving Ed and the children. Life at Troy Corner was the real cake and what Jerry and she got up to when nobody was looking didn't amount to much more than the icing. Of course she adored Jerry. The way he made love brought on a swoon of delight. He was so physical. She tingled for days after, felt and looked more beautiful, thought more highly of herself and was, as a consequence, all the more the understanding and devoted wife that Ed deserved. And the more loving mother to their children. Her family was the priority, all the more so now that she and Ed were trying to start another baby.

'You've got to keep your wits about you then.'

'How do you mean?'

They were lying side by side, holding hands and talking rather dreamily, on the double bed in the blue bedroom, called that because of the colour of the curtains and the carpet. Now that the cubicle at the Otmoor General had been turned into a private room for the terminally sick, they had tried an accommodating friend's flat in Banbury and (though this was sordid) the back of Jerry's car. Finally they had settled for the blue bedroom at Troy Corner. Jerry's fuzzy red hair (he had it not only on his head and cheeks but a real forest on his chest) clashed with the décor in a way that worried Harriet. Absurd to be bothered by aesthetic considerations at such a time but that was the way she was. The blue bedroom had the advantage of commanding a view of the front drive so that if a car swished in they could see what the trouble was straight away.

'I mean that if you're having it with a view to pregnancy with one man and with no end product in view with another you've got to remember your diaphragm drill.'

'Jerry, I've news for you. I've a fertility pill for Ed, a diaphragm and one of the other kind for you.'

'There's no such thing as a fertility pill. And as for the contraceptive pill I have to tell you, as a doctor, there can be side effects. Well, when I say there's no such thing as a fertility pill I don't mean that exactly. If you had fertility promotion it would have to be under medical supervision and I guess you're not getting that. So what you're buying is some quack medicament. You're probably just glueing yourself inside.'

'Jerry, you are a gullible fool. You just believe anything you're told. But I love it when you get scientific.'

'Hell, I wish you wouldn't joke about such serious matters. Dear God, I love you and you've got to admit that Edwin doesn't spark you.'

Harriet got up and languidly began to dress. 'You couldn't be more wrong.'

'But he's so morose.'

'He's a poet and it drains him a bit, you know. You don't see the real him.' He thought she was joking and began to laugh. 'No, writing poetry,' she went on, 'can be tough but you're too illiterate to understand.'

'Does he know about us?'

'There's a convention in such matters. Better for everyone concerned if he pretends not to notice. Pity your wife isn't up to doing the same.'

'Poor Olwen. Her trouble's a whole series of miscarriages and then a hysterectomy. No kids. Now she talks of reporting me to the General Medical Council.'

'But I'm not your patient.'

'Mark has been. Then that little girl you were looking after. The Council could strike me off if they thought I was exploiting the professional relationship. And I've that relationship with members of your family.'

'Being struck off means you couldn't practise?'

'Not in this country. Back in Durban I could probably bend the rules. If you came with me we could do well there.'

'Darling, don't be so adolescent. I've got a husband and I don't want a replacement. Nobody need get hurt. Don't wave your emotions at me. It's your body I want. Come on, Jerry. Get up and dress. Jessica will be home soon after four and I want you well off the scene by then.'

Jerry turned on his side to look at her. In her bra and undies she was sitting on a chair to draw on her stocking. She did not look her age, though her breasts sagged more than they should, across her belly were folds of flesh, the large thighs marbly, with blue veins.

'You take everything so romantically,' she said to him. 'There's no need to be like that at all. It's a game and you've got to see yourself as just another player. That's Ed's secret. He's a poet so he just knows he has to play.'

'I don't know what poetry has got to do with it.'

'You wouldn't, would you, poor darling, with your limitations. Poetry is a high form of play. Just take it that an affair is my way of writing poetry.'

'You sure it isn't your fix?'

'That's offensive.'

'Sorry.'

Jerry sat up and reached for his underpants. Slowly, reflectively, he began to dress. He stood, first on one leg and then on the other, to pull his trousers on. His shirt was banana yellow and it seemed to brighten his fuzzy red hair and side whiskers almost to a glow.

'You mean, you've just been playing with me?'

'Hell, no! Another thing. You ought to get legal advice on being reported to the GMC. I don't think they'd accept it from a wife. Suspect evidence. Open to too much twisting. And on the not being a patient bit. Where do you draw the line? I refuse to accept that the medical profession is taboo. Can you imagine the warning? "Put that man down, my dear. He's a doctor." '

When he had levered himself into his jacket Jerry lowered his head and peered chimplike at Harriet. 'You're extraordinary. I've never met anyone like you before.'

'There you go again!' Down in the drive Jerry's blue Maxi gleamed in the late sun (it was January) and as they watched its roof was scored with the copious white droppings of one of the collared doves that had recently settled in the neighbourhood. 'That's a sign of good luck.' Harriet turned and kissed him on the lips. 'It was lovely of you to come. You were heavenly.'

'You don't seem to understand,' he said angrily, 'that I love you. Yet all the time you seem to do nothing but laugh at me.'

'Laugh? Yes, but then you are a bit comical.'

'Where's it all going to get us?'

Harriet affected to think hard. She actually frowned and put a finger to her temple. 'I think you ought to get Ed to explain what a game is. He'd do it much better than I can. Games are what you play. They don't get you anywhere at all.'

After he had gone, in a huff, she sat at her dressing table touching up her face, her lips, her hair, examining herself in the mirror for signs of the recent encounter, thinking that one thing, at least, she had said to Jerry was perfectly true, that he was comical, but she rather wished she hadn't. It had been a put-down. She did not regret telling him he was illiterate, because it was not really true, he knew it, and she said it only for the pleasure of hurting him. But comical he was. What made him so hilarious was his round-eyed, hairy, vaguely simian appearance coupled with all that earnestness. The thought of Olwen in the background, looking like a plumper Olive Oil (from the Barnacle Bill cartoons), threatening to report him to the GMC made Jerry even funnier and Harriet wondered whether she ought to see him again. Probably. But she was bothered by Olwen's miscarriages and the hysterectomy. That was no game.

During the winter Ed took days off from the office to turn out with the hunt but this year the weather was bad. Snow fell on the two days before the February hunt and then, surprisingly, the sky cleared and the trees with snow plastered on their north-east sides now blazed a full fig of hoar frost in the sunshine and against a blue sky, empty but for a pale sliver of moon still hanging there, in a lost sort of way. Guy Budgen supposed they could hunt on foot but not enough members were keen and it was decided Jack Price should ride out with the hounds to exercise them. This was a tame response to the weather. Ed was all for hunting on foot so when the decision went against him he felt under no obligation to turn out simply to trot along with the hounds. Instead, he put on his riding gear and a saddle on his new mount Tabby, a big brown gelding with corky patches, and rode across the fields to Wood End.

Since the Ritters left the house had been empty. The agent had a key, a retired policeman in the village had a key, and the

Parslers had a key with the idea of keeping the house under inspection. The retired policeman went in twice a week. But it was an uneasy arrangement. Vandals could break in. The hard frost made Ed wonder what arrangements had been made to avoid burst pipes. The easiest thing would have been to ring up Ingham (the retired policeman) but Ed was glad of the excuse to get out in the tingling air on horseback. Most of the way he just walked Tabby who snorted and threw up his head from time to time in response to the cold, mist curling and twisting from his nostrils. In the drive were the wheel marks of a single vehicle, the mail van, no doubt, and the unmistakable tracks of a fox, cutting across the drive and making round to the back of the house.

Ed tied up the horse at a convenient tree and looked at the neglected garden made beautiful by the hoar frost. The trees and shrubs looked considered, like works of art. There were fountains of lace, knobbly, receding networks of whitest coral and marble lawns. Two starlings burst explosively out of the laurels, scattering diamonds but that was the only sound, except for the snorting of the horse. Icicles a foot long tapered from the guttering. So after the snow there must have been a thaw. Water dripped and then the frost pounced. The lower windows of the house were shuttered from the inside, the upper windows curtained. Probably not wise to let the house look so untenanted. He would have had time switches and lights coming on at assorted hours in various rooms.

He unlocked the door with the bronze Chubb key, stepped into the blackness of the hall and was glad that he had remembered to bring an electric torch. He needed it to find a light switch. The house was not so cold as he had expected. Ingham must have remembered to come in and switch on the night storage heaters. Ed put a hand to the one in the hall and found it hot. In the kitchen he turned a tap and water gushed out, so Ingham had not seen the necessity to drain the system. Probably he had not thought of it. Ed went from room to room, switching on the lights. Dawn Ritter had been right. The place was in a mess. In one of the bedrooms a square foot or so of floorboards had disappeared from one corner. He pressed the nail of his thumb against the bottom of a window frame. It was like soft clay.

The cold water tank would be up in the roof where Lisa had so joyfully gone exploring and he ought to have a look at it. He found the ladder in the boxroom, had some difficulty in forcing the trapdoor open. Once he was up there, shining his torch on the beams that rose in the great roof space, it was of Lisa he thought and her enthusiasm. Because a spiritual testament attributed to Shakespeare's father had been found in the Henley Street house she was confident that something of the sort would be found here too. Not a chance. He had been sufficiently curious about the history of the house to look for evidence of some Shakespeare connection. At Exeter College, the eighteenth and nineteenth-century owners, there were no records. He had come at the question from another direction. The standard books of reference, like Chambers's *William Shakespeare* and Schoenbaum's *Documentary Life*, made it clear that when Shakespeare's granddaughter died, childless, in 1670, the Harts were left in possession of the Henley Street property in Stratford-upon-Avon, where they already lived, and they were there until 1806. No mention of Wood End.

In the roof space it was arctic. Ed located the cold water tank and made his way towards it, balancing precariously on a beam, his torch occasionally picking out the shrivelled remains of small birds. The tank was cladded. Even so the water inside had a covering of thin ice. He was able to crack it with his knuckles. Back downstairs he searched for the main water cock, found it behind a panel in the boiler room, turned it off hard and set taps running, two in the kitchen, two in the boiler room, to drain the system. He wasn't clear which taps to turn off. Eventually it was the hot tap in the bathroom that did the trick. It seemed an eternity before the sound of cascading water ceased and then he went round flushing the lavatories. He thought it might help. As soon as he got back to Troy Corner he would report to Kim Suttle and suggest he sent a plumber in to check on what he had done.

But as he rode back he thought why the hell should Lisa be disappointed? Coming to England to live deserved an agreeable surprise. Wouldn't it be marvellous if some seventeenth-century relic could be found in the house even if (and he was so excited by the idea that he set the horse cantering where it should have been led on foot, along a snow-packed lane) the relic had to be planted there? He could just see the expression of amazed delight on Lisa's face and the brightening of those eyes, tears of joy perhaps. Of course she must have it. And it had to be arranged so that he would be on hand to witness it all. By the time he had reached Troy Corner he realized that to excite Lisa the relic would need a special Shakespeare impress. But no genuine Shakespeare relic existed, unless you counted an early folio of the plays, or an early edition of the poems. Any of these would come expensive.

Harriet agreed it would be fun to plant a house-warming present provided they came clean immediately and said they had done it. It wouldn't be fair to Lisa if she imagined there were other treasures to be discovered and pulled the house down to find them. The best Harriet could come up with was a battered book in cracked leather covers which she had inherited from an aunt, *The Young Man's Companion, or Arithmetic and the Arts Made Easy*, by W. M., 2nd edition, 1684. Printed for S. Clark in George Yard in Lombard Street.

'No, it's got to have an association. With Shakespeare himself, I mean.'

'Why don't you ask Hugh Cornish? He actually taught the subject, didn't he? Shakespeare studies and that.'

It was months since Ed had been in touch and that was when Hugh, as fellow emeritus of his Oxford college, had invited him as a guest to the gaudy, the annual beano, when they had talked politics (Hugh was a Labour supporter but feared the party was in danger of degenerating into a front for the Communist Party) and Shakespeare's *Tempest* which was much in Edwin's mind because of the Lisa-inspired poem sequence he was writing out of themes he detected in the play. It was quite untypical of the sequence but he had even written a cod rant for Antonio in pastiche Shakespeare. Ed had handed the lines to Hugh, thinking he would put them in his pocket for later perusal, but instead of that he began to read them aloud in such a loud voice that faces were turned in their direction.

'Won't do, my boy.' Hugh had handed the paper back and for the next few minutes concentrated on his food. 'I've spent a lot of time studying Shakespeare. Too much. But I still don't understand him. Not really. I don't pluck out his mystery. Those lines of yours, though, no, no, no!'

So, when Ed now phoned, Hugh was delighted and said he feared they might have fallen out because of his rudeness at the gaudy. The Parslers had not even sent him a Christmas card. After the reassurances and usual civilities Ed explained what he was looking for, and since this involved saying quite a lot about Lisa, Hugh sounded off about American literary criticism which had killed off the human British approach. The other side of the American coin was the naive and enthusiastic antiquarianism of which Ed's friend sounded a prime example. He then wanted to know all about Lisa. Was she pretty? Was she *svelte*, as he assumed? What kind of clothes did she wear? Blonde? Brunette? He hoped to make her acquaintance in due course. When it came to giving practical help all Hugh could do was provide the names of a couple of dealers who specialized in rare books.

'I suppose I could write my Antonio pastiche out in Elizabethan hand and stuff it under the floorboards.' Ed had cast his fly.

'Don't you do anything like that. Shakespeare forgery has been a disgraceful industry in the past. Forgers should have their hands chopped off, like thieves in Arabia.'

'This would only be a bit of fun.' Having succeeded in making him rise Ed tried to lead him into even fiercer denunciations but Hugh said he must be lusting after this young woman and therefore out of his mind. 'Admit it! You're crazy. She's driven you insane with desire. Only a lunatic would even think of producing a Shakespeare fake, even as a bit of fun, as you call it. Confess all to Harriet. Give her my love, by the way.'

During the night a soft wind rose, there was a rapid thaw and melting snow from the roofs slithered and slurped over the choked guttering. Ed managed to drive to the station through the slush, so he was able to put in a day's work at the office. Late that evening, when he was back home, Hugh telephoned.

'I've been giving some thought to your housewarming surprise. You realize it's no game for a novice. Paper is very important. Ink absolutely crucial.'

'But this, if it's done at all, is only a five-minute wonder. I wouldn't want actually to take Lisa in.'

'Nevertheless it's got to be carried out with a modicum of conviction. Otherwise it's a bore. I think I know where I can put my hand on a sheet of paper with a watermark typical of London in the 1580s. I mean, I've got it somewhere about the house. Filched from the Peters' Library when I was doing research there. The watermark? Some sort of animal, just what I can't remember. A porcupine, probably. Could be a bear. Well, that's half the battle. Then you'll want some oak gall ink.'

'Suitably faded because of the passage of time.'

'That'll be okay. Apply gentle heat. Now listen. To make oak gall ink you've got to procure oak galls. Oak apples, you know. And gum arabic, copper sulphate, alum and loaf sugar. Well, sugar cubes will do. Rainwater you will have already. I've been doing research on this in Bodley. We'll get together. Then we'll need a quill. There is some argument about which are the better, turkey or goose. In the interest of authenticity I'd go for goose. How will you know what Shakespeare's handwriting looked like?'

'There isn't any, is there? Just a few signatures.'

'Next time you're in the British Museum, turn right off the entrance hall and where are you? A display of literary manuscripts. And there you'll find *The Book of Sir Thomas More*. It's a manuscript play open at a section I'm pretty certain William wrote himself. You can buy a photocopy and blow it up to be sure of getting the detail absolutely right.'

'You threatened me with hellfire even for mentioning a fake?'

'Quite right, too. But it would be *very* interesting, Ed. As a scholarly exercise. Please don't try to foist that pastiche you wrote on anybody. Be less ambitious. Think in terms of a short letter. Make a draft. Then come over and we'll see what we can contrive between us. Not that we'd foist anything. Everything above board.'

Hugh was enthusiastic because he was bored. Faking a Shakespeare document was better than doing *The Times* crossword. He might even try the fake on a few scholarly cronies, just to sort out the men from the boys. Ed had been right to think in terms of a game but it was important to ensure it did not get out of control. Some academic dignitary would have to be let into the secret straight away so that if anyone did make a fool of himself and accept the forgery as genuine Hugh could protect himself, in part, from the guy's fury when told the truth by producing this

dignitary to testify that no serious deception had been intended. The truth was that anybody who swallowed the fake
would be miffed away. Meanwhile, pressure was brought to
bear on Ed to draft a letter that Shakespeare might, conceiv-
ably, have written. Hugh phoned at intervals to know how he
was getting on.

Edwin went back to Chambers and Schoenbaum. Harriet
became interested too and did her own independent background reading. It was she who suggested that the letter
should be dated from London some time in 1609 and addressed
to his sister, Joan Hart, in Stratford. That was the year their
mother died and the Harts, living in the Henley Street house
could well have been anxious about William's intentions. It was
the year, too, that Shakespeare's company, the King's Men,
had started playing in a new theatre, the Blackfriars. It was a
time when there would be to-ing and fro-ing with the Court.
King James would expect the special performances for the
Court to be as cheap as possible.

Edwin followed Hugh's advice and looked at the MS of Sir
Thomas More (finding it almost impossible to read), studied
genuine letters written at about this time (like Francis Bacon's
but they were too correct and buttoned up) and eventually
produced a draft which, after revisions suggested by Harriet
was as follows.

Dear Lovinge Sisster,
    I had spoken with you ere now but a matter keepes me
labouring here with what issue I know not. The Cowrte is
more curiose and important for my affaires. Our Brother Gil-
bert comes at this time happily and delivers this and other
papers and remembrances. The house in Henley Street you
can be secure in. Think me not other than I am tho all is
change. Be happy in youre sons. Be happy in youre husband.
Be happy in what does not alter. In all kindnesse and affec-
tion.

Yr brother Willm S ffrom the Cocke
in Silver Street the 25 November 1609.

This was conveyed to Hugh who said it would pass, just. The
letter when finished would have to be sealed with an impress
showing a spear. The merit of this particular letter lay in the

way it authorized Hart possession of Shakespeare property. It would be an heirloom and the sort of thing that might have been taken to Wood End if that property had indeed been gifted by Shakespeare's granddaughter Elizabeth. Lisa would see this straight away. There remained the task of writing this out in an Elizabethan hand.

Harriet's brother Tom, had a birthday in March so there was a dinner party to go to in Great Missenden where the Harts came up in conversation. Tom's interest in Aston dated from the time of Jo's illness and the part he had played in trying to make contact with her father. Since then, casually, Tom and his wife, Meg, had been updated. Meg, in particular, had been intrigued to learn that Aston (whom she had never met) was married again. But what she really fastened on to were the odd happenings in that Kenyan homestead. Meg had started borrowing books from the county library on hauntings, poltergeists and psychokinesis and was reading the subject up with all the scepticism that came naturally to her.

There were twelve people at the dinner, different conversations were going on round the table, laughter was thunderous in the low-ceilinged room, and Meg had to speak up for Ed, some distance away, to hear. 'From what I remember Aston Hart and his first wife, what's her name? Shirley, that's it. He and Shirley got on together all right?'

'So far as I know. Shirley was, well, full of fun. Aston seemed absolutely devoted to her.'

'And there was just the one child? Joanna. Is she unusual in any way?'

Harriet, from way down the table, said she was a lonely kid, much too old for her years. She found it easier to relate to her doll, called Miss Jackson, than to anything or anybody else. She may have been different when Shirley was alive.

'You know me,' said Meg. 'I'm not a sucker for anything. Tom used to give me jewellery for my birthday but I couldn't stop myself checking the stuff in Hatton Garden (couldn't bear the thought of Tom being conned) so I just get perfume these days. You can imagine how much salt I take with the spook literature. But I must say the different cases hang together. The same sort of thing happens. There's a pattern. But the Hart haunting is different. In one important respect, anyway.'

'What's that?'

'One requirement seems to be the presence of a young girl, preferably round the age of puberty. When Shirley died Joanna was what? Five? Six? Much too young. And another requirement is often a tense, anguished domestic set-up in the house. Parents getting a divorce, for example. But from what you tell me the Hart couple weren't that way at all.'

Other conversations, and the laughter, had dried up because everyone was listening to Meg. Her older brother Wilfred who, with his wife Nan lived in a fine eighteenth-century house in Amersham High Street, chipped in to say they had bought the place cheap because it was reputed to be haunted. But they had not seen or heard anything. Perhaps it was because they had no pubescent daughter. Their only daughter, Sonia, who had been on the shelf for years, was now marrying a Watford surgeon, and Wilfred's remark was prompted by relief.

'It's just as though, when there's a lot of stress about, the girl becomes a kind of medium and discharges an enormous amount of psychic energy. Into what? Well, I don't know. It's just as though it scatters out. It becomes available and in some way this energy lies behind all the raps, sudden cold air, exploding tumblers, things being thrown about. Anybody had any experience of this sort of thing?'

No, but it soon emerged that everybody accepted raps, cold air and exploding tumblers.

Nan said, 'You mean this energy is given off by this girl and really she's the one who is causing the odd happenings?'

'It's as though some' – Meg hesitated – '*entity*, some spook, just cashes in on this energy. Are you sure Aston Hart wasn't having everybody on, Ed? The family set-up wasn't explosive enough to bring about the hauntings. In which case he might have invented them to cover something else up.'

Ed said no. 'He's not that sort. Too unimaginative, for one thing. And what else would there be to cover up, anyway?' This was the moment he took a glass of wine too many. 'We don't know what other people were in his household. Presumably the Harts had servants and they might be behind it all in some way.

Perhaps the cook was beating his wife and had a pubescent daughter.'

'In that case,' said Meg, 'the poltergeist would have harassed the cook's family, not the Harts.'

'Those servants would be Kikuyu.' Tom was at the other end of the table. 'Witchcraft is a way of life with them.' He turned the conversation to East African politics and to Amin. 'President Amin's mother was a witch. It'll be interesting to see whether he turns up for the Commonwealth conference in London next year. He took the opportunity of Obote's attendance at the Singapore conference three years ago to stage his *coup d'état*. He wouldn't want the same thing to happen to him. I still think he's not so bad as some people paint him. He gets a bad press but you've got to take a strong hand in a country where there are so many murderous tribes and factions. One thing, you'll never get him turning to the Russians.' Tom's idea of a happy birthday dinner party was one in which he was allowed to drink whisky, not port afterwards, and talk shop. It was the whisky, not the shop, that did for the Parslers.

They were scarcely on their way home before they were arguing, then quarrelling, then plunged into the fiercest of rows. Normally they didn't row. They were both, deep down, horrified at what they were saying to each other. But they were too drunk to restrain themselves.

Harriet let fly about Jessica and an unsuitable boy-friend she had picked up. Then, in the way of fierce quarrels, the ground changed completely and they were spitting at each other over Lisa and the fake Shakespeare letter. Harriet seemed completely to have changed her mind about that prank. Said she was sorry she ever had anything to do with it.

'It's just a nasty, cruel joke. What do you want to do? Screw her? When she finds out she'll just hate you for a superior, patronizing' – Harriet couldn't think of just the right word – 'sick prig and she'd be right.'

At Verney Junction Ed was dazzled by the headlights of a car coming in the opposite direction; it had been masked by the embankment carrying the now disused railway track and it appeared, blazing like a sun, out of the blackness under the bridge. Ed shouted a warning, Harriet screamed, and the two cars had passed each other without making contact before Ed slammed on the brakes and the car skidded sideways. They were lucky. The rear near side wheel smacked over the grass verge, the engine stalled, silence fell and that was that.

'You trying to kill us or what?' Compared with the way she had been going for him the past twenty miles Harriet was surprisingly calm.

Ed got out and walked round the car with an electric torch. 'Seems okay.' He climbed back in, sat quietly for a few minutes and then drove off cautiously. 'It would help if you said nothing until we got home.'

Jessica and Mark were, naturally, in bed when they arrived and presumably asleep. Mrs Weedon, a neighbour, was watching television and had nothing unusual to report. While Ed was driving her home the telephone rang and Harriet found it was Tom calling to check they had arrived.

'You both seemed a bit merry, Hat. Meg didn't know you were going and rushed out to insist you stayed the night. But by that time you were half way down the drive.'

'Merry?'

'Well, you'd knocked a few back, both of you. I could have kicked myself for letting you go.'

'Oh, Tom! We had the most frightful, mad sort of row coming home. Something just got into us. There was almost a smash but we're okay. We just screamed at each other. God knows why. The drink, I suppose. I'm making some coffee.'

'A row? What about?'

'I must have been plastered. Can't remember. All I can remember are the lights of the car we almost hit. Now I'm stone sober. It was sweet of you to call.'

She was on her way to the kitchen when Jessica appeared at the foot of the stairs in her white nightgown, barefoot. Harriet blinked at her.

'I heard. What did you and daddy have a row about?' Jessica spoke slowly, staring at her mother who could have interrupted easily and sent her back to bed, but did not. 'You know, daddy won't come back now. He's had enough.'

'He's only running Mrs Weedon home.'

'He'll do that and then he'll drive on, and on! And he won't come back, ever.'

'Nonsense. I was just going to make some coffee. He'll be back to drink it any minute.' True, Ed had been gone rather a long time. The Weedons lived only half a mile away.

'I know what you had a row about. I've seen it coming a long time. It's about Dr Clutsam, isn't it? I've been lying awake just thinking about everything. I couldn't be like you. I couldn't do what you do. No, don't come any nearer. Well, daddy's left you and I'm *glad*. He'll be in touch and I'll go where he is.'

'I don't think you know what you're saying.'

They heard the car enter the drive and go round the house to the garage at the back. A few moments later Ed came in and looked at Jessica in surprise. 'What's all this then? Why aren't you in bed?'

Harriet intervened. 'Tom rang up to see whether we'd arrived in one piece. I just blurted out we'd had a row and Jessica heard me. So she jumped to the wrong conclusion. Probably I'm still sloshed. I don't know what's happening. Jessica, you didn't *really* think your father would drive away and not come back? I mean, tonight? You were teasing.'

After some reflection, and as though remembering that Ed was not only her father but a lawyer too, Jessica said, with dry precision designed to flick their nerves, 'It was possible.'

Jessica began to sob. 'Everything's awful. 'Course there might have been an accident. You might have been killed. I could just see it. That would have been more awful. Everything is hell.'

Ed went over and kissed Jessica on the cheek. 'You're a good girl. Your mother and I are okay. Don't let the maggots get in. There's nothing to be afraid of.'

'What maggots?'

'Oh, just a way of speaking. Worries you can't get rid of. Gnawing at the mind, like maggots in cheese.'

'What a revolting thing to say.' Harriet made for the kitchen.

Remembering he had to catch an early train because of a meeting at nine, Ed felt suddenly drained. 'Dear girl.' Each word was a boulder he was rolling up hill, slowly. 'There's nothing to be afraid of. Things are usually never so bad as they seem. Nor quite so good.'

If young girls giving out psychic energy could set up a haunting Jessica seemed to have a damn sight more potential than Jo.

9

When Lisa's father Willi died he left a will directing that his entire estate, a substantial one, was to be in trust for her. Her mother was to receive all the income from the trust and the right to treat the Cincinatti home as her own, except in one respect. She could not sell it. Helga Muller, who had married young and still in only her middle fifties, was to continue the enjoyment of her late husband's estate until her death when everything would pass to Lisa. If Mrs Muller remarried the whole estate would pass to Lisa immediately. It was the will of a man who wished to control his family even after his death, which happened before Lisa married George. The references to her were such ('In the expectation of her marrying a good and honourable man of German stock') the impression was given that Muller might have needed persuasion from his lawyer not to turn that expectation into a legal requirement. So marrying George, who had Irish and Polish roots, was no disqualification from inheriting though Lisa's mother certainly tried to insist it was. The lawyers gave her no joy and collected their fees.

Helga Muller was angered by the will. Eighteen months after her husband's death she met, while on holiday in Germany, a Frankfurt businessman who was a widower with grown-up children and married him, partly because she liked him and because he was even richer than Willi had been, but mainly out of resentment that Willi had tried to tie her down. They lived at Kelkhm in a gloomy house with a two-acre vineyard that produced an excellent dry white wine. Karl Wicht, the new husband, added a codicil to his will making special provision for Helga, and they led the kind of life that aroused in Helga no regrets for the past.

So Lisa was, though Aston did not know it at the time they married, rich. No sooner had they and Jo arrived at Wood End than contract gardeners were in to tame the wilderness and Kim Suttle was carrying out a survey of the building. The next stage,

Kim said, would be to invite estimates from a number of builders. But Lisa said no. She was not satisfied with Kim's recommendations. First of all she wanted the place checked by experts for woodworm, deathwatch beetle, dry rot, wet rot and rising damp. They would then be told to deal with what they found. She wanted an architect with a sympathetic interest in old buildings, not with the idea of making any alterations or additions but to take out the Victorian accretions she had noticed (one big room had been split into two, so the dividing wall would have to come down and the new space reconsidered. She wanted a 'seventeenth-century sense of space and simplicity', whatever that meant). And, of course, central heating and double glazing put in. She would buy antique furniture. All this work was actually under way by the summer.

There might be up to a dozen workmen in the house at any one time installing a new kitchen, stripping paper off the oak panelling in the drawing room, leaching tarry black paint from the beams and restoring some of their original light colour. Creaking floorboards were taken up and hammered down more firmly. Men were painting or papering walls and ceilings, laying carpets, hanging curtains (Lisa had spent days in London choosing fabrics and deliberating over sample books). She had been horrified to learn there was only one bathroom. The architect, a man from Oxford with a black beard who looked like Karl Marx, was instructed to make a second bathroom a priority. And an outside toilet for the hired gardener who would take over when the contractors had finished. The roof space, which held a special fascination for Lisa, she had partially boarded so that she could walk about up there (the rest of the floor had fibreglass packed between the joists for insulation) an electric light put in, dead birds and nests removed, the beams scoured and treated with preservative. One day she would have the entire roof lined, but not yet. As she looked around she could see chinks of daylight through the tiles. She rather liked that. It was a real period touch. Bigger holes down by the eaves were plugged to keep more birds from coming in and building.

The Parslers were kept informed of many of these developments and when work in the roof space started Ed lived in daily expectation of his forgery being discovered. He had planted it with care. Too much care apparently. No excited squeal came from Wood End. Harriet never mentioned the plant and gave the impression she had forgotten all about it.

In spite of all this restoration work what chiefly counted with Lisa was the well-being of Joanna now attending, with dignity, the nearest RC school. Her other preoccupation was with Aston's help, starting a baby. So far she had been disappointed. And now, she told Harriet, she was convinced she would conceive only in Stratford-upon-Avon. In a four-poster bed, with hangings. She had called the English Tourist Board to explain her problem. A young woman there seemed unsurprised and sympathetic. Yes, there was a hotel in Stratford that advertised it had a four-poster (it was the Bear) but as there was a lot of competition among the Americans to occupy it she might have to wait until the end of the season. That was not good enough for Lisa. Her need was urgent. She had a lengthy conversation with the manager of the Bear on the telephone and established that if there was an unexpected cancellation the Harts were to be given first refusal.

'But there would be no refusal,' said Lisa. 'We'd come immediately. My husband is a member of Shakespeare's own family. What do you think of that? Doesn't that give us a claim?'

Aston was not entirely pleased with the way Wood End was being renovated. He even found it difficult to know whether he could accept, in the relaxed way Lisa wanted, the fact that she had a lot of money. He had cast himself in the role of the unappreciated victim of the way Britain's empire was being allowed to slip away and it really hurt him that, as matters turned out, he was not being hurt much. He and Jo were benefiting from Lisa's money. Among the self-made men he now met and admired on his trips to the City, soft-speaking, smiling types trading in commodities and property development, he was made to feel a eunuch. Even Edwin Parsler, whom he regarded as a functionary, and his brother-in-law Tom, (when eventually he met him) with his job in the F & C Office and no better than lots of other clerks who sat on their big bottoms waiting for a pension, put him on the defensive. Would he have married Lisa if he'd known she had so much money? He used to think about this from time to time; but he was honest enough to say yes, he needed the money and she really hooked him. He did not understand her. She had interests, like this Shakespeare stuff, that took her where he could not follow. But he did not think she had fancied him just because of Cousin Will. He guessed she saw him as the romantic big white hunter who stopped charging elephants with well-placed shots. He was as keen as she was to have a child. Once that happened he might get her more clearly in focus. Until then he would be conscious of blurs and indistinct areas he could fill in only from his own imagination; this paradoxically presented her as a real, rounded person. More so than anyone else he had ever known, even Shirley.

He had come, reluctantly, to accept he would never make a home in Africa again. Lisa saw them living in England for the rest of their days and Aston more and more identified with her. Trips were different but England was to be the base. No matter he was a stranger there. But he had to hit out on his own account. He wrote letters, pulled strings and was lunched by the occasional tycoon with trading and commercial interests in Africa. Their empires were in southern Africa (not South Africa; Aston was wary of any South African connection), in Malawi, Zambia and Rhodesia (Zimbabwe), where Aston's experience was not worth much. He had the idea of starting an exclusive travel agency specializing in really first-class safari expeditions and was waiting in the outer office of one of the directors of LONRHO, to whom he proposed to sell the idea, when the great man himself came out, looking sly and amused at the same time. He was going to speak to his secretary. The appointment with Aston was plainly not uppermost in his mind but, as soon as he saw him, he said, 'I just remembered. Amin's a friend of yours, eh? You heard what's happened? The PLO have hijacked an Air France plane full of Israelis and landed at Entebbe.'

'That's bad.'

'How do you reckon Amin will play it? These hijackers say they'll blow the plane up and all the Israelis in it unless a lot of Palestinian terrorists are let out of jail. I can't see Amin storming the plane at the head of his troops.'

'He's unpredictable.' Aston thought again. 'His line is anti-Israel now so he'll be playing it to please the Arabs. That's my guess.'

Travelling back in the train Aston read the reports in the evening newspaper but Lisa, who met him at the station, had been listening to the radio and was that much more up to date. 'It's too terrible. Who do we know these Israelis are? They might be concentration camp survivors. After all they've gone through to be at the mercy of terrorists! You know Amin. Why don't you call him, Aston? You could fly out there. The Queen should step in. She's head of the Commonwealth, isn't she? She's Queen of Uganda. She should just put the screws on this fat bastard. Or are you telling me the Commonwealth just doesn't mean a thing.' Lisa was so angry and upset she said she couldn't trust herself to drive, so Aston took over.

'But if I called him and by some fluke got through what would I say?'

Lisa screamed at him. 'Let my people go!'

To please her, but knowing it would do not the slightest good, Aston rang the Presidential office in Kampala (he had key Ugandan telephone numbers in his diary) and as luck had it got through, to be told that the President was in Mauritius at a meeting of the Organization for African Unity. Aston tried to reach him there but all lines seemed permanently engaged. When he was not using the phone Lisa was calling Washington to speak to ex-colleagues in the State Department. By now it was known that the hijackers had set a deadline, 1 a.m. on 4 July and Lisa wanted these colleagues to know what was on their mind. There ought to be US paratroops in there within hours. Somebody said, 'Sure, ma'am, we'll put it in hand right away.' Lisa looked grim. 'Are they heading me off?' Aston said, 'What did you expect?'

But on 1 July the Israelis seemed to back down. They said (and this was for the first time) they would swap Palestinian prisoners for the hostages. The tension slackened. At 1 a.m. on 4 July an Israeli commando task force landed at Entebbe and, within minutes had shot four of the hijackers and were releasing the hostages in preparation for evacuation. Ugandan troops defending the airport were routed. When the news came through Lisa walked about with a shining face and tears of joy in her eyes. Why had she ever imagined the Israelis would give in to terrorists?

Though they talked about Hans from time to time Aston was incurious about Lisa's family background. The emotional storm that hit her before the Entebbe raid made him think there might be a Jewish grandparent in the background. He could not help saying, though, that the Israeli raid was an impressive operation but it was an infringement of Ugandan sovereignty. That's how a lot of people in Africa would see it.

'That's not your view, Aston?'

'No, I'm just saying that even anti-Amin Africans will just see it as whites cocking a leg at blacks.'

'But lives were at stake, for God's sake!'

'You can't expect Africans to see it that way. Don't get me wrong. What the Israelis did was okay by me. But it's got to be a one-off.'

'It won't be a one-off if there's another hijack like this one.'

Lisa's next outburst came when it was learned that one of the hostages, Mrs Dora Bloch, had been admitted to a Kampala hospital before the raid took place. She was no longer there after the Israeli commandos and the freed hostages flew out. All the signs were she had been murdered. 'She's British,' said Lisa. 'Yeah, she's Israeli too but she's British and if that's the way the British Government lets its nationals be treated it'll be one kick up the ass after another from now on. Why wait for things to happen? The only way is not to. You've got to be realistic. Get your own reaction in first.'

Aston laughed. 'That'd make a good family motto.'

'It's the sort of thing my father would have said. He was anti-Semitic as hell, which is why I'm so much the other way, I guess. Yes, if that's what you meant, Aston, you're dead right. It's the German flick response.'

'I didn't mean that at all.'

'What did you mean?'

'Just what I said. I thought it was funny. Why was your father anti-Semitic?'

'It was a generation thing. He thought Hitler was right.'

Aston realized the Jewish grandparent theory was out. He also realized he did not know as much about Lisa as he should.

Harriet's brother Tom was keen to talk to Aston about Amin and invited him to lunch at the Travellers' Club. They had not met before. Tom was quick to remind Aston, when he telephoned, that he had used his position at the Foreign and Colonial Office, to facilitate enquiries when the Parslers had been trying to locate him two or three years ago. The implication was that Aston was under an obligation.

Tom jumped up from a chair in the entrance hall of the club as soon as he heard Aston say to the doorkeeper, 'Mr Hubbard is expecting me.'

Tom Hubbard was an athletic, fresh-faced, stringy-looking man who ought to have been at least a stone heavier to be physically easy, but he jogged ten miles a day to keep himself screwed down. He was older than Harriet and the little hair he retained was silvery. Aston noted the round, metal-rimmed National Health Service spectacles and assumed they were worn, not because Hubbard could afford nothing better, but because they were a status symbol. Another hint that Aston had a lot to learn about living in England.

They had a drink in the bar where Hubbard wanted to know whether Aston had a London club. 'No, well, you'd feel at home here, old man. Some people call this the FO canteen. Sub is pretty moderate, all things considered. Good cellar. Useful library. But it's the chaps. That's the main thing. Never know who you're going to run into. I'd be glad to put you up for membership. Truth is, we need members.'

'I mightn't stand up to all the requirements.'

Hubbard slapped him on the shoulder, laughing louder than was necessary. 'I doubt that. You're not an unknown quantity to us, you know. Let's go and eat. I've booked a table.'

Hubbard had an austere lunch – consommé jelly and a rare steak with salad – but Aston had a plate of whitebait (the kind of dish, like kippers, he yearned for in Africa, but in vain) and duck à l'orange. Hubbard stuck to water but he insisted on Aston having a carafe of the club white Bordeaux which he said was quite drinkable. It was obvious he had not only FCO sources of information but gossip from the Parslers as well. Aston knew nothing that would be of any use or interest to Hubbard and his colleagues but guessed Hubbard liked to give the impression he had valuable personal contacts. 'Grainger' – he was the High Commissioner in Kampala – 'is bound to take that line. But I hear from a chap just back', etc. Aston could imagine him throwing out a remark like that. Hubbard knew about the refurbishing of Wood End, and that Lisa wanted to stay in England. Now he wanted titbits of information about Amin.

Aston said he had no idea how Amin would take the Entebbe raid. He had seen press reports that when Amin saw the hostages in the early stages of their detention at the airport he had greeted them with the Hebrew word '*Shalom*', and worn Israeli wings on his uniform. But press reports are just press reports. Amin was quite capable of having a dozen or so of his own *askaris* shot to ensure the survivors stood up to the Israelis next time they landed. He was also capable of praising the Israelis and saying they were the sort of soldiers he wanted his own men to be.

'Why did you stop working for him and get out of the country?'

'It was the time of the Hills affair. I put my oar in.'

Hills was a British lecturer in Kampala who had been sentenced to death by Amin for referring to him a manuscript (not published at that time) as 'a village tyrant'. After personal pleas for clemency by the Queen and the Prime Minister Hills was reprieved and Jim Callaghan, the British Foreign Secretary, flew out to bring him home.

'What happened?'

'Amin said Hills was a criminal and as I'd spoken up for him I must be a criminal too. I was next on his list.'

'You speak Swahili?'

'Sure.'

'How do you think the President will react to the break in diplomatic relations? It was announced at noon today.'

Aston put his glass down and stared at the remains of the Stilton he had been eating. 'Honest? Broken off diplomatic relations?'

'Personally I don't see what good this sort of thing does. But public opinion, you know. And MPs working themselves into a froth, each trying to outdo the other in patriotic indignation. Some of it genuine, some not. It was the Mrs Bloch tragedy that clinched it. But it doesn't make the job of looking after the interests of British subjects in Uganda any easier. Let's go into the library and have some coffee.'

Breaking off diplomatic relations with Uganda seemed daft to Aston. How could you break off relations with another member of the Commonwealth? Had it ever happened before?

'What interests me,' said Hubbard once they had settled in leather chairs with cups of black coffee on the table before them, 'is what happens next year. It'll be the Queen's Silver Jubilee and the Commonwealth conference, both in June. Interesting situation would arise if Amin insisted on coming.' During the silence that followed Aston was aware that Hubbard was studying him closely. 'So you haven't any particular job on hand?'

'Not yet. I've feelers out. Something will turn up.'

'A pity all that experience and knowledge going to waste. In the run up to the conference protocol department takes on extra hands to cope. Interested?'

'I can't look ahead that far. What's involved?'

'Not only the run up. During the conference itself.'

'Servicing the delegates, you mean? What's that involve? Blowing their noses for them, show 'em the loo, fixing theatre tickets. And women, no doubt. Not my line.'

'Not even if the President himself arrived? We'd need all the assistance we could get to handle that one. Say no more. Real work doesn't start until the New Year. Now, if you'll excuse me, I've got to dash. Please stay on and finish your coffee.' He hesitated. 'It's so far ahead. By next summer everything may be normalized. In diplomacy a year is a long time.'

Aston did indeed stay and finish his coffee. He also ordered a cognac and explained to the waiter that he was Mr Hubbard's guest. Diplomacy! A year was a bloody short time in diplomacy, not long. A man who talked as Hubbard did lacked firepower. Aston was so relaxed he even stayed and had a nap in that same leather armchair he was occupying, and did not leave until nearly four. No, he didn't want Hubbard to put him up for membership.

Lisa said there had been a visitor that afternoon – the Rector, the Reverend Paul Brough, who arrived without warning on a bicycle. He was a lean, tense sort of man with worried, or perhaps angry, expression on his cockerel-like face who repeatedly ran a finger round the inside of his dog collar. He wanted

131

to welcome the Harts to the local community. A difficult parish, he had explained, or two parishes really because of the amalgamation in 1947. So many of the men worked in Bicester or Banbury or Oxford. No sense of community. He was no longer a young man, pushing 50, he said and occasionally it got him down, the way his congregation was made up of elderly females. He, himself, had never married. No special reason for this. He was not against women. Just an accident of circumstance. Would it be too much to ask if Lisa and her husband were of any special religious persuasion?

Lisa explained she had been brought up a Lutheran but had lapsed. Her husband was an Anglican but he did not go to church either, at least not on his own account. He took his daughter, Joanna, to the Roman Catholic church in Bicester. Her mother had been RC. Lisa filled in some of the family background. At this moment Jo walked in and the Reverend Paul Brough, after examining her carefully, said, 'But I know you. You're the little girl who stayed with the Parslers. What a pleasant surprise.'

'I don't remember, I'm sorry.' Jo held herself so erect and so steady she might have been balancing a basket on her head. 'I was very ill and then my daddy came and took me back to Africa. He married Lisa to be my mother-on-Earth. My real mother is in Heaven.'

'Very well said.' The Rector pursed his lips, his face quivered and the invisible scarlet wattles shook. 'So things have turned out all right,' he said to Lisa. 'You're American.'

'We're okay. Once we get this house sorted out.' They were in the main sitting room where, in preparing the ceiling for papering, the workman had brought down several square yards round the central chandelier and then left early because it was sports day at his son's school, with plaster and other rubbish left scattered all over the place. Fortunately the carpet had been covered with protective sheets and the furniture draped. Lisa sat on the decorator's trestle and the Rector stood with his legs wide apart, bicycle clips still round the bottoms of his trousers.

'So you must know the Parslers,' he said. 'He writes poetry. Must say it's a bit deep for me. Well' – preparing for departure and with an air of having drawn blank in this household – 'I'm sorry to have missed your husband. Being an old bachelor I don't do much entertaining. Perhaps I should. Would you come? I mean, we could have a drink in my little garden one of these hot evenings. Isn't it incredible weather?'

The Reverend Paul Brough cycled the couple of miles back to his red-brick Rectory bungalow, humming tunelessly to himself and thinking of the Parslers. He had really done his best to cultivate them. Seeing that Ed was a fairly regular communicant he asked him to read the prayers at Family Communion but Ed said he was not a good enough Christian for that. Eventually he agreed to read one of the Lessons and, as luck had it, it came from the Prophet Hosea 11, verses 1 to 11. 'When Israel was a boy, I loved him; I called my son out of Egypt; but the more I called, the further they went from me.' Yet in spite of the backsliding of Israel God would not destroy her, 'for I am God and not a man'.

When Ed was leaving the church after the service he said to the Rector that he had not really understood the lesson. Perhaps he ought to read the whole book of Hosea and see the text in its proper context.

'Do that,' said the Rector quietly as the other members of the congregation waited to file past and shake his hand. 'The key to the whole thing is that Hosea was a poet (poet and prophet are the same in the Old Testament) whose wife deceived him. There is a parallel between God's love for faithless Israel and Hosea's love for his worthless wife. "Go again," said the Lord, "and love a woman loved by another man, an adulteress, and love her as I, the Lord, love the Israelites." ' The Rector hesitated and then went on. 'There is no doubt in my mind that Jesus was thinking of the prophet Hosea when he said to the woman taken in adultery, "Go and sin no more." We even know the name of Hosea's wife. She was Gomer. Perhaps I shall tackle this in a sermon one day. If God can love sinful mankind can not a man love a sinful wife? "How can I give you up? How can I surrender you?" ' For a bachelor this was uttered with surprising passion. Or, perhaps, not so surprising. Celibates must have a lot bottled up.

As the subject took hold of him the Rector's voice was raised, almost as though he wished to draw in those waiting to leave and make them listen to what was becoming an impromptu sermon. 'Perhaps it's a lot to ask, that we should love as God loves. But it is asked of each and every one of us.' He nodded at Ed. 'You read it beautifully. Of course, this would be a difficult subject for a sermon. On the whole, I think I'll duck out.'

That rainless and scorched summer the thermometer could be up in the 80s by midmorning and the razed fields, after the wheat and barley had been cut, stretched away feverish and brilliant. They were enormous, between the woods, savannah-like in the heat. After the cool of the church the open air glowed. A marble headstone flashed in the sun, too painful to look at. Ed, in the lightest of clothes, sandals, cotton slacks and shirt under a biscuit linen jacket, decided on the long walk back to Troy Corner, past the reedy, dried-up pond that had once been a fishpond for a long vanished religious house. He was tieless. How his father would have marvelled. How could you go to church and read the lesson dressed for the beach? Women no longer covered their hair. One woman wore a gauzy, flowered and backless dress that drew the eyes up the indented back and between the soapy-smooth shoulders to the great stalk, the column holding the huge sandy chrysanthemum of hair. That is how he saw her, voluptuously. Someone was coming to lunch. He could not remember whom, but it was still early and there was no hurry.

He climbed the stile. First in the wood was a dead elm, leafless and wintery against a background of summery green birches. Up the hill were two slumbering oaks, not a leaf stirring. But the wood was cool. The trees sucked heat out of the air. The shade was a cool breathing of air, next best thing to the water he was making for. Ed knew the wood best in winter. There were foxes here and one old dog fox in particular they were sometimes lucky enough to head into the open, two seasons running, but they never caught him; so he must be hereabouts still. Half a mile downhill, through ground that had now given way to fern, was the stream, just a trickle compared with normal but wide enough to need a plank bridge just above the natural pool where, surely, kids from the village would be splashing about. But no. Nobody. Silence. Instead of crossing by the planks he walked through the water. The bottom was firm. Mud. And pebbles he could feel through the soles of his sandals. The water did not come up to his knees but was astonishingly cold. He scooped up a handful and dashed it over his face and the shock set off a body sweat. After the first shock and, fully clothed as he was, Ed lay down in it, on his back, with his head resting on the ferny bank.

> Out in the brook I lie in bed,
> Heaven conspicuous overhead
>   In a windless summer dream;
> Forests of green have made complete
> The morning eucharist; my feet
> Point in the running stream.

It took some minutes of playing with words and rhyme until he arrived at something he could accept and then forget about. By then he was aware he was being looked at from the opposite bank.

'Oh,' said the boy when Ed raised his head. 'You all right then? I thought you might be dead, or something.'

Ed rolled over on to his front and, now completely sodden, stood up, the water streaming from him and his clothes clinging icily. The boy was in bathing trunks. He was joined by another boy and they became wide-eyed fauns with tails and hooves. But shy, because when he said, 'Just taking a cooler', they disappeared. Ran off. Where the eyes had been were now green leaves. Ed knew they were boys from the village. But at some profounder and unpersuadable level they were fauns and they would come back with more fauns to torment.

'Of course, I love her.' He actually muttered these words out loud. 'I don't hate.' He fought against the delusion that he hated Hatty. He stepped out of the pool and his shoes squelched. From time to time he had these mad stretches when the mind said, 'There's nothing wrong. You just have this delusion.' But it did not make the delusion go away. When Harriet had been pregnant with Mark they had gone to Vancouver to stay with her brother and his family. The last part of the journey they made by train from Calgary. During the night he became aware that Harriet was missing from the sleeping bunk overhead and when he eventually found her, she was in the observation car, a

135

dressing gown over her pyjamas, quite alone looking at what could be seen of the Rockies in the pallor before dawn, black rock faces and swooping grey emptinesses under a few tinny stars. Harriet did not see him. That's not my baby she's carrying, he thought. I'm not the father. That was the conviction that took hold as he looked along the car to where she was sitting.

'Couldn't sleep. And you were snoring so I thought I'd catch the dawn.'

What the hell's the matter that you have these crazy fears? Or are they fears? Aren't they wishful thinking? You just *want* to be cuckolded and that's why the delusion won't go away. What makes you so vulnerable, emotionally, anyway? You had a loving family. Dad and mum weren't demonstrative but they didn't neglect you either. Your father didn't stop kissing you until you were twelve and, of course, your mother never did stop. You never had any grounds for supposing you were unlovable. So, why now? Even when Mark was born and everyone said how like his father he was (quite true, this) Ed could detect the nerve tremor that told him the old incubus was still there. Now, years later, as he walked back to Troy Corner in his dripping clothes he could not remember how it was exorcized. Hard work and a more active life, perhaps. It was a plus he could think they would work again.

He was still working hard and taking more exercise than ever. What with tennis and riding he was fitter than in the early years of the marriage, when he and Hatty lived in London, so he ought to have grown out of delusions. Like this one about hating her. Why was it, too, he had seen fauns in the wood and was now sure they had disappeared to find, not other fauns to torment him, but Lisa. He was, quite suddenly, irradiated by her presence. Lisa! She was in the wood with him. That was put badly. He knew perfectly well that Lisa was not in the wood; but he could not help responding.

He took the footpath over the field called Wychall and there was no escaping Lisa there either. Arthur Crick had combined his wheat there the day before and now the straw lay in bands on the stubble waiting to be fired. Whole patches of the field where the full sun was reflected seemed already incandescent and puffs of hot air blew in his face and parched him. Parched his clothes too. His skin was quite dry already. But Lisa said it was no ordinary heat. Look at the little dragons with golden scales exhaling gentle fire, she said, through their quivering nostrils. Look at them and see how friendly they were. Look at the radiant day and see how it welcomes him. She stroked him with cool fingers. In spite of the heat she was so cool and reassuring he was uplifted. He was able to share some of that coolness and share her – well, it wasn't just enthusiasm for the whole world, visible and invisible, because she wasn't as naive as that. It was a largeness of spirit she induced. A kind of sanctity.

The heat made him reel. The icy plunge and then the heat again, all on top of the bread and wine sent him. The sacred meal worked inside him and now Lisa was leading him. Another delusion? Yes, of course it was. He was sent on the fiery field in which he stood, the dark wood behind and the empty blue serenity of the sky (how easy to fall into it!) and by the imagined presence of Lisa. He was so drunk with what he saw it all seemed new. Never before had he felt so alive.

Born again, in a way. He was the rejoicing heir of this created world, and (Lisa told him) Harriet too was a rejoicing heiress of this created world. They were all rejoicing. They were mortals leaning in the fiery, gentle breath of God. Yes, he was Hosea. Now he understood it. 'Go again,' said the Lord, 'and love a woman loved by another man.' Ever since his father died he had guarded himself against delusions until he now discovered himself victim to the really great delusion, that Harriet had not slept around. She had, and he had fought like all hell to con himself! The defence mechanism had played him false. Never, since his father died, had so much reality been thrown at him. And he could take it. He could take hold of it and rise like a bird with mud and straw in his beak and claws. Harriet was indeed loved by another man (he had fought against knowing this) and yet they were both there to love and enjoy the world, and each other. Lisa showed him how by running so lightly over the straw it did not even crackle under her weight.

The guests for lunch were Hugh Cornish and his sister Angela. When Edwin appeared Harriet rose from her garden seat.

'I could do with a drink,' he said.

'What have you been doing?'

'Came back the Wychall way.'

'But you're soaking and covered with mud.'

'Found myself in the stream, somehow.'

They were drinking white wine. Harriet offered him a glass but he brushed it aside and made for the house. She followed and, as he went up to the bathroom, darted to the drinks cupboard for whisky. When she reached him he was, still in his wet clothes leaning over one of the wash basins as though preparing to vomit. Harriet put the whisky down and undid his jacket. He had his eyes closed and made no resistance when she removed it.

'I don't hate you. That'd be a helluva lie,' he said. 'If anyone said I hated you.' Then his shirt, pants, everything. He stood there naked while she rubbed him over with one of her own personal, fluffy pink towels. He went to bed as he was and after a bout of shivering fell asleep in a hot sweat.

Hugh and his sister had gone by the time Ed came downstairs in the late afternoon. The heat was more intense than ever. Wearing nothing but shorts and sandals he sat in the kitchen drinking tea which set him sweating again and he dabbed at his throat and chest with a drying-up cloth that came to hand. No, he didn't want Brownlow, the local GP. He wouldn't come anyway, on a Sunday, except in a real emergency, perhaps not even a severed limb, it might have to be the head. Anyway, Ed felt fine. He'd had a spasm. It was all over now. He would take a shower and see if that helped.

'Where are the kids?' he asked.

'They're all right.' Harriet was studying him. 'You're not going to the office tomorrow. You know that, don't you? I'll make an appointment with Brownlow and drive you over. You just don't have spasms. So, you must get Brownlow to give you a checkup.'

'These days,' said Ed, 'GPs don't give checkups. You know that.'

'He could fix it for you to have it done privately at the hospital. You've been paying medical insurance all these years.'

'I must be due for my annual at the London Clinic anyway.'

138

Edwin took his shower, not a cold one, just tepid, and put on a very old, faded, navy-blue cotton shirt he had bought donkeys' years before in Naples and which he wore whenever he was off duty and felt a special need to calm down. That Naples holiday had been before he even met Harriet. So it was a very old shirt indeed, preserved for sentimental reasons, which Harriet knew all about. He was with a girl called Carrie who eventually married a soldier. They had had a good, relaxed, loving holiday, eating at restaurants on stilts in the harbour and taking trips to Capri and Ischia. Everything went just right and the dark-blue cotton shirt brought the calm of it back. Ed went down and rang Hugh to apologize for the way he had messed up the lunch.

'Are you all right? Angela and I were concerned, Edwin. What was it? You sound perky now, I must say. Heat stroke? Could be. You missed the most delicious food. Vichyssoise and escalope something or other. We sat outside and as your bedroom window was open we could actually hear you snoring from time to time, so Harriet didn't even have to go and check whether you were still breathing. Joking apart, we were all very worried. Might have been food poisoning. But Harriet said you went off to church without any breakfast at all. Not many people take communion with that kind of discipline these days, you know.'

'I just wanted to apologize for presenting myself in that state. This bloody heatwave just goes on and on.'

'Oh, Edwin. By the way.' Hugh was one of the few who called him Edwin.

'Yes.'

'What happened about that Shakespeare forgery?'

'It never surfaced.'

'Rum, that.'

'Yes, rum.'

Harriet prepared him some cold chicken and salad. As he sat with her, still in the kitchen, eating it he said it had been in his mind for some time to mention it, but they really ought to do something about CTT.

'What's that?'

'Capital Transfer Tax. What's been brought in to replace the old death duty. I ought to know. I should have done something

139

about it before. It's always the barber who's in need of a haircut. One of the great legal jokes is that the chap who wrote the standard book on Probate actually forgot to make his own will and died intestate. So I'm a lawyer and I don't do the right thing legally.'

'Why should you bring this up now?'

'It's been on my mind. You see, under the new rules there is no CTT between spouses, so whenever one or other of us dies the survivor gets the lot, free of CTT. But after the second death there's a whacking CTT to pay and the kids might find themselves stripped of as much as a hundred thousand quid or so. That would be payable immediately if, say, we both got bumped off in a car crash.'

'Like on that night.'

'Like on that night,' he agreed. 'The first £60,000 or so, as the rate stands, would go free of tax. But the rest, whoosh! So we've got to minimize it.' He went into detail about this. They could separately will £30,000 each to Jessica and Mark. Then they could formally divide the ownership of everything they had, the house, investments, cash, equally between themselves and formally will their portion to the other. He'd check on the insurance policies to see whether they were written in such a way they fell outside the estate so that Jessica and Mark could benefit directly.

'You sound as though you're getting ready for a divorce.'

'Hell, no! This is just to minimize CTT on the second death. It's just what any lawyer would advise us to do.'

'Because if it's Jerry you've got on your mind I have to tell you I gave him up for Lent. You'll remember that's how I managed to give up smoking.'

The words popped out and she rather regretted them because, although she believed that life could be so grim one's duty was to take it as lightly as possible, nobody wanted to be thought frivolous. Quite right, she had dropped Jerry at the beginning of Lent and it amused her to think it was her penance that year. It was coincidence, no more, but that was not good enough. Much more satisfying to think of it as religious observance. But now she had actually uttered the words, and to Ed, she could well (she thought) be kidding herself. She threw out the quip about

Lent to show what fun life could be for the unconventional and uninhibited. But it didn't ring true. More likely she was just a bitch, which was what her brother Tom told her now and again.

Jerry certainly thought she was a bitch and so did his wife, Olwen, which made three of them. To Harriet's amazement she had been telephoned by Olwen one day and told she was behaving very badly to Jerry. He had become moody, drank spirits heavily (Olwen could not bring herself to mention which), quarrelsome to the point of violence and, Olwen feared, suicidal. Olwen sounded not the slightest bit hysterical about all this. She was calm, even jokey about a conversation she'd had when she called the Samaritans and found herself talking to a woman who said her husband was just the same and what the hell could they do, just the two of them? Olwen forced herself to come to the point. She had long since got over the shock of Jerry's infidelity. The physical side of it hadn't wounded her as much as it might . have wounded some women because she had never had sex drive. Being an ex-nurse she thought it came into the same category as administering or receiving an enema.

You don't know what you're missing, Harriet wanted to tell her, but didn't. An enema! It was like saying music was catgut scraping. In spite of being Welsh Olwen was probably not musical either.

Olwen said it would help her if Harriet would see Jerry, even if it was just to have a talk. He was at the end of his tether. His life, Olwen's life, their life together, could not go on in this way. Harriet could not suck him dry, like an orange, and drop what was left in the compost bucket. Give him a ring right away. He's at the hospital. Just to hear her voice would set him up. Olwen wanted them to get on with whatever they were doing before Jerry had this breakdown.

'Breakdown?'

'Yes, breakdown. You heard.'

'Poor lamb!'

'So you will phone him, won't you, Harriet? I don't think your husband can have much objection judging by what he said and the way he behaved when I spoke to him about you and Jerry. He seemed very understanding.'

'Did he?' Harriet pondered this. 'I don't think it's much good you getting in touch with the Samaritans. Why don't you get Jerry to do it himself? This woman you spoke to might find some way of telling him how to pull himself together. Then *you* might speak to *her* husband and tell him a few home truths too. In counselling it's a bit like surgery. No surgeon should take out his or her spouse's appendix. It isn't only the knowledge, it's the detachment you need if your therapy is going to be effective. What a bit of luck you hit on this particular Samaritan woman. Sounds like you've got yourself a ready-made therapy group.'

And she put the phone down. Yes, she was a bitch. And hard hearted. She could see that now; so what with her brother Tom and the two Clutsams that made four of them in the secret. Only Ed, among those closest to her, did not think she was a bitch. Jessica probably did. Mark had started to write poetry and there was no knowing what went on behind those preoccupied eyes. So he was out. Why could she be sure Ed wasn't critical and potentially hostile? Because he wasn't like that. The day he had come home after lying in the stream with his clothes on he had made that clear. He said he didn't hate her. They were – well, living the way it was now. She a bit more than Ed. But there was Lisa. She was better than nothing and now Ed had started along this path in his fifties there would be other muses later on to quicken his old bones and restore some of the fading vision.

So when Edwin's lecture on Capital Transfer Tax made her blurt out that she had given up Jerry for Lent Ed had, after blinking twice and looking at her sharply, merely become even more emphatic he wasn't softening her up for divorce, that the course he proposed was the one any sensible couple should follow when they were getting on in years, or given to drunken driving, she was able to say, 'All right! I'll buy it. But you've got to admit you've got a poor sense of timing. I'd come straight home from church in future and not through Wychall, if I were you. When you walked in you looked like the raising of Lazarus. You know that? You were really frightening. Why do you treat me like this?'

'Because I love you,' he said.

As the front door bell rang so the cat brought a live mouse into the kitchen, released it and with rare detachment watched it scamper away. Harriet screamed. To her the mouse seemed huge, even though commonsense told her it was just a field mouse and harmless. Normally the cat just killed these field mice and left them lying about as virility symbols so what did he mean by letting this one go, and in the house? She had never known him show this kind of malice before. There were holes in the skirting board and once he was through there the mouse had a free run of all the tracks and tunnels hidden behind plaster and panelling. If he was a he. A female mouse, pregnant, and the house would be infested. Harriet was terrified of mice, even field mice and she had no idea what to do but scream.

'Anything the matter?' A man in shirt sleeves and jeans was standing just outside the back door and she guessed that he had come round from the front of the house because he had heard her screaming. He was young, immensely tall and hairy; long, fair hair that covered his ears and a moustache that drooped over his mouth. He had a ruddy complexion, sunk cheeks and blue eyes. A Viking raider, she thought, not knowing whether she was glad to see him or not.

'There's a mouse. He's gone into the cupboard under the sink unit.'

'Would you like me to deal with it?' The cat slunk off, in his white gloves and tuxedo, like a disappointed conjurer, deciding that his trick was not going to pay off, and in a matter of minutes the Viking was down on his knees with the mouse in his huge, cupped hands. 'What shall I do with it?'

'Take it as far away as you can. Out into the middle of the field and let it go.'

When he came back Harriet was waiting for him at the back door.

'Seems I came just when I could be useful.' His voice had a

crack in it. 'Here's my card,' he said tunelessly, flatly, slowly but with a grin as though he did not expect Harriet to believe what he was about to tell her. She read that he was Abraham Henderson, Architect and Surveyor, with a business address in Aylesbury and a private address in Brill. 'I must apologize for calling without an appointment but it's the most practical course. I'm an inspector, part time, for the Department of the Environment and I'm checking to make sure there are no buildings that should be listed but aren't.'

'A likely story.'

'You've seen my card. But there's this as well.' He produced a photograph of himself affixed to a Department of the Environment identity card. 'I'll go away, if you prefer and call again on appointment. I've been driving round inspecting buildings from the outside. This is an interesting looking place but it isn't even mentioned in Pevsner's guide. I wonder why.'

At this point Arthur Weedon, Mrs Weedon's husband, a pensioner who did odd jobs, came into the yard carrying a couple of buckets of oats and looked quizzically in Harriet's direction. She had forgotten it was one of his mornings and was reassured.

'What do you mean, listed?' Harriet still kept Henderson in the yard. It now turned out he was one of those matter of fact, loquacious men who, when it came to the exposition of matters near to their heart lost all sense of time. He just went on and on, with tuneless deliberation. Under the 1971 Planning Act, he explained, buildings of special historical or architectural interest could be listed by the Department. This meant they could not be pulled down or drastically altered without special permission. 'Have you any exposed beams?'

Harriet said no but he was welcome to come in and have a look round for himself.

Henderson said he was all the more grateful because he had just been turned away from another house in the neighbourhood.

'Where was that?'

'Over there. On the other side of the hill. A place called Wood End. It's been much added to but I think a bit of it may be very old indeed. On one elevation I could see cruck beams.'

144

'What are they?'

'Crucks? Bent timbers resting on the ground and rising to meet at the ridge. Could be medieval. Unusual in this part.'

Henderson went over Troy Corner with Harriet and said it was a charming and desirable house but only the shell was more than two hundred years old and even that had been extensively rebuilt. The windows were Victorian and out of keeping with the stone walls. Basically, it was an eighteenth-century farm house that had been gentrified. He did not feel he ought to take up more of her time. 'I'd guess even its name is modern. It's fanciful.'

Harriet rather took to Henderson. She gave him a cup of coffee and, when he revealed that he had been turned away from Wood End by an American woman offered to ring her up and see whether there was any chance of her changing her mind.

'You know her? I suppose it's natural for people to be cautious, particularly if it's a woman on her own. But there were workmen in the house.'

So they went over there, to Wood End. Lisa said it was all right by her if this guy was some kind of Government inspector but when he called she had been putting flour and fat into the food processor, making one of Aston's favourite puddings and she wasn't going to be interrupted. If Harriet said he was on the level, sure, why didn't they come over, both of them? Aston was up in town trying to fix some deal or other. Yes, she meant both of them because the workmen had packed up for the day, she was alone and felt vulnerable even if the man was what he claimed to be. You never can tell.

Henderson had a bottle-green Dyane, one of those little French cars, and when he folded himself into the driving seat his knees came up to the dashboard. He was so wedged that Harriet offered to release the handbrake for him but he said he would be okay once he'd got his breath back. He had taken the inspecting job to raise extra money. His wife was going to have a baby and they would have to get a bigger car. Not an expense they had foreseen. Life was tough for architects, these days.

At Wood End Lisa was upstairs, changing her dress and putting her face in order. She opened a bedroom window and, once Henderson had levered himself out of the Dyane, like a mollusc escaping from its shell, shouted an invitation for them to go right in. Minutes later she appeared in sandals and a pink trouser suit with finger and toenails painted to match.

'Sorry about the way I told you to get going,' she told Henderson, 'but what do you expect, the way you operate? What's this about a listed building?' She listened to what he had to say. She smiled. 'If there was ever a listed building this is it. You know what its historical associations are? It was gifted to my husband's ancestor by his cousin, Lady Barnard who was William Shakespeare's granddaughter. And he was Shakespeare's great-nephew.'

Henderson asked if he could walk round the outside of the house. When he came back he wanted to inspect the main sitting room which, he said, was pretty well the whole ground floor of the original farmhouse. Incidentally, he had been wrong about the cruck beams. Must be confusing it with another house. But it was quite old. Those great beams making a cross in the ceiling and, being supported at either end by the bearing walls, were original.

'We've been told in the village it was once four rooms,' Lisa said.

'Might have been in Victorian times but in 1640, or thereabouts, when it was built it could only have the beams put that way if one big room was intended. A farm kitchen and living room combined.'

'That figures,' said Lisa. '1640.'

'This room and what's over it and the roof are the only interesting bits. All the rest of the house is eighteen and nineteenth century addition. Quaint but ordinary from the Department's point of view. Mind if I see the beams in the roof?'

'What about the Shakespeare association?'

'I don't know anything about that. I'm just an architect.' Henderson pointed out where the original staircase must have been. 'Pity about the windows.'

'What's wrong with them?'

'Victorian, like at this lady's house, Troy Corner. If he could see this room now Shakespeare's nephew wouldn't recognize it. What's under the carpet?'

'Concrete. Used to be a cellar but it was all filled in years ago.'

'You see?' But Henderson just loved the beams. He was tall enough to caress them. Upstairs in the main bedroom there were unpainted oak beams in their natural state and Henderson went about kissing them. When they finally arrived in the roof, with Lisa's newly installed electric light switched on, and were able to walk up and down on the boards Henderson said the roof space was so huge it must have been used for storage. Hay, maybe apples and pears had been stored up here. 'I can see this boarding is new but there's this old, original planking too. From a barn possibly. Or even a ship. And there, look, with their feet resting on the bearing walls are symmetrical crucks. They were made by slicing the trunk of a bent tree along its length. That's really beautiful. There's some muck here.'

'Muck? Shouldn't be any muck. I had the place cleared out.'

Henderson drew out a handful of dirty-looking hay and feathers plugging a cavity between the beam and the wall but so high up neither of the women could have reached it. He grunted, put his hand in again and produced a piece of worn sacking. Finally, he extracted a wad which, when examined in the light, turned out to be thick folded paper. 'Hm! There's writing on it. Captain Blackbeard's treasure map, no doubt.' He handed the paper to Lisa. 'Looks pretty old to me. Might be interesting.'

Lisa asked him to check whether there was anything else in the cavity. When he said no she smoothed the paper out. 'Yeah, there's handwriting but you just can't read it, it's so squeezed up and wiggly.'

Henderson went on talking ecstatically about the beams and explaining why, in spite of their quality, he was not going to recommend listing the house.

'So why don't we get out of here?' Harriet had not exactly forgotten the bogus letter Ed had planted but it was way down below the conscious level. Now that it had surfaced she was not amused. 'Lisa, you ought to let me take it and show it to Ed. He might be able to make something of it.'

Downstairs, in the little bedroom that Lisa had converted into a study she examined the document with the magnifying glass that went with her Compact Edition of the *Oxford Dictionary* and began to squeal. 'But you *can* make it out! This calligraphy comes back to me. Say, there's a date. Jeez, oh no, my God, look,

147

"Twenty-five November, 1609." ' She gripped the paper fiercely and Harriet, glimpsing her face, just could not look away. It had lost all colour. She might have been white porcelain. Then the colour came back in a great flush of excitement. 'Do you know what, folks? Do you know what I hold here? It says, "Your brother, William S", and who do you think that is? Oh my God, tell me!'

'I wouldn't jump to conclusions, Lisa. Just let me take it over and show it to Ed.'

Henderson asked if he could see the letter. Lisa would not let him take it from her. She held it up to the light of her reading lamp and he bent to study the writing over her shoulder. 'Can't make head nor tail of it. I can see the date, now you point it out.'

'See that "Willm S"?'

'1609. But that's before the house was built.'

'So what? When the Harts moved in wouldn't they bring old letters?'

Henderson shrugged. 'And conceal one of them in the roof?'

'There are lots of ways it could have ended up there.' Lisa was still poring over the letter, picking out words. ' "Dear loving sister!" There! It's a letter to his sister Joan. And look, look! "The house in Henley Street." That's where the Harts were living at one time. The birthplace.'

'You're smarter than I am if you can read that.' For Henderson it had all become something of a joke. He began scratching his head and laughing. 'I just chance in and pull this out of the wall. Funny, that. Makes you think, doesn't it?'

'I did a course in Tudor calligraphy at college,' said Lisa.

'You did?' This surprised Harriet. 'That's a bit specialized.'

'For years I've just prepared myself for the possibility of something like this, Harriet. It is my fate.' Lisa was less agitated now and seemed to be sailing into the calm ecstasy, with radiant face and parted lips, of a transcendental experience, as it might be, the Vision of the Blessed William standing before her with a quill pen in one hand and one of his 'foul papers' in the other. 'Of course, we'll have to get it checked by the experts but I just know it's authentic. Nothing is going to persuade me it isn't the real thing. I just know by the vibes.'

Seeing there was no more for him to do Henderson made a

move to go and Harriet followed him down to the hall. He thought she was going to ask for a lift back to Troy Corner.

'No, it isn't that. I'll hang on here a bit. But what I want you to do, Mr Henderson is to keep quiet about this.'

'Switched her on, all right, didn't it.'

'Mrs Hart needs protecting. It can't possibly be what she thinks. Sounds more like somebody playing a joke, if you ask me. Anyway, don't tell anybody.'

'Not even my wife? It's a bit of a story. I just put my hand in. I didn't expect anything, only that muck.'

'I've got your card so I know how to get in touch. If there are any developments I'll let you know. I can't make you take a vow of silence. But I hope I can rely on you.'

'I won't tell anyone if you don't want me to.'

'When is the baby expected?'

'Next week.'

'Your wife will be thinking of other matters. So don't bother her with this just now. Don't tell her. Not even her. I'll give you a ring later on to know whether it's a boy or a girl.'

Back in the study Lisa had mastered enough of the letter to be convinced it was authentic. 'What he says about his sister's sons is really poignant. His own son died. You know that, Harriet? "Be happy in your sons." He's envious, you see. Well, it's understandable. The last years must have been a bit gloomy for the guy. *The Tempest*, he must have been turning it over in 1609, and what does he get Prospero to say? "My ending is despair/ Unless I be reliev'd by prayer." Oh, Harriet! I want to throw up. I'm so excited I want to throw up.'

Lisa had too much style to be capable of anything so lacking in elegance as throwing up. She might take off, though. Harriet could imagine her lifted by invisible hands and floating up to the ceiling. That was the way Ed saw her all the time, as a seraph, as innocence, purity and happiness made visible; this was the creature who shook poems out of him.

'What were you talking to that architect about downstairs?'

'I asked him to keep quiet. You've got to be realistic. Just sit on this thing for a few days. Don't say anything to anyone. Allow time for the temperature to drop. Then get Ed over and ask him what he thinks you should do next.'

149

'Why Ed?'

'Why not? The chances are this letter is a fake and if it is Ed may have something to say about it.'

'But it *isn't* a fake. I'm not going to be talked out of it.'

Harriet wanted Ed to meet head on the consequences of planting this letter. 'Ed has contacts in Oxford who can vet the thing quietly. That's the main thing. If you go screaming out into the open brandishing a supposed letter from Shakespeare the media will just set about you. So don't. Have a quiet talk with Ed. You know you trigger him off?'

'Trigger him off! Me?'

'Don't get alarmed. It's nothing sexy. Well, I suppose it is really but Ed doesn't see it that way. Just what it was about you I didn't know, not until I saw you react to that letter. I think that's the way Edwin sees you all the time. Transfigured is the word, I suppose, and it just gives him ideas and sets him writing poetry. You're his muse. Mind you, it isn't the first time it's happened. I was his muse once. And then there was Betty Grable, though he never actually met her.'

'A muse? You're fooling. Well, I never thought I'd be any kind of follow to Betty Grable!'

'I'm just telling you this because I think a girl's got to know what she's surrounded by. You mean he hasn't dedicated any poems to you? No? Well, that surprises me. You might take it up with him when you meet. But the main thing is to get him talking about this letter. I wouldn't even mention it to Aston until you've done that.'

When Ed arrived home that evening Harriet told him that Lisa had found the letter, and how. He ought to do the decent thing and see her straight away to explain why he had set up this mare's nest. 'She's running crazy,' Harriet said.

Ever since he was 40 Edwin had an annual check-up at the London Clinic, the firm paying. After the first few years and he had been given a clean chit each time he came quite to enjoy the routine. He was given a key to a locker where he put all his clothes except his underpants, socks and shoes, and then emerged in a scruffy cotton dressing gown to be weighed, his height measured without shoes and his blood pressure taken.

He couldn't imagine why his height had to be checked. Surely that was a constant. 'Oh, no,' said the nursing sister. 'After a certain age people get shorter. Cartilage dries out. And bones curl up. Where do you think those little old men and women come from?'

The bit he liked best was the cardiograph. He lay on his back while the sister put greased metal discs on the parts of his thorax where it mattered. These were connected by wires to the machine which, once he was relaxed, the girl switched on so that it hummed soothingly and excreted, he gathered, (though he could never see it) a tape that recorded his heart beats in a line of jagged waves. The quietness of the cubicle, the patience with which the girl parted the hair on his chest, the oily kiss of the discs, were so relaxing he could doze off.

But not this time. Lisa just bugged him. He could think of nothing else but the phoney Shakespeare letter. He had wanted to make an impression on her. He wanted to see her eyes light up. He could just imagine her incredulous delight. But what sort of a house warming gift was it that had to be declared worthless as soon as it was delivered? He had imagined being actually present when she found the letter and somehow sustaining her happiness even when he told her the truth. She would see it as a flattering tribute to her obsession. That was the line of thinking, or non-thinking, rather. How could he have been so naive? Now it was too late. He was ashamed but he didn't want to own up. There was no need. As soon as Lisa showed the letter to an expert it would be exposed as a fake and everyone would suppose it had been in the roof for years. Probably planted there by the eccentric uncle who collected Coronation mugs.

'You're all tense,' said the nurse. 'You've got to let yourself go. I can see what your heart's doing on the screen but I don't think it's characteristic and I won't start printing till you settle. No hurry. You sure you're okay?'

'I'm okay.' The trouble was he couldn't keep his mind under control. Everything that surfaced came up with stress. Please God! Not Harriet. If he had to think of her let it be at a stage in the checkup when his emotions did not show up on a screen.

But Harriet might help him through the bit he liked the least. This was later when the doctor in charge of the unit, a Chinese who said his name was difficult for Europeans but could be written Ng, made him lie on his side and lift his right leg so that the man could explore his anus with a finger in a plastic sheath. Every year it was Dr Ng. Edwin judged by his ancient, sage-like, appearance that he was given this job after normal retiring age to make his pension up. Edwin intended to ask for this part of the inspection to be skipped. It was too uncomfortable, but he never did.

So what about Harriet? He was incredulous about her too. Or, rather, about the way he had suppressed what he knew about her. He had managed to deceive himself. He had gone over to automatic pilot at some stage, possibly when Olwen walked into his office. No, it was long before that. What she said had come as no surprise. It was as though he had given the automatic pilot wrong instructions, and deliberately, so all this time he had been off course. Or the Ed of everyday life was off course while the real man was drugged and dreaming in the cabin. What was the real he? The poet? That would involve Lisa.

Now he had snapped out of the trance he felt just great about everything and everybody. He was large. He contained multi-tudes. He was better than he thought. He did not know he held so much goodness. When a thing had been well said once it can stand a lot of repetition. What if Walt Whitman had been there before? Whitman never married, which only went to show you didn't need an adulterous wife to bring out the best in a man though there was Hosea to demonstrate how it helped. That was the way Ed talked to himself while Dr Ng tested for haemorrhoids and rectal cancer. Between the cardiography and the invasion of his rectum, there was the blood test, the provision of a urine specimen, the brain scan, and the chest x-ray. Ed then had to stand erect and twist this way and that while Dr Ng tried to decide whether there was anything visibly wrong with his spine.

'Your weight is constant,' said Ng. 'Well, that seems to be about everything. When I get the results of the tests I'll do the usual. I'll write to you. Oh, I forgot to do what I should have done right at the beginning.'

'What's that?'

'Ask you if you were okay. I take it you are? No complaints. Eating well. Sleeping well. That sort of thing.'

Ed hesitated. 'I don't take this hot weather the way I used to. Actually, I nearly passed out the other day.'

The sage seemed to think this amusing; he gave a tinny laugh. This surprised Edwin. He thought a doctor would have wanted to know more. But not Ng. He took Ed's hand and shook it. 'You may go and get dressed now and sister will give you a cup of tea. I'll be writing to you.'

When the letter came the wording was different. Instead of 'I am pleased to say the routine tests showed no abnormalities and trust you will continue to enjoy your present satisfactory health', Edwin opened the envelope to find Dr Ng saying, 'The tests were all satisfactory with one exception. The blood test did not seem quite right to me and I wonder if you would telephone so that we could arrange for it to be done again.' It was Friday evening (mail came after Edwin had left for town in the morning) so he had the weekend to wonder what Ng was getting at.

'Can't be anything serious,' said Harriet, 'or he'd have rung you at the office. Tell you not to make any abrupt movements, or something.' Later on she said Lisa had phoned to report she had been in touch with someone at the British Library who specialized in English literary manuscripts and been told that if she brought her Shakespeare letter in she (it was a Mrs Hawkins) would look at it. But that would have to wait because Jo had been laid low with the most appalling hay fever, was on antihistamine and prostrate in her darkened bedroom where she was visited by the apparition of Miss Jackson whose mortal remains had been consumed on a funeral pyre before they left Nairobi.

'The sooner they carry out tests the better.' Ed's mind ran on tests.

'Allergy tests? You mean it may not be pollen?'

'I'm talking about the Shakespeare letter. The sooner it's exploded the better. Then we can forget about it.'

'So you're not going to own up?'

'No. I think she'd probably attack me.' Ed helped himself to another drink. 'Sorry about Jo. Hope Lisa's getting her looked at by somebody good.' He took particular pleasure in pronouncing Jerry Clutsam's name. After all, Jo had been one of his patients.

'Not his field. Jo needs an immunologist. Lisa talked of flying one in. She still thinks she's in the Third World.'

The long spell of hot, dry weather was broken up by thunderstorms. Driving rain explored roofs, walls and windows for weak spots and at Wood End the down pipes couldn't cope. Tattered sheets of water fell from the guttering. Doors slammed. The loose carpet in Jo's bedroom rose as though some long, lithe animal was trapped beneath it. Her father had to come up and walk about on it to reassure her.

'It's just the wind getting under the floorboards,' he said. 'How are you feeling?'

To help her breathing Jo was sitting up on her bed, supported by pillows. 'Awful,' she said. 'Have you got any sherbet suckers?'

'What are they?' Lisa had come to see what was going on.

'Little yellow packets of some sweet powdery stuff you suck up a liquorice tube.'

'Where do you come across those?'

'At school.'

No, they hadn't any sherbet suckers and it was too late to go out to buy any, the shops in the nearest town would be shut. Lisa went and fetched the next best thing which, Jo said, was a glass of effervescent fruit salts. But she was not to put the fruit salts into the water until Jo was preparing to drink it. In that way she would get all the fizz in her nose and mouth. To keep her company Lisa and Aston sat talking about the Shakespeare letter, while the wind grumbled and snored in the roof space overhead.

Aston thought it would be a good time to go up and inspect the place where the letter had been found. Jo wanted to come too but Aston said there would be a lot of dust flying about up there and that would be bad for her. That turned out to be wrong. When he climbed the ladder, pushed open the trapdoor and switched the light on the dust was less in evidence than the wet. Rain glistened on the underside of tiles where the wind had blown it. Even as they looked (Lisa had joined him by this time) there was a tight whine and rain was forced in two, three, separate jets of fine spray through the leaky roof.

154

'You'd think we were at sea,' said Aston. The house was shuddering under the blows of the storm. The beams, the bare boards, the damp as seen by the electric light swinging on the end of its cord did indeed seem to be working up to some sort of shipwreck. Aston was not tall enough to look into the place Lisa indicated so he fetched a chair and an electric torch.

'There's some wet mud, or clay, or something.' He peered and put his hand in. 'What did you say that fellow pulled out? I mean, as well as the letter.'

'Just some muck and feathers. You've seen the bit of sacking.'

'Where is this muck, then?'

'Does that matter?' Eventually Lisa identified what she was standing on as the dirt and feathers Henderson had pulled out and Aston came down and fingered the stuff. 'Quite dry. You don't get a storm like this all that often but if you ask me that letter, and the sacking and this stuff couldn't possibly have been there very long. One lesson we've learned. This place needs a new roof and a proper lining or it won't be here much longer.'

Back in Jo's bedroom they found her requiring a full report. She had seen the letter once, and the piece of sacking, but now she asked to see and handle them again. The effervescent health salts had cleared her head, she said; now she wanted to be entertained. 'I don't see why you're so grim about this letter,' she told her father. 'You're really annoying Lisa.'

'For one thing, this is a bit of jute sacking and I don't think jute sacking has been around all that many years. You see, it's dry. And the letter's dry. But up there it's wet. My guess is that whoever set this up did it since the last big storm. Anyway, the last big storm with wind driving the rain from the south-west.'

'But that doesn't mean the letter isn't genuine,' said Lisa.

'If it's genuine who in his right mind would stuff it up there?'

'I can think of lots of reasons.'

'Name one.'

'For one thing Drew Ritter might have been up in the roof one day. He might have come across this package in some dry spot and used it to plug this hole, without looking at it too much. That's the sort of guy he is.'

'Well, if it wasn't for one thing I'd say have your fun. Kid yourself.'

'What's the one thing?'

'Somebody's setting us up.'

'Who would do that? Who would want to?'

'There's your ex-husband George to start with. Judging by what you tell me he's potty enough for anything. And yes, I can imagine George going to all sorts of lengths.'

So could Lisa, for that matter.

'But George isn't literate enough for that kind of fake.'

'He doesn't have to do it himself, does he? He just dreams it up. He's bright enough. And mean enough. And rich enough to pay a forger, somebody who knows a bit. But it couldn't have been much. Shakespeare freaks are two a penny.'

Edwin put off calling Dr Ng to make that appointment because he felt so fit, the way he was on a crisp winter morning with the hounds running well, and he bumping along on Tabby, but this was late summer and, the storm over, the parching returned. The commuter trains ran with windows down to let in a breeze and men with the *Telegraph* in front of them slackened their ties. Dr Ng had made a mistake. A chap feeling robustly healthy as Ed didn't produce unsatisfactory blood samples. He was in flower. He showed understanding of Harriet's affair with Jerry. He dispensed love and understanding with the generosity of an old-time pasha distributing meat, sherbet and alms. Immersion in the stream was a baptism. He was born again into love and understanding. The world was real. He didn't just dream it. It was there! He observed it carefully for the detail – the smooth, seal-like, muscularity of the plum, for example, when he rubbed the bloom off. And the long clouds drifted high over the garden, snowy above and edged below with just that same plum dust on his thumb, powder blue.

Eventually he did call Dr Ng's office where he spoke to a woman who denied all knowledge of his case. 'Oh, you're *that* Mr Parsler,' she acknowledged under pressure. 'There's no need for Dr Enjee to see you. You just go to the path lab.' She fixed a time. No argument about it. The path lab worked to a tight schedule. So did he, said Ed, and an eleven o'clock appointment meant he would lose a whole morning in the office. But she could not be moved. Not worth going into the

City at nine and coming all the way back to the Marylebone Road.

'Any idea what's wrong with the blood sample?' he asked.

'Not my job. But it's fairly routine people coming back for a second check. Not to worry.'

At Bicester station he met Lisa wearing a crisp, oatmeal-coloured suit, a milk chocolate cravat and a narrow-brimmed straw hat that might have been spun sugar. Not only, to his eye, was her get-up edible but Lisa herself; peachy, wholesome, confectioned in one of the sparkling kitchens of paradise. As he looked at her Ed wondered whether there was anything erotic in cannibalism.

'I've heard of the English making a late start in the morning, Ed,' Lisa said, 'but this is ridiculous.'

He explained about his appointment at the Clinic and she wanted to know what was wrong.

'Ed, tell me honestly now, do you feel flaked out, sort of despondent?'

'On the contrary, 105 per cent.'

'So you're not anaemic. Maybe you've got too many red cells. You been eating spinach?'

The train came in and as luck had it they found a couple of seats with nobody sitting opposite, so they could talk without being overheard, or could have done if only Lisa had kept her voice down. She was too happy and bubbly to care. He noticed the tiny wash of happy tears he had seen in Lisa's predecessor all that time ago. He'd have to ask her about Shirley. Out in Kenya Lisa may have gathered a bit more about the way she died.

'Oh, Ed, I've been having tests too. You know what? I'm pregnant! Aston and I have been trying so hard but it wasn't until we made it to that hotel in Stratford with the four-poster we did the trick. I'm just convinced of that. The dates fit. We're both just ecstatic.'

'What marvellous news.' In fact he did not know what to say. It was as though he had been coming down a flight of stairs with his eyes shut and there was one fewer step than he had expected. 'Harriet will be thrilled too. Congratulations! Aston must be kicking up his heels.'

'Jo thinks it'll be a reincarnation of Miss Jackson, even if it's a boy, and I know it's going to be a boy, another William, because Jo says in reincarnation sex doesn't come into it. Ed, the books she reads!'

By the time they were approaching Princes Risborough Edwin realized he was genuinely pleased about Lisa's news. Pregnancy would make her more unapproachable, and therefore more mysterious and magical. As though it were a sign of divine approbation the great and ancient cross cut in the chalky hillside above Whiteleaf slid into his view. He drew a deep breath. The muse would now be maternal and the Whiteleaf Cross signalled its approval.

'So, you're off shopping to celebrate?'

'Oh no, Ed. I'm not going shopping. I'm going to see a Miss Hawkins at the BM with my Shakespeare letter.'

'I thought we'd decided it must be a fake.'

'No, sir. The reasons for thinking it a fake are entirely circumstantial. Sure, George could have gotten somebody to fix it for him. Sure, Aston may be right about that dry hole. But it still doesn't mean for sure it's a fake and I don't believe it is. Too trivial. If George had wanted to make a fool of me he wouldn't have been satisfied with this. Not sensational enough. I know George. He'd have to be telling us who the Dark Lady was.'

'You mean you've got the letter with you?'

'Sure, I've got it strapped over my belly.'

'A body belt? For security?'

'No, it's as near my unborn child as I can make it. I want all the right influences for this kid.'

'A sort of phylactery?'

'What's that?'

'You know. A sacred text in a case. Jews wear them.'

'Sure, then. It's a what-you-said.'

They thought about this until the train approached High Wycombe and then Edwin said, 'You don't suppose the heat of your body and the humidity might, you know.'

'It's in a sealed polythene envelope.'

'Still, I'm told temperature is critical so far as old manuscripts are concerned.'

'So you see, Ed, you *do* think it's genuine, or you wouldn't say things like that. That's real nice of you.'

'You're kidding.'

'Don't forget I'm your muse and muses don't kid whoever it is they're trying to inspire. Sure, I've got that letter strapped to my belly. Would you like to look?'

'Who said you were my muse?'

'Harriet. I think it's an oversight not telling me yourself.'

'I'd never have guessed you were superstitious, Lisa.'

'I'm not superstitious but when it comes to my kid's intellectual and artistic endowments there's no stratagem I'm prepared to overlook. What've we got to lose anyway?'

'You mean you really are wearing this letter?'

'*I've been telling you.*'

'I thought you were sending me up. I'm appalled.'

'Appalled?'

'It's so primitive. It's like believing in spells and magic.'

'Aston does. That's what comes from Africa.'

'Did Aston put you up to this?'

'Hell, no. Sometimes I think I'm really going down in that man's opinion. He says you can come away from Africa but you can't leave the place, not definitively, and it's got me sort of worried all this stuff arriving. The drink wasn't so bad. But a tusk, I ask you!'

She had to repeat it all for his benefit. For some time mysterious unsolicited gifts had been arriving at Wood End. To begin with they were left outside the front door, presumably during the night, because they were there first thing in the morning: cases of Johnny Walker Black Label, of Southern Comfort, boxes of Havana cigars, and bags of green coffee beans. At first they thought the postman was bringing the stuff, but that seemed unlikely when they realized the packages were not addressed. They asked the postman one morning and he knew nothing about the deliveries. The following day a black man drove up in a Cortina with something long and curving, wrapped in sacking which, when Aston cut the string that secured it, turned out to be a yellowing tusk. From a young elephant, Aston had said. He was furious. The way elephants were being slaughtered for ivory the beasts would be extinct as the dodo before long.

The black man said his name was Mr Otim. He was a small, not very black man, said Lisa, who seemed so nervous he would not get out of the Cortina.

'What did Aston do?'

'He wouldn't accept it. He pushed the tusk back into the car and told Mr Otim to beat it, which he did.'

'So what's it mean?'

'Aston says it all comes from Uganda. The drink is diplomatic corps duty free but the tusk must have come in a diplomatic bag, probably the Libyan bag now that there are no direct diplomatic relations. Aston says it's Amin keeping in touch.'

They arrived at Marylebone soon after 10.30 and Ed had time to walk along the Marylebone Road to keep his appointment but he helped Lisa find a taxi and then, on impulse, climbed in after her. She thought he would ask the driver to drop him at the Clinic but no, Ed said, he was giving the Clinic a miss. He'd ride as far as the Museum with her.

'You mean you're not having the check? Say, is that wise? You're not scared, are you?'

'I'll drop in some other time.'

'You plan to come and see this Miss Hawkins with me?'

'You can tell me all about it later.'

He paid off the taxi at the gates and watched Lisa walk across the forecourt to where the great columns were marching the pale portico into September cloud. She radiated joy. Her step was quick and springy. On either side the lawns glistened with last night's rain. When the sun came out the stone turned biscuity. A baroque painter would have shown her, he thought, all innocence and love, like a winged soul floating with arms outstretched and confident of heaven. Nothing he could do to break the fall. Too late for that. He hoped she would not take the disappointment hard. Her climb up the steps was taken as lightly and airily as though supported by the extended finger tips of rejoicing cherubs. No human being was entitled to knowledge about another that gave her every move such cruel irony. That was for the gods.

No human being? A bit far, that. Poets never admit it but they do, on occasion, manipulate the muse.

Aston had smoked several of the Havanas and lowered the level of whisky in one of the Black Label bottles by the time the tusk arrived, asking no questions. He had other things on his mind.

160

Living in Africa he was used to receiving presents, those given with a smile as broad as the daylight, and those left on the back doorstep. Sure it was bribery but what was wrong with that if you weren't influenced? But these gifts delivered to Wood End were different. Only one person would send him a tusk and that was Amin. So the presents were in no way a bribe disguised as tribute. Amin paid no tribute. These were gifts of a more sinister kind. They were designed to compromise, even intimidate.

The mail van drove up to the front door one morning, the bell rang and Aston had to go down and receive a package in brown paper. It was addressed to Mr and Mrs Hart. As Lisa loved opening mail there was an unspoken agreement that any addressed to them jointly should be regarded as hers to open. So Aston took the package through to the window seat where newly arrived mail was deposited. But there was something about this particular delivery that aroused his curiosity. It was tied with particularly hairy string, the knots sealed with blobs of red wax and, as though even this was not secure enough, brown adhesive tape had been given a turn round the length of the package. Aston felt the package and guessed it was curtain material or furnishing fabric. The Hart name and address was typed on a white stick-on label. The postmark could not be read. Aston knew it was just the sort of delivery that should be left for Lisa but she was out, having dropped Jo at the school and then driven on to Banbury to do some shopping.

After some hesitation he left it and went off to his room to carry on studying the catalogues of garden machinery he had now determined to go in for. Lisa must have found the package as soon as she arrived back from Banbury because it was only a matter of minutes after he had heard her car turn into the drive that she was in his room with a mass of black silk and white silk, in great patches, like some kind of fancy dress. She was looking at him with a puzzled expression on her face, as though her memory was jogged but only in a tantalizing way. What she was carrying meant something special, she did not know what.

He looked at the silky back and white flowering over her arm and stood up to take it from her.

'This was that parcel that came? I ought to have opened it myself.' He turned it over and over, looked at it this way and that, examined the cloth backing, almost as though he did not know what he was handling. But of course he did. 'Is there a note or anything in the parcel?'

They both went back to the hall where the wrapping paper and string were still lying on the floor but there was no accompanying note. Postmark too smudged to make out. Probably London. Not that it mattered.

Aston began wrapping the skin up again. 'I'd have thought anyone who knew me well enough to send me a present would know I wouldn't want a colobus monkey skin.'

Lisa now realized she had known it was the skin of that monkey as soon as she undid the parcel.

'That's what you found in the house. That day.'

'Prettiest monkey in Africa,' said Aston, wrapping the skin up again. 'You remember. Yes, it's what we found in the house. Somebody's having fun.'

11

Aston was never at ease with Jo – not only because of the Miss Jackson talk but because her mind moved quicker than his but also, and this was worse, she would listen to him and Lisa in discussion or argument and then bring up a consideration neither of them had thought of. Sometimes it had no real bearing but usually it did. Aston found it irritating but Lisa used to say, 'That was real smart of you, Jo, to think of that. You'll sure make a fine prime minister one day.'

Sometimes she would say nothing but look at Jo incredulously.

They were talking about visiting Lisa's mother in Germany, Frau Wicht as she now was. Aston hardly knew her. He, Lisa and Jo had spent a long weekend at Kelkhm soon after they came back from Africa but the visit had not been a success (they argued about everything, politics, German white wine compared with French, Lisa's habit of coming down late for breakfast) but Lisa was not giving up. Aston was so much against the trip that Lisa was now considering going alone. That was fine by Aston.

'Oh, no,' said Jo. 'She would think daddy and I didn't like her and that would be awful. Ask her here. And her husband? They've never been to England so she'll want to see the house and everything. It'll be her grandchild that is born in it.'

'Babies are not born at home any more,' said Aston.

'She's right! Mine will be.' Lisa actually danced over and kissed Jo. 'My, you do think ahead!'

This was one of the times Aston could almost hear Jo's mind rustle and it wasn't his kind of rustle. His didn't rustle at all, to be honest. So where did Jo's come from? Who did she look like? She had a nose as straight you could have put a ruler along it. Now, a ruler on his nose would not make contact all the length of the nose. It would stick up one end because his nose, seen in profile, had a curve. Shirley's nose had been on the broad side with a slight knob on the end which went white when she was angry. Perhaps, genetically speaking, cross a slightly aquiline nose with a knob nose and a straight nose is what you would get. He doubted it. And where did she get those steady brown eyes? And so wide apart. Aston's mother had brown eyes but they weren't set wide apart like this. Jo had some kind of presence that didn't quite belong to Shirley and him. She was getting smarter all the time and that was why she unsettled him.

Judging by the questions Jo asked she thought he knew everything. For example, what were dreams for?

'They're not *for* anything. You just have them.'

'Are they real?'

He hesitated over this. 'Look, Jo, when you're asleep your brain sometimes goes on working. And it seems things are happening, but they're not, it's just in the mind.'

'But if your brain tells you something is happening you can't know it isn't because there's nothing else but your brain to tell you.'

'There's a difference between the way your brain works when you're dreaming and the way it works when you're awake. When you're awake you can check up on a dream and know it didn't really happen.'

'I mean you see things in a dream and it seems real at the time.'

'Seems is right. It's just your brain playing tricks.'

'But you dream something. Then you wake up and it's really there.'

'Do you dream a lot?'

'All the time. I dream when I'm asleep and I dream when I'm awake. The same dream, sometimes. Well, there's a black man with nothing on coming with presents. He comes out of the wall. Or through the window but I'm not frightened any more. He used to frighten me but now he brings presents.'

'What sort of presents?'

'One thing was this big black and white warm furry cloak. It was so smelly and warm when I put it on. Then I woke up and got out of bed and there this cloak was, lying in front of the door. As I looked at it it seemed to curl up and fade away.'

'You were still dreaming.'

'No, I put my slippers on. I was going to walk over and pick it up. Then it was gone.'

Aston was sure Jo had not seen the monkey skin. He had rewrapped it almost at once with the intention of getting rid of it somehow. But he had not actually done this. The package was locked in an old cabin trunk (the one with his father's name painted on the side) in the boxroom. But of course Jo might have heard Lisa and him talking about it. And she might remember seeing colobus skins in Kenya where the whites used them as pram covers. He could think of natural explanations for Jo's dream.

'These antihistamine tablets she's taking must have a dopey effect too,' said Lisa when he told her. 'She's imaginative and she gets excited. I don't actually like her going to this convent school. I know you've got to do it. It's what Shirley would have wanted. But I just don't trust nuns. They could work on an impressionable child. See visions. I get this feeling sometimes when I pick her up from school she'll say she's had a vision of the Virgin Mary.'

'Jo gets that from Shirley's side of the family, that dreaming and fantasizing. And the asthma and the allergies. I don't dream much, not that I remember. I'm not bothered about that black. White girls in Africa always have nightmares about blacks.'

'You know all this might get worse when she starts her periods?'

'Why?'

'Chemistry.'

Aston grunted. 'Thank God I was born male.' After further thought, he added, 'And white. When will that be? Periods, I mean.'

'Any time now.'

'Christ! Am I glad I'm a man!' They thought this over in silence. Then Aston followed an earlier scent. 'I see what you mean about nuns. If Jo had a vision of the Virgin Mary that could be the start of a cult in these parts. That could be good business.'

'You ought to relax, Aston. Forget about money. You don't have to do anything. You're just who you are and that's more than enough. Gee, *do I love you*! Say, how do you know what white girls dream about? Is this the first thing one of them tells you about when she wakes up?'

'I've never slept around. Anyway, I love you, sweetie.'

165

'I don't get it why this black man was naked. Why should she say that? I mean, why did she know he was naked.'

Aston looked at Lisa, puzzled. 'She meant he had no clothes on.'

'There was more to it than that, brother. There was more to it than that.'

'So far as I'm concerned, Lisa, she was just dreaming.'

'That's fine so far as it goes but in my book it doesn't go far enough. You've got to remember I'm pregnant. And pregnant women see things differently.'

From time to time over the years Aston had thought of that Mau Mau gangster who had come so damn near to spearing him. The little dreaming he did was of the Mau Mau years. Aston had not the slightest intention of telling Lisa there was a naked black, shining with mud and blood, who popped up in his dreams from time to time too, to give him that dead man's curse. There were only two men in the world who knew about that curse and it was a bond between them. Amin thought Aston was under threat and had offered to round up some powerful witch doctors to lift the curse but Aston would have none of it, not even after Shirley died.

Aston kept Lisa in the dark about all this. He thought it would make him look a fool.

'It is, of course, a forgery,' said Miss Stella Hawkins of the Renaissance and Modern Manuscripts Department of the British Library. She gave a merry toss of the head. 'And not a very good one at that.'

Lisa had taken an instant dislike to her and was quite determined to believe nothing she said. She had straight black hair and a fringe with a line of white scalp showing just where it started. And, incredibly, she wore a monocle which previously Lisa had seen worn by no one but the dandy who appeared from time to time on the cover of the *New Yorker*. 'Suspect phrases just *leap* to the eye. Note this, for example "Be happy in your sons. Be happy in your husband. Be happy in what does not alter." Note the cadence of that. Very calculated, as though the forger was wondering how a poet would write a mere domestic note. Spelling, of course, was chaotic in the period but I've never seen a double ff in "from". So you see, Mrs – ?'

'Hart.'

'Mrs Hart, there is no *prima facie* case for thinking this is an authentic document and, frankly, I don't think the expense of scientific tests on ink and paper would be justified. The forger would naturally have covered himself in those respects. Did you do it yourself?'

'No.'

'We get all sorts. The motives of literary forgers, and I have seen many examples of the genre, are interesting. Not financial. Psychological. You think I'm jesting?'

'My husband is a descendant of Shakespeare's sister, Mrs Joan Hart.'

'That's fiddle-faddle, isn't it, my dear? How many generations are involved? At least twelve. More likely a lot more, expectancy of life being what it was. So there is a dilution of the genes. Quite significant. It is of no more importance, genetically, to be descended from Shakespeare's sister than it is to be descended from – well, who shall we say? Any other tradesperson of Stratford. In any case, does this have a bearing on the forgery?'

'It is not a forgery and it was found in a house, and I happen to live there, which was gifted to my husband's ancestor by Lady Barnard, no less, Shakespeare's granddaughter.'

'That's out of the question,' said Miss Hawkins, not quite snorting. 'Lady Barnard didn't gift any houses to anyone. I would have known about it. But one can't help feeling sad the real family died out.'

'My husband is a direct descendant of Shakespeare's father.'

'Even if this were true, which is unlikely, descent through the female line, I'm sorry to say, is not normally described as direct. Not real family, I would have thought. That died out with Lady Barnard. What would you like me to do with this?' She pushed the paper back across her desk in Lisa's direction.

'I'll take it to a real expert,' said Lisa.

'You're American?'

'Sure.'

'Send it to the Folger in Washington.'

'I might do that, Miss – ?'

'Hawkins.'

167

To cheer herself up Lisa took herself off to Harrods where, in a lavatory, she replaced the letter in its plastic envelope and strapped it comfortably where, she thought, it mattered, on her belly. As she considered fish to be good for the developing embryo she had smoked salmon with brown bread and butter in the snack bar and then went off to buy Aston some shirts. She spent a good two hours examining cots, pushchairs, nursery wallpaper and taking advice on what would be needed for the layette. The assistant was doubtful whether it would be possible to incorporate the Shakespeare crest and motto, *Non Sans Droict*, in the lace drapes that Lisa had set her heart on, even if ordered as much as this in advance, but gave her the address of a small firm in Olney who might do the unexpected. For Jo she bought some pearl earrings and then, to kill time before the train, went to the Wallace Collection to look at the paintings, particularly the Rembrandts, and marvel that's how they were when they were painted over three hundred years ago and that was the way (because they'd been cleaned) they were now. She guessed she had a fixation about time. She just wanted to reach back and *be* back. When Aston asked her what she wanted for her birthday she would say, and it would be a sad and hopeless joke, 'A time machine, please.'

It belatedly occurred to her there was a fallacy in Hawkins's view on the generations. The normal expectation of life did not necessarily affect the gap between the birthdate of one generation and the birthdate of the next. Children were normally conceived by parents in their early twenties, and if the parents subsequently died early there was still going to be, what? Twenty-four, twenty-five years between their birthdate and that of the offspring. The way Hawkins talked you'd think seventeenth-century girls had babies only in their teens and twentieth-century women had them in their forties! Lisa wished she had been quick-witted enough to point this out. She would write to the woman.

There were not many Bicester trains so it was not surprising she should see Edwin on the platform and travel back with him. She wanted to know what they had told him at the London Clinic.

'I'm all right. Something to do with the viscosity of the blood. Changes show up if you've been under stress. But it's back to normal.'

'You mean they looked at the sample straightaway?'

'He's Chinese, the doctor. He speeded things up. Thought I might fret, I suppose. Which wasn't the case. I knew there was nothing the matter. I just feel particularly fit. He's asked me to drop in one day and he'll show me slides of blood under the microscope and explain this viscosity business. I might do that too.'

'But you've been under stress?'

'Well, that's life, isn't it. What happened at the BM?'

Lisa told him about Miss Hawkins and wanted to show him the letter so that Edwin could give his opinion too. She would go into the toilet and remove the envelope. But Edwin said that would not be necessary. In fact, if she didn't mind, he'd much rather not see the letter at all.

'Why ever not?'

'I can see what it means to you. And I wouldn't want to say anything unwelcome.'

Lisa looked at him, laughing in a way that gave him the usual gut tremor. Her eyes were swimming with fun. She had this secret source of joy that set her apart from ordinary mortals and, like no one else, she could set him going too. He could feel the lines on his face relaxing, his eyes begin to water. Then, as unexpectedly as in Washington, she kissed him on the cheek. They were sitting side by side and she moved her head on its long neck (like a swan, he thought) but his own neck was too short and creaky to let him respond in the way he would have liked. He couldn't kiss her back, so he sat holding her hand for twenty miles, all the way to Wycombe Marsh.

She removed her hand. 'You're sure right about that letter, Ed. It gives me a permanent, non-alcoholic, no-dope high and that's for sure. But I'm sorry you won't even look at it. What you said wouldn't matter at all, any more than the Hawkins female. Nothing anyone said against it would matter. There's no way I'm going to miss out on it, this feeling I've got right here of awe and magic.' She put a hand to her stomach, indicating either the Shakespeare letter or her unborn child, but probably both.

Aston was amazed when Lisa told him about Hawkins. 'You mean an English expert on an English subject actually said there were people in the States who knew the job better than she did?'

'It was her way of giving me the air.'

'Why do we have to run ourselves down? It's the British death wish.'

'Actually the Folger Shakespeare Library in Washington isn't such a bad idea. They're Americans there and they'll be real receptive, I guess. Maybe I'll send them a photostat first. Then if they're interested I could fly over with the real thing.'

'You could look up your ex-husband,' said Aston. 'Ask him what he means, planting this letter. Might save a lot of time.'

'Are you serious?'

'He's sending you up. Perhaps I'd better come along too. He's that screwed up he might need attending to.'

Lisa prepared to go off and meditate in her cell. 'No, I wouldn't want to see George. This letter has nothing to do with him. It's genuine. Can't you accept that? Say!' She raised her voice. 'Don't you want me to have a genuine Shakespeare letter, or something? Why are you so against it?'

'I just think you're wrong to go on kidding yourself.'

'Hell, Aston! Why can't you be generous and let me have this letter? Anybody would think you were ashamed of your family background. You got to remember, it's mine too now. Or soon will be. Through our child I'll be linked by blood. My genes and the Shakespeare family genes brought together. Okay, I know what you're thinking. It's the German in me coming out.'

Aston raised his arms level with his shoulders, as it might be preliminary to flying. His eyebrows set high. 'What the hell has being German got to do with it?'

'Taking things seriously,' said Lisa. 'You know, it's an awful thing to say. But genes matter. The Jews know that. That's one of the reasons I'm so pro-Jewish.'

As part of the refurbishing of the house Lisa had taken over one of the spare bedrooms and hired an interior designer to give it an Elizabethan look. The designer, a square-faced woman with a moustache, had managed to lay her hands on some oak panelling salvaged from a derelict Victorian vicarage. The walls of the little room were now lined with it and, what with the oak table (also Victorian) in front of the south-facing window, the pewter mugs and the tall bookcase with a leaded glass front like an old cottage window (not lead, in fact, but painted wooden strips, another Victorian touch), stepping into what Lisa called her cell was a bit like stepping into a stage set.

A small roll-top desk was kept locked most of the time and Lisa carried the key on a ring together with the house and car keys; here were Hans's letters, his notebooks and his poetry manuscripts which, at some time, she intended editing for publication herself, now that she had reconciled herself to Ed Parsler's lack of interest. Below the roll-top, in the upper of two right hand drawers was the plastic envelope containing the Shakespeare letter. Sitting and just staring at it was the most restful experience Lisa had ever known. It emptied her mind, even more than the hairdresser's. She heard nothing, thought nothing, saw nothing but the squiggly, worried-looking writing and she just sat there cocooned in serenity.

The determination grew that Edwin must come and look at the letter, in spite of his show of reluctance, and to hell with what he said. Ever since Harriet had told her she was Edwin's inspirational muse she had wanted to put it to the test. What did that mean? What it meant, she decided, was seeing how much she could hypnotize Edwin into seeing the letter just as *she* did.

The opportunity arose at Jo's thirteenth birthday party which, Jo insisted, was no kid's affair. A few girls from school were invited but the main guests were the Rector, the Reverend Paul Brough, (Jo had struck up quite a friendship with him, she had plans, which she had discussed with Sister Tabitha, the Latin mistress, also present, to bring him over to Rome), Jessica Parsler and her boyfriend, Eric, (Jo admired him because he looked like one of the Saxons in her illustrated *Hereward the Wake*) who arrived on a thunderous Suzuki, Mark Parsler (he gave her a large fossilized fig his father had brought back from one of his foreign trips; it had been much coveted by Jo when she had stayed with them), Edwin and Harriet Parsler themselves and, most unexpected of all, Olwen Clutsam. Jo had invited both the Clutsams. Looking back over the years she had come to the conclusion that Dr Clutsam had saved her life when her window had blown open at the Parslers and she had those terrible pains in the back. Even now, when he appeared in some of her dreams, he was friendly and reassuring, standing between her and very rude black men. But no, he was sorry he could not come to the party. Olwen had seen that the invitation was addressed to both of them and decided to come on her own.

'Can I help you?' This was what shop assistants said when they caught you browsing around. Jo was going through a phase of imitating shop assistants and she had not set eyes on Olwen before. 'Oh, isn't Dr Clutsam coming?' she asked when Olwen introduced herself. 'That's very disappointing. I owe him ever so much and I dream of him. He's really dishy.' This was a word one of the girls at school had used and been warned never to use again.

Lisa did not know Olwen either and came over. Like Jo she was sorry Dr Clutsam had been unable to come but she was sure he must be very busy.

'He's not busy at all,' said Olwen. 'He's in one of his moods.' She had seen Harriet Parsler and was quite unable to resist the strong pull in her direction. Indeed, the reason she had come to the party was in expectation of seeing Harriet.

'Jerry's going back to South Africa for a year,' she told Harriet once the conversational preliminaries had been gone through. 'But I don't know whether I ought to go with him. What do you think?'

'But the sunshine, Olwen.' Harriet was wearing a dark green trouser suit, obviously expensive. Her shoes were unusually high-heeled and she towered over Olwen. 'It would do you both good.'

'Don't patronize me. He can go to hell for all I care. Never liked South Africa anyway.'

She snapped the words out but there was a warmth in her manner towards Harriet that was almost amorous. It was something to do with the way she held herself, tensing her body, holding herself tall to look up into Harriet's eyes. Harriet thought of all those miscarriages and wanted to feel sorry for her. But the truth was that Olwen was beginning to give her the horrors. She was pushing her face up to Harriet's, as it might be to kiss.

'Men are hateful, Harriet. Be honest now. You think so too.'
'Why do you say that?'
'Because of the way you behave. You take men and use them. Oh! It's marvellous. I wish I'd known you years ago. I'd really have understood what goes.'

'My dear,' said Harriet, 'I don't know what goes.'

'Oh you do, Harriet. You do. That's just what you do, and I'd like to be what you are. I'd like to crush men. But I'm not attractive and sexy like you.'

'You're very sweet and fetching. You've got – mm, I dunno. Put it like this. There's a sort of, well, Amazonian challenge about you and a lot of men go for that. Jerry did, didn't he? There's just one thing – ' Harriet hesitated.

'What's that?'

'Let me be the candid friend. It's the make-up. You've used too much eyeshade. Your lipstick isn't actually limited to your lips proper. Why don't you be nice to yourself? Be really kind to yourself. Love yourself a little and buy one of those Elizabeth Arden beauty treatments. You know, full body. You've got nice skin. But it doesn't glow the way it should. Perhaps you need more fibre in your diet. I'm all in favour of regular bowel movement. It's a matter of getting the right breakfast cereal, Olwen, believe me! You've got to smell right too. Chanel 19 would be just right. Your hair. Spend a bit of money and go to a real stylist. Antoine Mercure in Chelsea would love to work on your gorgeous black locks. Do away with that fringe. Then clothes. Splash out a bit. Jerry can stand it.'

Olwen looked at her with shining eyes. 'I just love you, Harriet. You've got style and everything I haven't got. But I will. You're right. I'll run the bugger into an overdraft. And, by God, I'll just set about men.'

'You do that, Olwen.'

'And Harriet.'

'Yes.'

'I'm going to do all this and I'm going to Durban with him and I'm going to live so that he gets screwed into the ground. He'll come crawling.'

Harriet looked around. 'You haven't seen that husband of mine by any chance?'

Ed was talking to Aston about horses. Drew Ritter had gone, a few others had dropped out too, so Hunt membership was down and Guy Budgen, the Master, had set up a recruiting drive. Aston seemed an obvious candidate though, big man as he was, he'd need a strong mount and Ed happened to know

173

just the horse, hard, short-legged and spirited. He was in the hands of a dealer in Aynho.

'I'm too old to start that caper,' said Aston.

'You'd soon catch on.'

'I'm forty-four. A man who starts fox hunting at my age is a fool. Don't see the point of it anyway.'

'Good exercise, for one thing. Still, if you're not interested.'

They had been down to inspect a spot in the garden where Lisa wanted a pond (a lake, she called it) with a stone dolphin vomiting water and heron standing about. Jo, Jessica and one of her school friends were carrying round trays of iced mint tea which was what Jo insisted her health should be drunk in. It was generally understood that at four o'clock she would cut the cake, when Aston would say a few words and Jo would perform a mime while the Beatles, on a tape, would be heard singing 'Strawberry Fields'. Jo's intention was to interpret the song in a way that would convey her initiation into puberty – a sort of quivering, upward unfolding like an extraordinarily speeded-up film of an opening horse-chestnut candle. To conceal her flowery white dress she was wearing a brown cloak which, she said, represented the sticky bud.

But none of this happened. Lisa suddenly appeared on the terrace, looked around for Aston and, when she saw him, came almost at a run holding her keyring in front of her.

'It's gone!' She fetched up squarely, almost accusingly in front of Aston, chin up, eyes wide and weepy. 'I was going to get the letter and show Ed. But it's not there!'

Aston took this calmly. 'It must be around.'

'What letter's this?' Edwin had never seen Lisa in such agitation. To think of her as always serene was important to him. So he was upset she was not serene.

'The Shakespeare letter. What else? It's gone. I kept it locked up in my desk and I was going to bring it down and show you. Because you've never seen it, Ed. Oh God, I so wanted you to see it. Why, for hell's sake, wouldn't you look at it? I hate you for not wanting to see it. I hate you. You know that? But when I unlocked the desk and opened the drawer, nothing! Not even the envelope. Am I mad!'

'You've got it strapped round your middle.'

'No. I thought of that. It's gone. Somebody's taken it.'

'You sure of that?' said Aston. 'Wait a minute.' Aston wanted to reassure. 'Lisa, you say you unlocked the desk?'

'Sure. This is the key.'

'Any sign of the lock being tampered with? I mean, you don't think it might have been forced?'

'Nothing like that. Anyway, who'd want to do a thing like that to me?'

'Let's go and have a look.'

Ed was just entranced that Lisa had said she hated him.

They went, all three of them, Aston, Ed and Lisa, up to Lisa's panelled room and it was just as she said. The top of the desk was rolled down, the top right hand drawer was open and empty. Though the two men stood by while Lisa went through the other drawers there was no letter. Ed said documents were sometimes absentmindedly put in books and he began examining a few of them at random. Aston screwed his eyes up at the lock but there were no signs of it having been forced.

'The only way of opening that desk would be if somebody had a duplicate key,' said Lisa. 'A duplicate could be made easily if somebody borrowed the original for a few hours. But I don't just leave the keys lying about. Either I'm using the car keys or I've got the bunch in my handbag.'

'You sometimes leave them lying about, Lisa.'

Ed had been crawling on his hands and knees, looking under the desk and under bookcases. 'I don't know why it is but I'm always losing things these days too. Papers, books, letters. The other day I even lost a gin and tonic halfway through drinking it. I just put it down somewhere. A way of telling myself I'd had enough, I suppose. You don't really lose things unless you want to, some people say.'

'You think I might have lost it deliberately?'

'Not deliberately. But I don't believe anyone has taken the letter and you are the only person, really, who could have put it in another place. Absentmindedly, of course. Totally without realizing what you were doing.'

'I'm not a zombie. Why should I hide something so precious to me?'

Aston did not understand Ed's theory and said he was going

to look up the local locksmiths in the Yellow Pages.

'You can't do that, Aston.' They must think him interfering but Ed had a hunch a lot was at stake.

'Why not?'

Ed hesitated. 'I think you should have a talk with Jo first.'

'Jo? You don't think she's responsible? Why should she do a thing like that?'

Lisa looked even wilder and waved her arms about as though there was a bat in the room and she was terrified it would get in her hair. 'I don't know what to think.'

Ed took her on one side when they had gone downstairs and into the garden. 'I know about losing things. You could say I'm an expert. The chances are you put that letter somewhere yourself. Just think. When did you last see it?'

'Must have been yesterday evening.'

'You've got to reconstruct the occasion. Did you have your handbag with you? That sort of thing.'

Lisa looked at Aston's receding back. 'I remember locking the desk, that's all. It's just as though the letter has been spirited away. But you're right. I don't think we ought to bring Jo into this, not yet.' And she hurried after Aston to say so.

The autumn afternoon was warm and humid. Yellow and tawny flowers, chrysanthemums and marigolds melted into one another. The beaded fruit of a crab apple hung in amber ropes. The low, thin cloud diffused the sunlight like vapour among the trees and bushes, brightening these flowers and these crab apples and a few early fallen leaves as a wet cloth brightens an ancient, dusty mosaic. That was how Ed saw it all. Lisa's almost hysterical reaction to the disappearance of the letter shocked him. It did not help that Lisa's torment was absurd. It would only not have been absurd if the letter were genuine but not even Lisa believed that now. He was sure she knew it was a fake but equally sure she would go on saying it was not. If anyone was ultimately responsible for this nonsensical situation it must be him, Ed. But, honest, he had never imagined that his innocently intended little 'surprise' would trigger such an irrational response. He never dreamed she had such a need. So was the responsibility all his?

He saw Lisa hurrying after Aston in the mellow afternoon, trim, eager, passionate and, he thought, marked down in some way he still did not understand, to conspire in her own deception. As a muse she was flawed, as a woman she was all too human and more fascinating than ever.

'Don't play the fool, Jo.' Mark sounded a bit shrill, as though he was frightened. 'It's not funny.'

'Jo, come over here, darling. I want to show you – ' It was Lisa speaking but she broke off and rushed over to the child who, everyone could now see, was behaving in an odd way.

Jessica was laughing. She stood straight in front of Jo. 'You look as though you're all spooky.'

Jo, in her brown cloak and her loose, silky hair seeming to stand out as though responding to magnetic forces, was white faced and shivering, her hands clenched at her sides. Her eyes were turned up, the pupils almost disappearing under the upper lids, so she looked shockingly blind. Aston thought she was putting on an act and walked away, embarrassed.

Mark really was upset and screamed at Jo again, 'It's not funny. You look awful!'

Only Olwen, with her nurse's training, understood what was happening and went over to put her arm round the girl. 'You're all right, Jo. Now, I'm going to help you lie down on the ground. That's right. Just let yourself go. Lucky you've got this nice cloak to keep you warm.'

Jo was as stiff as a board. Olwen let her fall back on her heels and Aston, looking back and realizing there was something wrong, rushed to help. Between them Aston and Olwen lowered Jo to the ground where Olwen turned her head on one side and slipped her little finger inside her mouth as though searching for something to remove. Momentarily Jo had stopped shivering but now a current of electricity might have been running through her. She vibrated, and so freely she could have been floating just above the ground and not actually on it. No sign of breathing. Her body was light, almost insubstantial, to the point where she would be nothing but vibrations and fade like an exhausted pulse of energy into the absorbent afternoon, just disappearing.

With her free hand Olwen, kneeling at Jo's side, stroked her face. 'Has she had this sort of thing before?' she asked Aston.

177

'No, what is it?'

'Just a convulsion. It looks more alarming than it actually is. She'll be okay. Any history of this sort of thing? In the family, I mean.'

'I reckon we get a doctor to her quick,' said Lisa. 'Eh?'

'You do that,' said Olwen.

'What'll I say?'

'She's had a seizure. But look. She's coming out of it.'

Jo's face was still chalky and she still had her hands clenched but she lifted them to her chest. The pupils of her eyes were dead central. They looked straight up at the sky. Her nostrils pinched and quivered. Aston was now supporting her in his arms, his lips pressed to her forehead.

'Jo, listen to me, Jo. You're all right,' he murmured.

By the time Lisa had come back from the house to say she had phoned Dr Brownlow's surgery in the village but there was no reply Jo was sitting up, still supported by her father. He had been trying to get her to sip some Coke but Jo would have none of it. She clenched her teeth. Nor could he get her to say anything.

'We'd better get her to bed.' With some assistance from Edwin he managed to pick Jo up and set off for the house. 'You're fine, Jo. It's over now.'

'You could try my husband,' said Olwen to Lisa, and gave her the number. 'I know he's just mooching around at home and this is the sort of kid's illness he knows all about, when all's said and done. He's treated Jo before. He could be here in half an hour if he really gets his skates on. He may want to take her into hospital for observation.'

Aston heard this and turned. 'Jo's not going into hospital,' he shouted back. 'She's staying with me.'

The clerical collar of the Reverend Paul Brough winked in the sunlight as a ray struck through the foliage and caught it. 'Wouldn't the quickest thing be to take the child to your husband?' he said to Olwen.

'She'll be all right in a couple of shakes.'

For some reason Olwen was playing the attack down, perhaps because that was the way she always behaved in a crisis but a stronger reason might have been the sight of Aston's face. The man looked not just concerned about Jo but actually frightened. She could not understand why and she wanted to be a steadying influence.

'A highly strung little girl,' said the Rector. 'In the way exceptionally intelligent people sometimes are. It's almost as though they've come from a different world. Anyway with insights clods like me are incapable of. I do hope she'll be all right. Her mother dropped dead, you know.'

Olwen stopped and faced him. 'I didn't know.'

'Oh yes, Mrs Hart told me the whole story one day. I don't remember the details but I can quite see this attack, or whatever it is, brings back memories for the family.'

The Rector hesitated. 'I'm sorry I should not have said that. Breach of confidence. Please put it out of your mind.'

'I might do that,' said Olwen.

'What made the occurrence all the more horrifying was that a priest was involved.'

'How do you mean, involved?'

'A Roman Catholic priest. He had been called in by the Harts to bless the rooms in the house. Sprinkling with holy water and all that, no doubt. They had got it into their heads the place was haunted. And so he blessed the rooms and poor Mrs Hart, the first Mrs Hart that is, just collapsed and for all the world as though some evil spirit had expelled from its refuge and taken violent possession of her.' The Reverend Paul Brough tightened his lips and raised his eyebrows. 'Nothing of that sort has been going on here. If there were occasion for a blessing I am sure Mr Hart would have asked me.'

Not having met the man before Olwen inspected him curiously. 'I didn't know people still had primitive ideas like that.'

'Oh, it wasn't here. It was in Africa.' Realizing that he had talked too much the Rector said, 'Excuse me!' He had caught sight of Harriet and set off to remind her that the first time he had met the little girl was when she was in the Parslers' care. 'And she had an attack then, didn't she? But not like this one. No? What a thing to happen at a birthday party. Now she was looked after by a very splendid doctor on that occasion. What was his name? Ah, yes.'

179

'That's his wife you've just been talking to.'

'She's Mrs Clutsam? I could see by the way she tended to the little girl there must be some connection.'

Harriet, with Sister Tabitha's assistance, had been rallying the other guests, particularly Jo's school friends, with a feeling that *something* (a large crystal egg came into her mind) had been shattered and she was going round, picking up the pieces. Rallying meant encouraging them to drink mint tea and tackle the sandwiches and cakes. 'Jo's just been over-excited. But she'll be all right. You'll see.' Now she told Ed she was going indoors to see if she could make herself useful there.

Lisa was on the telephone, arguing (obviously with Jerry) and not to much effect. The excuses could be imagined. He wasn't a GP. Patients had to be referred to him by a GP. That was how specialists operated under the National Health Service. And so on.

'Let me talk to him,' said Harriet. Surprised, Lisa surrendered the telephone and Harriet weighed in. 'Jerry, this is Harriet Parsler. You're to come immediately. Do you understand.' She gave directions for finding the house. 'Is there anything we ought to be doing? Hell, Jerry, be helpful for once. Okay, we'll do that.' She put the phone down and turned to Lisa. 'He's on his way. You must have given him a pretty clear indication of the symptoms. He said keep her warm and put cushions under the legs. So that the blood runs to the brain, I suppose.'

'Friend of yours?' asked Lisa.

'Sort of.'

As they went up the stairs together Lisa said she just couldn't get over the fact that in England everybody seemed to know everybody else. And they went on knowing each other in spite of the occasional fit of must.

'Must? I like that.'

'It's the word they use in Kenya when elephants go on the rampage.'

'I see. Well, I like the ordinary sense too. A fit of must. That describes it fine.'

Jo was lying on the bed, a light blanket thrown over her, looking surprisingly normal. Lisa found some pillows and stuffed them under Jo's legs. Aston was standing with his back to them, gazing out of the window. When he turned his face was blubbery and puffed up, almost as though he had been crying. But it was rage that made him look that way, a face red as a cock's wattle. He opened his mouth but no words came out. When Lisa told him a doctor was coming he brushed the information on one side. He did not want to know. He stood there with fists clenched so tightly in front of him he might have had little rows of white pebbles under the skin.

'It's another bloody attack,' he said.

'Jo's all right. I don't know what you mean by another attack. She hasn't had one like this before. You know that, Aston sweetie. There's no need to upset yourself. She's fine. Nothing to get worked up about at all. And Harriet here has a special paediatrician friend who looked after Jo when she was sick before.'

'I meant we've been attacked again. Us. Through Jo.' Aston looked at Harriet. 'That South African?'

'I know you don't like him but he's a good doctor.'

Aston stretched out his hand. He wanted to tear something up. Or even to tear something out of himself; an agony he could not explain, perhaps. He would have hated to say he was afraid. The two women could not understand what had got hold of him. Then suddenly he relaxed, calmed down and even smiled. He went over and knelt by Jo's bed. 'You're okay, kid. What came over you?'

'I am so glad Dr Clutsam is coming after all,' said Jo. 'He's really dishy and I know Mrs Parsler thinks so too. Can I go back to the party now?'

'You're staying right there, kid.'

'But I can't neglect my guests.' She sat up and threw off the blanket. 'What's that smell? Oh, I know. It must be a barbecue. It wasn't part of my plan. It's a surprise. Oh, Daddy, you're marvellous. That's what is nice about birthdays. Surprise!'

So it was Jo who first detected the fire.

Aston opened the door and went out on to the landing but he soon came back. 'Come on, quick! Everyone downstairs. Go on, Lisa, for Chrissake! It's all we wanted. The bloody house is on fire.' He picked Jo up from the bed and stepped through the doorway into a drift of blue smoke, followed by the women. The

181

smoke was drifting from the far end of the landing. Lisa took a few steps in that direction and yelled. 'Gee! Look at that!'

'Get on downstairs.'

'But it's the cell. There's smoke coming under the door.'

And not only smoke to tell them a fire had taken hold. There were thumps, hisses and sharp crackling as though someone in there was dancing on a lot of brittle sticks. Sharp snaps, then hisses and sighs gave way to low grumbling. It wasn't just fire on the other side of a door at the other end of the landing. There was an animal presence. It slobbered about, mumbling up bits of furniture. The room was possessed.

The fire had been noticed from the garden. Out there people were shouting. Aston was half-way down the stairs with Jo in his arms when Lisa was still on the landing, looking into the smoke with streaming eyes, saying, 'My room is burning. Hey! I've got to go in there and get my things.'

'Like hell you are!' Harriet grabbed her arm and Lisa tried to fight her off. The two women struggled together. Seeing what was happening Aston handed Jo over to Edwin at the foot of the stairs, asked the Rector to dial 999 for the fire service, and then rushed back upstairs to grab Lisa, still yelling and protesting she wanted to get her things. The smoke was so thick it might have been night. The house whined.

All three of them – Lisa, Aston and Harriet – made it downstairs and into the hall where there was less of a smother. Aston was now gripped by the idea someone might be upstairs trapped in a bathroom or lavatory but Lisa was sufficiently recovered to point out all the plumbing was at the other end of the house away from the blaze. So there were no loos that way. The last thing she wanted was for Aston to go back up those stairs. He went round shouting for people to check there was no one missing. 'Just make sure everyone is here. I mean, if you were with someone see where they are.'

It was out of proportion. A block of flats or a skyscraper blazing, yes. But not a two-storey stone house with lots of windows and exits.

Then he went off to the kitchen for an extinguisher kept on a bracket there in case a pan of cooking oil caught fire. The Rector sat calmly in the hall with the telephone at his ear waiting for a reply which did not come. Harriet ran out with a small oil painting which looked as though it might be valuable and this was a signal for others to rush in and pick up chairs, cushions, books, ornaments. Ed had handed Jo over to the care of Jessica and returned to the house to help Lisa carry out a sideboard, still with a bowl of fruit, a decanter of whisky and glasses on it. The window of the room where the fire was stood partly open and the smoke came out in puffs and veils as though the fire animal lurking there, the dragon, had to draw in air before expelling the flame from its nostrils. The smoke curled up to the eaves and then, caught by the light wind, followed the slope of the tiled roof, to curl up in a broad, unsteady spiral into the milky sky.

Jo's schoolfriends were frightened and Lisa distressed but nearly everybody else was pleasurably excited by the fire. This included Jo who was sitting with her back against a tree, legs and arms spread out, like a big open-mouthed rag doll just tossed there. The whole late autumnal afternoon was spicy. The air throbbed with smoke. Nobody was more excited than Jessica's friend, Eric, who became an even greater hero in Jo's eyes by finding a ladder, setting it against the side of the house and going up it with a garden hose that shot out an impressive spray of water when Mark, on his instructions, turned the tap on down below. Eric was able to spray through the open window into the room which almost immediately began to hiss like snakes and exhale a different kind of smoke, white with occasional crackling sparks.

Aston came out of the house and ordered Eric to come down.

'I'm okay.' Eric turned his shiny, sweaty, face to see who was shouting at him.

'Don't you see he's trying to put the fire out,' said Jo. To her Eric had become a Saxon warrior attacking a Norman bastion from which she herself had only just escaped. That is what it felt like. Something really unpleasant had happened to her and she had managed to get away. Eric undoubtedly was responsible for her escape but she could not remember the details. All she knew was that Eric was returning to the attack.

Aston did not see it that way. He shook the ladder and made Eric come down, to be accidentally drenched by the hose. Aston took his place with the extinguisher and was soon directing the flow of suds through the window (the glass had now shattered) and the whole upper side of the house was hidden a dahlia-like efflorescence in yellow and white.

'My God,' said Lisa. 'Why does this have to happen to us?'

By the time the firemen arrived on a couple of spotless red vehicles the fire was out and the officer in charge looked both disappointed and annoyed when Aston gave him the news.

'We'll check,' he said.

The men in yellow helmets and waterproof slacks ran a ladder up to the window and the officer said he would make an inspection himself.

'We only took delivery of this pump yesterday,' he informed Aston. 'She's a beaut, eh? Her first outing. Well, it's an exercise, I suppose.' He was on the ladder peering into the still fuming room. He sent a couple of men into the house to see if they could enter the room that way. One of the men soon after appeared at the window and, after a brief discussion, the officer climbed in to join him. Other firemen went into the house and looked around. It all seemed casual and possibly dangerous but Aston assumed they knew what they were doing. When a man took a hose up the ladder he said, 'Do you have to do that? I tell you the fire's out and we don't want any more water pumped in than we can help.'

'You can't be sure, sir. You've got to 'ave training to know when a fire's out. Can be cunning. Lie low, like a fox in a nole, then before you know. Whoosh!'

Inside the house men began shouting and a woman screamed. Aston looked around and could not see Lisa in the garden. When the scream came again he realized she was up in her cell and that the fire officer was angrily ordering her to get out of it and to safety. Aston would have climbed the ladder but the fireman with the hose blocked his way so he followed what must have been Lisa's route, raced up the stairs and along the landing where the door was open, one fireman outside, another inside and Lisa beyond him in the acrid, wet, stinking, beetle blackness of the cell, trying to get past the officer to the window and beating at him with her fists.

'Lisa! Come out of there.'

At the sound of his voice Lisa turned. She was excited to the point of frenzy. Her voice cracked. 'Oh look, Aston. Look, it's there and it's safe and it's not harmed at all. What do you know about that? Isn't it a miracle?'

Lying on what had once been a small carpet but was now a slick of carbon was a piece of paper, brilliantly white in contrast.

'It's my Shakespeare letter and this guy won't let me get at it.'

The scorched and blackened room was no place for white paper. If Lisa was right about it being her lost letter it could not possibly have been in the room when it burned. The letter must have been planted afterwards. But by whom? Only the firemen and Lisa had entered the place.

Aston made for the paper but the officer put an arm out. 'As I've been telling the lady the floor isn't safe over there.'

'Okay. But my wife wants that piece of paper.'

Aston did not understand how the letter was where it was, nor more profoundly, did he understand why Lisa attached such absurd importance to it, a fake anyway, and his ignorance was unbearable. It made him so helpless. So he lit up with a special rage against his own inadequacy. Anger was what he wanted and nobody could stop him enjoying it. He went for it wholeheartedly, in rage and fury.

'To hell with it,' he shouted and pushed past the officer. 'I can go through a floor in my own house, can't I?'

The charred surface of the boards crunched under his weight but they were thick old elm and stood firm.

'This is crazy. It isn't even scorched.' Aston came back with the letter but when Lisa tried to take it from him he held it away from her.

'Give it to me, Aston. I want to kiss it.'

'It isn't even charred. Must be asbestos.'

'I want you out of this room.' The officer was cross, too, because not only had the fire been out before his men could get to it but there was an argument he could not understand about a piece of paper that ought to have been burnt but wasn't. 'You'd think somebody had thrown a petrol bomb. I've never seen anything like. It's a funny sort of fire. If you ask me. Was there any smell of gas?'

'No gas,' said Aston. Lisa was jumping about.

'But let me see it, Aston. It is the letter, isn't it?'

Aston had been looking at it. 'Sure. And now I want to see whether it'll burn.'

'Where's the plastic envelope?' Lisa was recovering from her ecstasy to realize just how odd the survival of the letter really was. If it wasn't planted then it had simply survived. But how? 'Aston, *please*!' She wanted him to hand the letter over but he muttered something about having had enough of all this bloody nonsense and bundled her out of the room.

'*We'll see*.' He could say no more, he was so furious.

Not being a smoker Aston had no matches about him and it was not until they were down in the hall that he was able to borrow a box from one of the firemen. Aston was so much taller than Lisa that when he held the letter as high as he could she was unable to reach it; and she was not strong enough to pull his arm down as he took a match out of the box and struck it.

'Please!' she wailed. 'Please, Aston. Please!'

Ed had come in from the garden. 'What's happening?'

'He's going to burn my letter. You must stop him, Ed.'

'You mean you found it?'

Aston put the match to the letter. 'You see, it burns!'

Now that the incineration was taking place everyone fell silent, even Lisa. The letter flared. Aston turned it so that the flame had more and more white paper to lick with its striped yellow and red tongue. The upturned faces flickered in the light, Aston with his lips parted and wide-eyed as though he was carrying out some momentous gesture, some act of ritual defiance, like the burning of a national flag or firing a cross. Lisa was both miserable and furious. Tears on her cheek winked in the dancing light and she made impotent reaching gestures as though she still wanted to catch the fire. As Aston held it away he burned his fingers. It all seemed crazy beyond belief. Did he think that the moment Lisa's fingers touched the flame it would be doused and the paper, white and unharmed, flutter to the ground as if in some conjuring trick? He could not hold the letter until every bit of it had been consumed so he let it go and the charred paper with a blue flecked flame at the one remaining white corner, floated in the air. Then it was blank, no flame at all. The writing could still be seen, paler against the black of the consumed paper just before Aston caught it, rubbed it between his two hands, before making the gesture of flinging the ash away from him.

'So much for that.' He turned on Lisa. 'I had to do it.'

'What are you talking about?'

'You lost the paper, the room caught on fire. Then you found the paper and it wasn't even scorched. You know what? If I'd hired a witch doctor instead of a priest Shirley would be alive today!'

'Shirley? What's she got to do with it?'

'I had a Mau Mau curse put on me. This is it. I'll get a witch doctor flown out from Kenya before anything worse happens.'

'A witch doctor in England?'

'Sure! Really nasty black magic can travel.'

The fire officer had come downstairs in time to see Aston burning the letter. 'That's a bit dangerous. Is that how the fire started upstairs?'

'Of course not.'

'Well, I can't see why the room went up like that. What to say in my report I don't quite know. Usual thing is an electric fault. Seeing you wave that burning paper makes you think, don't it? There are people as actually like starting fires. Know what? That's arson. I'm not saying anything. But I've got my report to make. And you'll have your insurance claim to think about.'

He ordered his men outside and they made preparations for packing up and moving off. A police car came up the drive with its amber light flashing and the officer not getting out of his seat was soon in conference with the fire officer who took his helmet off and bent down, revealing the seat of the navy blue pants he was wearing under the yellow waterproofs. A voice could be heard crackling over the police radio. The officer lifted his gloved hand to his mouth. 'No, everything's okay. No casualties.'

Seeing how upset Lisa had been Ed wanted more than ever to come clean over the letter and explain there was nothing to grieve over because it was phoney and if it gave her any satisfaction he was quite ready to concoct a replacement. There were a number of reasons why he did not. In the first place this was obviously not the right moment. For all he knew Aston had stage-managed the letter burning to shock Lisa out of her cranky obsession. He might have been so far out of his depth, that he'd tried even that. If Lisa felt defeated Ed did not want to increase her humiliation. But the other possibility was that she would not believe him. She so needed the letter to be authentic she just would not accept any other view of it, lunatic as that might seem. And, in any case, he hadn't the guts.

But there was more. Aston had upset Lisa. Seeing her under stress, with real, pearly tears on her cheeks Ed had an almost irresistible urge to put his arms round her, there and then, in front of everyone, and kiss those tears away, saying, 'You just make me love all God's creation.' These were the wild words that went through his head. He knew Harriet was looking at him. So what? He was in tune with her too. He was in tune with everybody, thanks to Lisa. In spite of appearances she was just herself, unchanging, as radiant as ever. Even when he shut his eyes he could still see her serene, reassuring face. Pins could have been stuck in him and he would not have felt them. He could have walked on fire. He could have thrown himself over a cliff and soared away like a bird.

All he said was, 'I don't understand about the letter. What happened?'

The firemen were still there when Jerry arrived. After he had examined Jo he wanted to know which had come first, the fire or her little attack.

'I didn't have a little attack,' said Jo.

'You mean you had a big one?'

'I didn't have an attack at all. I was just enjoying my birthday and suddenly everything went phizz. It was lovely. There were lights and things.'

'Well, which was it?' Jerry asked Lisa who was standing at the foot of Jo's bed, while Aston fidgeted in front of the window. 'The attack came first,' he said. 'We brought her up here. She was lying on the bed and then I went out and saw smoke. Matter of fact Jo smelled it and thought we'd got a barbecue.'

Still watching her carefully Jerry asked Jo what presents she'd had.

'Oh, a kitten. He's sweet. He's an Abyssinian. I want a real

Abyssinian name for him. And a super bicycle. But the best thing was this fire.'

'You don't think the fire was a present, do you?'

'Of course it was a present. No birthday party is a real party without a bit of the house on fire. When we have presents we ought to give something up too. What I mean is, actually lose things. And you lose things in a fire. It's like giving them back to God.'

For the second time Jerry looked closely into first one of Jo's eyes, then the other. 'You could call the kitten Tafari. That's an Abyssinian name.'

'Tafari. I like that. There was this fire and now *you've* come. So what more could anybody want for a birthday?'

'You're pleased to see me?'

'I wouldn't have sent an invitation otherwise.'

Downstairs Jerry seemed more interested in medical etiquette than anything else. 'I think you ought to call your GP in. What's his name? Yah! Dr Brownlow. Then if he wants to refer her that's okay by me. She needn't stay in hospital. But I'd like to see her there for tests. Yah! Explain to Dr Brownlow I only stepped in because you couldn't contact him and you knew me because I'd treated the girl before.'

He was interested in the fire too and, before he left, was taken along by Aston to view the damage.

'Jeez!' He looked round in amazement. 'Some blaze. Surprising the roof didn't come down. Funny about the desk. Just carbon. I suppose if you touched it the whole thing would crumble. Lucky. The whole house could have gone. I suppose an old place like this is flammable as hell.'

They did not enter the room. They stood at the door peering in.

'You been about much in Africa?' Aston asked him.

'Here and there.'

'Then possibly you wouldn't pee in your trousers if I said we're being got at here. Long distance.'

Jerry said nothing about this, possibly because he thought the remark too eccentric for sensible comment. 'Hope your insurers cough up without too much hassle.'

'Why shouldn't they? We changed our insurers not so long

ago anyway on the advice of a friend of ours. Ed Parsler. He's in the insurance business. Do you know him? Got a pretty wife.'

Jerry, being tall and with no fat, had a way of wriggling when he was really concentrating his mind. He went through this performance, grunting and not knowing what to say.

'As a matter of fact they're downstairs now. But of course you know them. So much going on I get confused. They were looking after Jo when she was your patient two or three years back. Ed found me new insurers. What impressed me was it wasn't his own company. You'd have thought he'd want to sell me one of his own policies. He's got integrity. Know what I mean? I don't think there'll be much trouble over the claim. If they want to know what caused it I shall put down witchcraft.'

'Witchcraft?'

'I had a curse put on me.'

'You don't believe that sort of thing?'

'I do and I don't. But a fire and Jo foaming at the mouth and the letter not being burned puts me on edge. Yeah, I do believe in witchcraft. And do you know what?' Aston's manner turned threatening. 'If I'd had any sense I'd have gone in for it myself. Yeah! I'd have made a hell of a good witch doctor. And I'd have known what to do in present circumstances. You talk about giving Jo tests. You know what? You won't find anything, brother. I know what I'm talking about.'

Jerry had recovered from the question about the Parslers. 'You don't really mean Jo foamed at the mouth? Nobody told me that.'

'No,' said Aston. 'It was just a manner of speaking. Can I give you a drink?'

The landing outside creaked and Ed appeared. It was the first time he had come across Jerry in months. Well before he had taken that ducking in the brook. He thought of the brook a lot. It was a divide, a kind of profane baptism into knowing something he had fought against knowing. The encounter was unexpected because Ed had not expected to find anyone in Lisa's cell, certainly not Jerry.

As though he had just come along to check up Ed said, 'I still don't get it about that letter. Being picked up after the fire, you know.'

Aston said, 'You're an insurance man, Ed. I'm putting witchcraft down as the cause of the fire. How do you think the insurers will take that?'

'Speaking for myself I wouldn't take it at all.'

And then, without warning Ed had clenched his fist and struck it backhanded across Jerry's face. He hoped the cheekbone and jaw hurt as much as his hand did. Anything and everything was now possible. The charred floor could at last collapse under the combined weight of the three men so that they descended in a black smother into the room below. Just anything. Not even too crazy to think of backslapping and laughter. If you slug anybody you just don't do it that way. You make a great bunch of fives and just go for where it hurts most, in the guts. But Jerry was lean. He probably took the right kind of exercise and had tight muscles over his guts. So the jaw and a knee into the crutch. Failure to do just that would naturally raise a smile and Ed's blow had been almost ceremonial, a mere slap across the face. But anything was possible. Murder was possible. Ed could not think how to kill with just his hands. He looked around for something to hit Jerry with but there was nothing, just hate flaming from out of nowhere like a psychic gas leak that had ignited.

Aston was bigger and stronger than Ed. He wrapped his arms round him. 'You see what I mean about witches, Ed. He's got into you of all people. Sure he was the firebug. Insurance companies have got to get updated on witches.'

'I'll be going,' said Jerry. He had a red patch on the side of his face.

'You do that, doc,' said Aston. 'The devils bite at the back of the neck so keep your coat collar turned up.'

When Jerry had gone Aston asked Ed if he was okay.

'I'm okay.'

'That really was a bad attack. I'm flying in a witch doctor. No kidding.'

From the outside of the house the only sign of the fire was the smashed windows, though the firemen had left their mark. They had trampled over the chrysanthemums and the air was charged with that odour, a kind of bitter incense, and with the smell of a dead fire. Hard to know whether the haze was due to the smoke or a rising mist. It was wild mushroom and blackberry weather.

Lisa was amazed she could walk into the fields and pick mushrooms. She had never seen anything like it. Several mornings she and Aston had walked out and picked enough to fry up with bacon for breakfast. There were different kinds. Some the usual size, with the sweet tangy pink gills under the white button heads that grew out on the hillside where the cattle grazed. And others, in the danker ground on the other side of the garden fence, were huge. Horse mushrooms, Aston called them, as big as cowpats, so they could be seen from quite a distance. As now, through a gap in that fence, where Lisa was sure there had been none in the morning. She thought of telling Aston she was going to pick mushrooms and then walking out of the gate and disappearing. Not coming back.

'The chances are it's nothing to worry about.' Jerry had approached so silently over the grass he startled her. 'Children have these occasional convulsions and then grow out of them.'

'Thank you for coming at such short notice.'

Jerry shrugged. 'Give me a ring at the hospital and we'll fix it so I can take a closer look.'

He was on his way to his car. Harriet came over and squeezed his arm. 'Hope I did the right thing. We were all a bit scared.'

Jerry walked faster and straightened his arm in the hope she would let go. 'That's okay.'

Olwen was already sitting in the car (she had come to the party by the country bus and then walked the mile or so from the main road) and when the couple arrived Harriet said, 'Olwen tells me you're off to South Africa.'

'That's about it, I reckon.' Jerry glared down at her. 'Any objection?'

'Oh, don't be like that, you bastard.'

'Harriet!' Olwen gasped.

'Well, he is, isn't he? The way he treats you is bloody shameful.' To Jerry. 'A lovely wife like you've got. If I were Olwen I'd lead you a real dance! Well, you can kiss me.' He bent down and kissed her on the lips. 'Now, kiss Olwen.' After some hesitation he put his head through the car window and kissed Olwen too. 'Why do I always have to do what you tell me? Your husband just struck me.'

'Ed? You did rather ask for it, didn't you? You lecher, you. Well, that's great for both of you. It's been what you might call a real party this afternoon, hasn't it? Something out of the usual. Though how much? Hard to say. Might be a lot.'

The convent minibus arrived to pick up Sister Tabitha and the girls and the Reverend Paul wheeled his bicycle out from behind the garden shed. Eric's Suzuki, from half a mile away, was still making a lot of noise and people had to lift their voices to be heard.

Like Ed and Lisa. 'What a queer business, that letter,' said Ed. 'I hope you weren't upset.' He was still out of himself because of the way he had gone for Jerry.

'Upset? I'm hysterical. You can't have a fire in the house and Jo having this attack and not be really gone over, you know? Hysterical, is it?'

'I meant about Aston destroying the letter.'

Lisa thought for some moments and then turned to him with immense seriousness. He guessed she was exploring him for the poem he was hiding and as still she looked and still she did not speak so the words began to form. But they were nonsense. 'Ripe in the elastic teeth.' What had that to do with him or her? 'A helmet of indifference.' Sounded like a quote from an old poem. Again, no relevance. 'Quiver river.' He liked that. Now you've got the rhymes, and the helmet and the elastic teeth think back to the poem buried there. The rhymes were the teeth of the poem. How far back were the tongue and heart?

'No, I was not upset by Aston destroying the letter,' said Lisa. 'I was glad. Say, when he put that match to it I got a real kick. You know that? Well, I thought, he's my husband and if a husband can't do things that gives his wife kicks what sort of a husband is that? So far as I'm concerned it's just great.'

'You don't really mind?'

'Fire purifies. You know that, Ed?'

Deep down in the poem the heart was a burning coal.

'You know you set *me* on fire, Lisa?'

And she laughed at him, as she had laughed in the train on its way to Wycombe Marsh. This time she didn't kiss him. She turned and walked away. Ed guessed he was looking odd, because that was how he felt. It showed and Lisa must have decided she'd had enough oddity to be going on with. He really did look wild.

12

During her pregnancy Lisa had bouts of feeling so ill she thought she was going to die, or at least have a miscarriage; and there were other times when she felt so blazingly well she wanted to sing and laugh a lot. The staff at the local antenatal clinic were marvellous and Lisa could not get it into her head that the service was free. After one session she said to the sister-in-charge, 'Well, okay, I accept this is a government health service but there must be something I can pay for. Don't you have a welfare fund?' There wasn't so she took to placing a ten-pound note in the spastics collecting box every time she went.

Aston was finally taken on as a temporary officer in the Foreign and Commonwealth Office to help with preparations for the 1977 conference (he was won over by Tom Hubbard saying they were desperate for help) and spent days every week up in London. Lisa already had a woman who came in for the cleaning but now, in the absence of Aston, she felt in need of more support and started to employ Mrs Buck who answered her advertisement in the *Bicester Advertiser*. Mrs Buck (at all times she had to be addressed in this way) was a widow in her fifties who rode a Vespa. With her hollow cheeks, hawk nose and dyed black hair she looked a witch and Lisa was a bit frightened of her. She spoke in the strong local accent which Lisa found hard to understand but she cooked passably well and, more important, could ferry Jo to and from school in the Peugeot when Lisa did not feel up to driving it. She also did shopping. Lisa developed yearnings for strange, exotic foods – at least, strange by Mrs Buck's standards – swordfish cutlets, octopus, tortillas, New England baked clams. Mrs Buck, not the least surprised, looked for them in the local supermarkets. They had none of these things. Lisa began asking for bear steak. Ever since she had read a Yukon adventure story as a child where the hunters shot grizzlies and grilled steaks over their camp fire she had always had it at the back of her mind that one day she would eat bear.

Mrs Buck drew the line at this. She wasn't going to ask at the butcher's if they had such things. Nobody in England ate bear.

'Okay. Venison is English enough. Try that. You know, deer meat.'

Mrs Buck found some venison in Oxford market but when it came to dressing the meat and getting it ready to roast she said, 'No, Mrs Hart. You'd a better do that an' you like that sort of muck. It's make me throw up.' She added the information that once, when pregnant, she had sucked coal. The fancy just took her that way so she understood Lisa's whims. Lisa didn't fancy coal but she did, a bit, become addicted to charcoal biscuits.

Soon after her visit to the British Library Lisa had had photocopies made of the Shakespeare letter (the idea was to send one to the Folger with an exploratory letter) and from time to time she would take out the sole survivor of the fire and study it. This particular copy had been in her handbag. Even allowing for the fact it wasn't the magic letter itself the scrutiny of it ought to have aroused stronger emotions than it did: amazement at the way the original had been lost, incredulity at its subsequent strange and inexplicable survival, but now she was apathetic about it. Being pregnant had a lot to do with the way she was switched off about the letter but what really wiped the slate, if not clean at least obscured whatever message it bore, was the way Aston apologized. Poor dear! He had been terribly upset. He told her about the curse put on him by an African tribesman just before he died and how he'd always felt Shirley's death might be the result of it. Now, here in England, it was all happening again. Jo having this fit. The fire! The letter that went missing and then should have been burned in the fire but wasn't! It was a deliberate provocation. In the frame of mind he then was in he could just imagine some hostile presence throwing the letter down in contempt as a way of demonstrating power, not only to destroy but to preserve. And, in doing this, to demonstrate the presence was privy to their thoughts, not only his thoughts but Lisa's too. It had cottoned on to the importance of this letter to her. All this had gone through his mind and he lost control. What did he mean by presence? Something like a devil.

Lisa did not know what to think of this curse stuff. What was for sure was the hold it had on Aston. She had to recognize he thought it was for real. She just had to accept that and not allow herself to get too worked up about the fire and the loss of the Shakespeare letter. She had to get a grip of herself. Her father would have said there was a need at all times in the life of the individual, as there was in the life of the people as a whole, for control and discipline; otherwise tests and trials which might seem bad, even hard to bear, would only become worse. Chaos was always round the corner. She had a hunch he would have been pleased to know he was going to have an English grandchild. He had always thought well of the British, particularly the old British, before there was so much immigration. After the Germans and the Scandinavians he had been ready to grant the British a place in the hierarchy of nations. Yes, of course he was a bigoted old fool, but he was her father and he was dead, and Hans was dead too, and she, Lisa, had a kind of responsibility for carrying the family tradition on and this meant respecting at least some of her father's views.

Another reason Lisa thought her father would be pleased with her English marriage was that her mother, Frau Wicht, plainly was not. She and her husband paid their visit (first time in England) and Frau Wicht asked lots of questions about the house. How much had Lisa spent on doing it up? And so on. It was Frau Wicht's money by rights, was the implication, and it had been thrown away. All mere show! Fundamental maintenance, such as checking the electric wiring, had been neglected. So naturally there had been a fire. She spoke to Lisa in German but Lisa always kept to English.

The Wichts got on surprisingly well with Jo and invited her to come and stay with them in Kelkhm the following spring. By that time the weather would be warm enough for her to go walking in the forest and have picnics. Herr Wicht had a grandson a bit older than Jo and a granddaughter who was younger. They had lots of friends and he was sure they would love to make her feel at home and try out their English on her. Jo was excited at this prospect. German was not normally taught at the convent but Jo persuaded Sister Agnes, who was Swiss, to give her lessons. She was growing fast, bright-eyed, alert and developing such a concern about her weight and living largely on lean meat, rye biscuits, cottage cheese and apples, that Lisa feared she might be heading for anorexia. Jo had never heard of this affliction and when it was explained said, 'Oh no, I just don't want to be fat, that's all. When I grow up I'm not going to eat any meat because it's wrong to kill little lambs. But I won't give it up yet because I like it so much.'

She had another convulsion when the Wichts were there. When she recovered she explained there was nothing to worry about. Dr Brownlow the GP had been very pleased to pass her on to the specialist. So Dr Clutsam was in a sense, legitimized. He talked about electricity in the brain but he didn't really know, he only pretended to know why she had started having sparks there. So Jo said. She was fond of him because he had such sad droopy eyes but he didn't really respond to her as a person. She was just another patient so far as he was concerned and this disillusioned her. The truth was he didn't understand her case at all. He wasn't as dishy as she had thought. He said the convulsions were just something that happened inside her. She knew perfectly well they came from outside. She was receiving messages. From whom she wasn't sure. Her first thought had been Miss Jackson, an old friend who had been burned at the stake for her religious beliefs. But that wasn't really possible because when you came to think of it Miss Jackson had only been a doll. When you really came to think of it. Perhaps it was her dear departed mother because she was jealous of Lisa. That was out, though, because when people passed over jealousy was left behind. No, it was much more likely that whoever was signalling was in some far off world in another part of the galaxy. It might well be her destiny to be the first earthling to make contact. *Dr Who* was kid's stuff and so was *Star Trek*. They were just made-up stories but she really was receiving something. This was fact. She was gradually being tuned in. When she was really spot-on. Whoosh! Contact! One thing she was clear about. If they came to get her she would not go.

Herr Wicht was an amateur astronomer with a 75mm refractor telescope set up in a garden shed with a sliding roof back home in Kelkhm and he had the bright idea of taking Jo up to the Planetarium in London. Lisa vetoed that idea (as she vetoed too much watching of TV) because Jerry had said bright, flashing lights could stimulate the optic nerves and trigger off responses

197

in the brain. Jo was probably susceptible to visual stimulants. Until she grew out of the attacks it would be better if she avoided them. Psychedelic lighting effects in discos were absolutely forbidden. If Jo was kept quiet for a couple of years there was no reason to doubt the convulsions would fade out.

Frau Wicht learned all this at second hand and remarked that Dr Clutsam sounded a bit of a fool. Babies had convulsions but not young girls. If Jo was still having them when she came to Kelkhm Kurt's cousin would see her. He was an excellent specialist in Freiburg who was not only a medical doctor, a paediatrician, but a psychiatrist as well.

'Kids don't go to psychiatrists,' said Lisa.

'If their parents are Herr Professor Schnürer's patients they do,' said her mother.

Workmen were in the house most of the time, either restoring the fire damage (new joists, new floorboards, a whole beam in the roof to be replaced plastering, papering) or turning one of the small bedrooms into a nursery with new built-in cupboards. So there was hammering, sawing, and pop music without pause on the transistors brought in by the workmen. They smoked cigars too, which was another irritation to Lisa. She was against smoking. Now that Aston had this important job at the Foreign and Commonwealth office he must, Lisa decided, have an office of his own. All the furniture was of solid Brazilian mahogany (no veneer); a work surface on legs (not a desk, Lisa insisted) built into the bay so that Aston could sit there and gaze out of the window at the copper beech hedge and the bridle path leading down into the valley: on two sides of the room were bookshelves (she would take a real interest in his work and help him choose all the books that would be needed to fill so much space) and on the remaining wall, yes, a real desk to take a computer with drawers on each side of the kneehole and shelves over, at eye level, to support the computer screen. She had been reading up on computers and was determined Aston and she would be in on the game, all set up for a computer terminal they could use to plug into the real hardware in London and New York, when such things were technically possible.

'What would I need all that for?' he complained.

'How do you know what you need? When I first heard of electric toothbrushes I thought, well, there's a useless gimmick. How wrong can you get! I just couldn't *live* without an electric toothbrush. And you'll be the same with computers.'

Lisa had told her mother nothing of the supernatural part of Aston's life nor of the Shakespeare letter and it was not until towards the end of their stay that Jo explained to the Wichts that Daddy had been cursed by a black man a long time ago, so the whole family, and that included Lisa, was pursued by an evil spirit. It had chosen a special torment for Lisa because it had first of all invented a letter that Shakespeare was supposed to have written, then it set Lisa's room on fire and caused the letter (which Lisa had lost) to reappear in the ashes in such a way that Daddy had been annoyed and destroyed it. In this way the evil spirit was working everybody into fits. Undoubtedly the evil spirit was getting ready for something really awful. Jo had a lot of confidence, though, in the intelligence from Outer Space. At the last minute It would intervene and save them all.

Herr Wicht, in particular, was enchanted with all this. His spoken English was painful to hear but he could understand all right. Frau Wicht was not quite so enchanted. They knew all about highly imaginative girls. Until married with their sex problems straightened out some girls didn't know the difference between their private fantasies and what was going on in the real world. Nothing to worry about. Frau Wicht told Aston he had a clever daughter. One day she would be a great actress, or possibly a writer, but anyway an artist. Her son Hans had been like that. Lisa was more like her father, excitable but not really intellectual. This had led him into prejudice and meanness and suspicion and jealousy. Even of her! But he had great qualities. Nobody dared to talk about eugenics these days. All women knew that good stock was what counted, even when in one generation it failed to flower. The good genetic inheritance was sleeping but in the next generation, in Lisa's child, it would wake again. Aston would have two gifted children. Lisa's son (no question, it would be a boy) would be a poet like his Uncle Hans and his remoter uncle, the playwright William Shakespeare. So, yes, the boy would be a poet. Jo was such a performer, though. The way she held out her hands in gestures of despair, the way she held her head on one side to show she was thinking – and her body! Such grace! She moved so beautifully. Jo's destiny lay in the theatre. What more could a father want? A son a poet, a daughter a great actress. What better way for the Shakespeare inheritance to express itself?

'To be honest,' Aston said, 'so far as I'm concerned he's boring. Just can't see what the fuss is about. On my side of the family they just thought he was only interested in number one.'

'What I always wanted,' said Frau Wicht, 'was for Lisa to marry a German professor. There is no dignity like a professor's in our country.'

The Wichts took their leave, repeating their invitation to Jo, and the contrast between the banging and sawing during the daytime and the quiet of the evenings at Wood End became even more marked. When the Wichts were there a row could break out between Lisa and her mother during supper, and rumble on afterwards (dogs fouling the pavement, English plumbing, the copyright in Hans's poems, arrangements for tending his grave, the strengths and weaknesses of Lisa's first husband, George, Soviet Jews wanting to emigrate, the climate of California compared with that of West Germany) so that except when everyone was actually asleep the house seemed in constant uproar. But now, particularly when Aston was spending the night up in London, and Lisa and Jo were alone with TV viewing strictly rationed, there was often no sound in the evening but the tap of rain against the window and, if the wind rose, the creak of timber under strain.

A man who turned up with some regularity that winter was an officer of the fire service called Percy Sharp. He was in the Fire Investigation Branch which went into action after a fire only if the officer in charge reported something suspicious. Arson was meat and drink to Percy Sharp. He was a heavy man with a reassuring manner – slow speech from the back of his throat, a readiness to smile and nod, while he waved his tobacco pipe which he sucked but, because it was empty, did not smoke. That first inspection had perplexed him. He could not be sure how the fire had started. A wiring fault in all probability. Carbonization at this point in the skirting pointed that way. But *everything* was carbonized! What puzzled Percy was why the fire had taken such quick hold. A lighted match thrown in a waste-paper basket containing something particularly inflammable, rag soaked in nail varnish remover, might have done the trick. Or some other highly volatile substance might have been spilled on the carpet. Such as what? Well, alcohol for starters. In the right circumstances the contents of a bottle of vodka could set things going nicely. He knew of such a case. But there was no evidence to go on. And it was so quick. There didn't seem much of a motive for arson; such as collecting insurance or of malicious intent or the irresponsible incendiarism of a child, a phrase he had seen in an official document. When it came to studying fire you had to plumb the depths of human nature. Percy was a churchwarden and turning over the possibilities he was left so uneasy that he took to calling at Wood End. For him it had become a moral issue of some importance. Aston did not have to let him in and was annoyed by the visits but he allowed Percy to mooch around. The insurance company had paid up. There was nothing to hide.

Eventually Aston told Percy to stop coming. Nothing more could be established about the cause of the fire.

'Uhuh!'

'Well, why do you come?'

'You never know with fires.'

'Anybody would think you hoped to catch some fire raiser on the hop.'

'Who said anything about fire raisers, sir? I've no cases of very mysterious apparently spontaneous combustion. But they occur. I've always wanted to be in on one from the beginning.'

'So you might strike lucky here?'

'You never can tell, sir.' Percy removed his pipe to smile and salute. 'I'll be on my way then. Always be prepared for the unexpected.'

Aston took his job as temporary civil servant seriously and read up some of the recent history of East Africa. Some of it he vaguely knew about but a lot of it he didn't. For example, just why Delamere's name was always coming up in his father's talk. Aston had reacted against his father in many ways and at that name a shutter used to come down in Aston's mind. He knew that Lord Delamere was the first white settler in Kenya seventy or more years ago but hadn't realized what a great guy he was.

Later he had led the resistance to British government policy which aimed at ensuring that the black native population were as independent of the white settlers as possible. Delamere and men like Aston's father were against this and said the blacks would be better off working for them, not independently, and Aston remembered his father being proud of the fact that, with Delamere and other settlers, he had stayed up all one night in the mid-twenties arguing with the then governor, Grigg. The talk was wilder than Aston had imagined. It explained why, later, his father could say, 'Every time a white settler is murdered it's men at Westminster I see with blood on their hands.'

Tom Hubbard presided over the morning meetings in Protocol Department where progress was reported on preparations for the Commonwealth Conference. As he was only a temporary official Aston could not sit at the table itself. He was given a chair some two yards back from the table, immediately behind Hubbard's PA. In the minutes she put him down not as one of those present but as merely as being 'in attendance' which made him feel a bit of a flunkey. His contribution to the discussion was, by way of compensation, irreverent and aggressive. Junketing, he was heard to say. That's what they were organizing. The old Empire had been something real but the Commonwealth didn't exist. Those heads of state who did come, and some wouldn't because they were afraid the rug would be pulled from under as soon as their backs were turned, didn't want an opportunity for a serious exchange of ideas. Before they went back home to do another deal with Moscow they just wanted a piss-up.

The conference would be held in Lancaster House. Radio and TV studios were being built in the basement and, a bit to his surprise, Aston was given the job of reporting to the Commonwealth Secretariat on the progress of the work. 'Nothing technical, of course,' Tom said. 'There's a project manager but he's from the Ministry of Works. Needham, his name is. Our experience is that Works can play you up. It would do no harm at all if you gave Needham the impression you were a qualified TV engineer. Needham isn't and it would keep him on his toes.'

This was the part of the FCO work Aston came to enjoy. He ate his sandwiches with the workmen at lunch time, picked the brains of BBC engineers who dropped in from time to time, and got to know people from the various High Commissioners' offices. Right from the beginning he could tell which of the Commonwealth countries would make trouble about the technical facilities they were offered. In Green Park the drifts of snowdrops gave way to daffodils. He went walking when the rain was not actually belting down, wearing a deerstalker hat and blue quilted overcoat he had bought from Oxfam, to check that the trees really were breaking bud. The English spring seemed dramatic as ever to him with the outcome always guaranteed. Would this be the year it didn't happen? Not a serious question. In Africa, though, there was always a chance the rains wouldn't come. That was in his part of Africa. Further north the odds were heavily against their coming. The English talked about a place in the sun. They were lucky. What most people wanted was a place in the rain.

Mainly, Aston thought about the future. Once the Silver Jubilee and the Conference were out of the way he was a man without even the pretence of an occupation. He had fantasies about some long lost friend running across him in the street and saying he was just the man he'd been looking for to manage a chunk of his business. Or the High Commissioner for, say, Canada taking him on as an adviser on African affairs. Was it too late to go into insurance? He was always hearing of retired officers selling insurance but that didn't seem much of a job to Aston. Nor would it seem much to Lisa. Her opinion of what he did was crucial. He'd asked Parsler whether there was any opening in his firm that meant a foreign posting. Lisa might be open to suggestions. In an indiscreet moment Parsler had said something about trouble in the Nassau office. Insurance was such a racket the intervention of an intelligent outsider like himself might bring some welcome fresh air. No, he didn't think his lack of experience was the slightest disqualification.

Tom Hubbard rang through to ask him to come up to his office. When Aston appeared Tom said, 'We've just heard the Archbishop has been murdered.'

Most men in his position would have thought of the Archbishop of Canterbury but Aston knew immediately it was a man he liked to think of as a friend, Janani Luwum, Archbishop of Uganda. The official story coming out of Amin's Uganda was that the Archbishop had been killed in a car accident but the British view came to be that the Archbishop had been murdered because he'd been taking a stand against Amin's slaughter of the tribes he regarded as a threat and of Christians, too, because he thought they, or their clergy, were hiding arms and ammunition.

Aston continued to be awkward. To begin with this was his instinctive reaction against minute taking, and meetings, and bureaucracy in general but it developed into real cussedness when he detected Tom Hubbard and others helping themselves to what he called smug sauce. What was there in Britain to be smug about? Rapes and muggings in the cities, horrific murders, and then there was the drug scene. 'Do you know' – he was being recognized as a bore on the subject – 'it's actually safer to walk the streets of Kampala at night than it is the streets of London? And pleasanter. You know, bright stars in the sky and flower smells. Yes, I know the place is corrupt but they haven't got the Mafia. The place gets a bad press. Christ knows why! Do you think there's no other country where tribes cut each other up? Take Northern Ireland.'

Official information of what went on in Uganda came at second hand, through Kenya, because of the break in diplomatic relations and because there were no foreign correspondents there. So Aston began collecting the misinformation dished up by the press. Take the stories about the massacre of students at Makerere University; anything up to a hundred murdered by Amin's troops and bodies left lying all over the place. That's what the *Observer* said. Just lies. Everyone now knew there never had been a massacre. Sure, students were beaten up but nobody was killed, no women were raped. This was accepted. What got into journalists? Was it just horror was so saleable? Take this latest story about the Archbishop. Let's wait until we get the truth about that too. Why was it such fun to believe President Amin had shot the Archbishop himself? Ask yourself! Aston was sure this was another lie. Seriously. Why is it such fun to believe these lies?

Tom Hubbard was beginning to regret taking Aston on as a temporary pair of hands but in spite of his bluff manner he was too timid to call the arrangement off. There was more to it than that. Aston had a contract that provided for his employment until the end of the Commonwealth Conference and if he were told his services were no longer required he could claim, and would receive, payment for the full period. Hubbard had been responsible for the terms of this contract and Administration would complain if the FCO had not been given value for money, by which they meant delivery of so many man hours. Hubbard thought the best he could do was give Aston another lunch at the Travellers' Club where he could urge him to be a bit more careful about what he said. Aston was upsetting the permanent staff.

Instead of talking about Commonwealth relations they found themselves discussing more domestic matters – the Parslers. Ed had taken a tumble when hunting and there was some trouble about his back. He could not move his legs and was in Stoke Mandeville Hospital, the spinal injuries section.

Aston put two and two together.

'Of course, Harriet's your sister.'

'She's bearing up terribly well. But I thought you ought to know, being neighbours. And looking after Jo, and all that.'

'Poor sod. You know he wanted me to join the hunt too. I said for real game, yes. You know, gazelle. Something you can eat. But foxes? It's absurd. He was at our place the time of the fire. Got excited. Possessed, to be technical. Hit that Boer doctor. Ed was really taken over. Fancied my wife, you know.'

Hubbard was startled by this. 'Harriet and Ed's marriage is a very happy one. I don't know what you mean. Is it some sort of joke? Like the way you talk about the Archbishop?'

'It's nothing serious. He's just a poet.'

'Ah!' said Hubbard. 'I see what you mean.' The two lay back in their chairs as the waiter poured the wine, rather as though this were a ritual that had to be endured stoically. 'Do you really think President Amin will attempt to come to the Conference? It would be most confoundedly embarrassing in the circumstances. You know him. Can't you head the bugger off?'

Aston drank his glass of wine at a draught. 'I'm really upset about Ed Parsler. I must go and see him. Where's Stoke Mandeville?'

Lisa was upset too when Aston gave her the news. She was on the telephone to Harriet immediately and Harriet said she was very grateful but Ed was in the very best hospital in the country for spinal injuries and the children, Mark and Jessica, were at that very moment with their father. Harriet was sure Lisa would be glad to know that the horse was okay.

Jessica and her boyfriend Eric broke up because of her father's accident. It happened just a fortnight before they were due to set off on a camping holiday through France and, they hoped, across the Mediterranean to Tunis, with no more gear than could be carried on the Suzuki. Ed and Harriet were dead against this but as Jessica pointed out she had taken all the pre-university exams she could, failed her 'S' level in economics, failed a couple of college entrance exams in Oxford but had done sufficiently well in 'A' levels to get a place reading Economic History at York. She had time on her hands. Harriet said that was not the point. There were tremendous rows but neither Ed nor Harriet really felt they could forbid Jessica to go. She would go anyway.

Ed's accident changed all that. Jessica told Eric she could not possibly go off on this jaunt when her father had broken his back. Eric became quite wild. He had set his heart on this holiday, had saved up something like £500, made route maps, bought a Michelin guide, and even tried to follow the French lessons that went out on TV on Sunday mornings.

'It isn't as if ya dad was dying, Jess.'

'We don't know what's going to happen.'

'Look, we've got to go, Jess. I've been really working at this. It'll be just about the greatest bike ride I've 'ad, ya know? See what I mean? Won't cost you a penny.'

'Can't we put it off?'

'No, I'm all fixed up to go, ya know. I fixed it with the boss. Anyway, I'm all set. You Dad'll be okay.'

'He's paralysed. You know that?'

'Only part of 'im. 'T ain't the end of the world. Look, Jess. We're going. I mean it. Ya gotta live a bit. We're not putting it off. We can't.'

'I'm not going,' said Jessica.

Eric roared off on his Suzuki and Jessica watched him go feeling it really was the end of the world. No one had been through a crisis as big as this one. No one had suffered as she did. Her quite unique misfortune (which nobody else could understand) was brought home to her even more sharply when sometime later she had a postcard with a picture of Rouen Cathedral, saying, 'Ella said she'd come and we're okay, Eric', Ella being one of the other girls who turned up at moto-cross on the back of some chap's bike to eat hamburgers, drink Coke and scream piercingly as the riders went round the track. Jessica cried a lot and her mother drove her up to London and bought her some new clothes. They called in at Stoke Mandeville which was conveniently on the way back and found Lisa and Aston already there.

They had been there sometime. There were screens round Ed's bed when they arrived and they had to wait in the ward sister's office until he was fit to receive visitors. He was lying flat on his back, his head resting on a slim pillow. A board, with the page of a newspaper pinned to it, was positioned at an angle some two feet over his face so that he could do *The Times* crossword puzzle. He had allowed his beard to grow and it was disconcerting to notice that it was darker than his hair, a curling, wiry growth, so that the hair falling back from his forehead and lapping at the pillow seemed all the whiter. Lisa had brought him some freesias because they would sweeten the air. But he seemed well supplied with freesias already. Ed turned his head to look at his visitors and waved his arms about. He wanted them to come so close he could embrace them.

'I've just had the bedpan routine. It's so disgusting it's absurd. I'm lucky. It's only the bottom end of me that's not functioning properly. But it's enough. I couldn't stand any more mortification. I've had enough to feel some of my sins have been purged away. Just one or two.' He laughed. 'I hate being inspected in bed.'

'We're not inspecting you,' said Lisa. 'You look like – say, I know what you look like, Edwin. You look like a saint on one of those old Russian ikons!'

Aston was interested in what Ed had said about the bedpan routine. 'You mean no trouble in performing?'

'Copiously. Never thought about bodily functions much. What I've been taught here is that legs don't matter. You can get on without them. But not the bowels and bladder.' He closed his eyes. 'Nice of you to come.' He waved his arms again and, impulsively, Aston bent over him and allowed himself to be hugged. They were all a bit emotional and talking with more abandon than usual. Then Lisa. She kissed him on the cheek. Edwin gave her a special hug.

'Aston, you know Lisa switches me on. The polite word is muse. She just makes putting words down on paper seem *really* important. Because there are times I don't.'

'So what? She's sexy.'

Lisa attacked him. 'Edwin wasn't operating on that level. *Have-you-said-the-wrong-thing*! This is literary inspiration Edwin's on about and it just makes me feel terribly unworthy and honoured.'

'You could have fooled me.'

Lisa ignored him and turned to Edwin.

'What's the prognosis?'

'They don't believe in telling you anything in this place.'

'Okay. But does it hurt?'

Ed hesitated. 'Only when the words don't come.' They all knew this was bravado.

'What happened?'

'A hedge I hadn't jumped before. There was quite a ditch on the other side I wasn't prepared for. The horse just boobed and I came off, and that's all there is to say. Bloody awful experience.'

Lisa picked up a black notebook from the bedside table and, not quite realizing what she was doing, opened it and began to read aloud.

> 'Feelings refract, like water.
> For the prey at the bottom
> Aim off, aim shorter.'

'Hey, Lisa! That's my journal. What cheek! Hand it back.'

'Sorry, Edwin. You mean it's a kind of diary? But I *love* reading other people's diaries.'

'No, it's where I jot down ideas.'

'Is there anything about me in it?'

'*Please*, Lisa!'

'Okay. Here it is. But what d'you mean, "feelings refract"? Don't you trust your own feelings?'

'All I mean is you've got to allow for the possibility you're

208

deceiving yourself about something pretty important. Not all the time. But now and again.'

Long silence. Nobody quite understood what was being said.

'You think I deliberately hid that Shakespeare letter, don't you, Ed? Then planted it again after the fire. Maybe you even think I started the fire myself.'

They said nothing for quite a time, listening to a tea trolley bashing against the ward door and an engine being revved up outside. Ed lay with his eyes closed. 'No, I don't think anything of the sort. Lisa, there's something I think I ought to tell you.'

Aston stood up. 'Time we went. I've just seen one of the sisters signalling.'

'What do you want to tell me, Ed?'

Aston insisted. 'I said we're going.'

'But – '

'Come on, Lisa. We're putting pressure on.'

It was at this moment that Harriet and Jessica arrived. Ed opened his eyes and gave a glad shout. The talk was then all about Jessica's new clothes. Aston took the opportunity to take Lisa by the arm and steer her out of the ward.

'What goes on? What's got into you? He wanted to tell me something?' Lisa put up a fight.

'Well, what could it be? I thought things were getting tight. Tell you the truth, I was a bit bored. Can't stand hospitals anyway. I didn't get what you read out.'

'When you poke a stick into clear water, or a spear, it seems to change direction just under the surface. You've got to allow for that if you want to stab a fish.'

'So what?' said Aston. 'Let's go.'

Lisa's baby was due at the end of May, well before the Commonwealth Conference when Aston reckoned he'd be seeing most action, particularly if President Amin did what he was entitled to do and attend. The Queen's Silver Jubilee was different. He had no right to present himself for that without an invitation and there seemed no chance of his getting one. The conference was the problem. The death of Archbishop Luwum, following the murder of Mrs Dora Bloch after the Entebbe raid meant, at the mildest, demonstrations against the President if he turned up. He was top ogre in 1977. The FCO broke into an even bigger rash of meetings when Amin announced he was not only going to come to the conference but he intended to bring 250 tribal dancers with him to add to the general entertainment. Aston was asked if he would make a private trip to Kampala to find out what Amin's real intentions were. He refused, saying his wife was pregnant and he was not prepared to do anything to add to the strain on her. As it was, the household had been at panic stations because of a feared miscarriage.

'She's okay now,' Aston told Hubbard, 'but she's been in bed for three weeks and the doctor says she'll probably have to stay there. There's only one thing more likely to bring about a real miscarriage than my going to Kampala and that's Lisa's mother coming to stay with us.'

'But where can 250 tribal dancers be accommodated?'

'Calm down, man. That's not our problem.'

'Of course it isn't. I'm just trying to read the man's mind. He even mixes up the ex-Prime Minister Edward Heath with the band leader, Ted Heath. He's invited Mr Edward Heath to visit Uganda with his band. Did you know that?'

'Well, he's got a sense of humour, man. At least grant him that.'

Mrs Buck moved into one of the spare rooms at Wood End during the last few weeks of Lisa's pregnancy and took breakfast and lunch up to her in bed. For supper Lisa crawled cautiously downstairs. Harriet took to dropping in regularly to relieve the boredom and report on Ed's progress. Or lack of it. There had been a couple of surgical operations in an attempt, as Harriet understood it, to reduce the pressure on the spinal cord. The net result of all this was Edwin's ability slightly to twitch his right toe. He was frantic to get out. And then he got these spells of depression. Jessica was marvellous though. Edwin had been really touched by her not going on that holiday with Eric. And so Harriet rattled on.

Lisa interrupted her. 'Don't you think in all honesty, Ed ought to let me see those bits in his notebook about me? I mean, there ought to be some payback for being a muse.'

'Edwin's so furtive,' said Harriet. 'Just nobody sees his journal. Say. Do I envy you. I just yearn to be pregnant again.'

'I never knew it involved a personality change. Would you say I was neurotic, Harriet?'

'No.'

'Neither would I. I don't seem to get anxious like some folk do. D'you know what? If it wasn't for this personality change I'd be real hipped right now.'

'I don't understand.'

'Being pregnant. I just take it for granted everybody's got to hand out niceness to me. Cosy, fluffy, niceness. And they do. So I'm sort of cocooned with the stuff and what with the passivity of it all I just lie here and think, hell, deep down you're in an anxiety state. But because you're cocooned, you don't feel it. Harriet, you know that Shakespeare letter?'

'Yes.'

'Ed faked it, didn't he? When we were talking at Stoke Mandeville he was just on the point of telling me something and Aston hiked me away. Now that's not like Aston. It was soon after you and Jessica came in and you must have thought it strange we beat it so quick. Ed said to me, "There's something I ought to tell you", and that was the moment Aston went all heavy on me. Now what else would Ed want to tell me about? He sounded so confessional. I knew it was bad.'

Harriet was collapsed in a too comfortable chair and she had to pull hard on the arms to escape and stand up. 'The rain's coming in,' she said and shut the window. 'You've got me confused, my dear. You said Aston marched you off when Ed was about to tell you something. The implication is he didn't want you to hear whatever Ed was going to say. But how could he know what Ed was going to say?'

'Gee! Aren't you rational! Aston's always believed the letter was a fake but he thought George did it. Then we were with Ed and he put on his special confessional voice. I just guess we both knew straightaway and Aston thought I'd be upset.'

'Haven't you talked to Aston about this?'

'No, there's so much been happening and suddenly it didn't seem all that important any more. That's partly what I meant about a personality change. You know I'm two people now. And the other one kicks. Ed did fake that letter, didn't he?'

It was some time before Harriet answered. 'Yes, I'm afraid he did.'

Lisa's eyes filled with tears. 'Why ever should he do that to me? I've known him ever since I was a kid.'

211

'I was dead against it. I guessed it would backfire.'

'It's so hostile. What have I done he'd want to be so hostile? Then he has the gall to try and confess in a hospital bed. I guess he felt safe. He thought I wouldn't take a swing at him.'

Harriet agreed. 'He's had his problems.'

'I've got news for him. You can tell him as soon as I laid eyes on that letter I knew it was a fake and I knew who'd faked it not just out of instinct but because the only man I knew with the knowhow was Ed so the darned letter just screamed at you I'm Ed Parsler's shot at being smart but I'm not as hot as I should be and it makes you sort of sorry for the guy who dreamed it up and I decide to string him along okay I'm not letting on I know he's tried to set me up so I set him up and see what a snake with all those twistings and turnings and he's the one who was set up.' This had become quite a yell, but Lisa had to stop to blow her nose which she did very loudly before passing the tissue to Harriet so that it could be put in the wastepaper bin. 'He's the one with the finger up him, not me.'

It was one of the days Aston did not go to London and, as Mrs Buck had taken the afternoon off, he picked up Jo from school and prepared to cook the evening meal himself. When Lisa broke it to him she had forced a confession out of Harriet over the letter he sat down and said, 'Funny that!'

'How long have you known?'

'Didn't *know*. Didn't give it much thought. Then when he said he had something important to tell you – '

'Spot on. Well, I knew from day one. I was stringing you all along.'

'You were?'

'I sure was. What do you think I am? Just gullible?'

'That's fine, then. No problem.'

When he saw that she was going to stick to this line about never, for one moment, having been taken in by the letter Aston thought he'd get something special for supper, put on his blue and white striped butcher's apron and took three salmon steaks out of the freezer. Lisa loved grilled salmon but she rationed herself because it was so nourishing and she thought the baby might be enormous as a result. Aston persuaded her this was a special occasion. When the steaks had thawed out he put them under the grill with a knob of butter on top of each one. He served them up with Jersey new potatoes and mayonnaise sauce which he warmed up, out of a bottle. A mixed salad, but no wine, because Lisa was off alcohol.

'Hey! I've been smelling that,' said Lisa when she sidled into the dining room with Jo holding the door open.

Ed was a subject he wanted to keep off but Aston could not help saying, 'He's not a bad chap. I'm sure he only meant it as a bit of fun.' Lisa would not be drawn and started Jo talking about her latest plan for the future, which was to train as an astronaut. She just wanted, to start with, to go to the moon.

Dear Ed,

I've been in bed as you'll know from Harriet. Or I would have been over again to see you. So, as one bedbound creature to another, greetings! What a way to enjoy the spring. The only cuckoos I've heard before were in clocks but I have my big bedroom window open this warm weather and I seem to hear cuckoos all day. I can just smell the spring, all green and juicy. The wind is so warm. The trees bend and sway, they've gotten themselves so many leaves now. I just lie and watch these white clouds skidding across the blue sky. When they cover the sun it's like a light being put out. Then it's switched on again. The cuckoos go at their cuckooing like crazy. One comes quite close to the house, judging by the noise it makes. But has anyone ever seen a cuckoo? There are other birds and I've gotten myself a bird book so that I can check who they are, thrushes and blackbirds and whatever. My baby is fine. He kicks me, so I know he's going to be big and strong. In all this lovely spring world there's only one person I hate. You! Yes, you!

I oughtn't to take the trouble to say all this but pressure builds up. You know that? You're twisted. What did you say to yourself? Find out where she's most vulnerable and work on it. What the hell! Did you think I was so ignorant I wouldn't know a fake when I saw it? Why did you do it? What sort of kick does a literary guy get out of socking a girl where he thinks it hurts? Are you frustrated, or something? Anybody would think you'd been after me and I told you to get lost. Harriet warned you against sending me up, so what got into you? Maybe we're all crazy. We've all got spots in the brain and this is the way yours break out.

I knew all along. I really did, you know, but I thought why should I give the guy so much satisfaction. Better play it quietly but all the time I was seething. What made me really snap was the way you magicked the thing into my burnt cell. Don't deny it. I guess I ought to relax. The one guy I knew, so I thought, who was not power crazy was that English poet I met on the steamer, all those years ago, Edwin Parsler. But was I wrong! He wanted power. And he wanted power over me. He was like a witch after a lock of my hair and my toenails to brew up his potion. For poems. I wasn't your muse, you just wanted to plug into my psyche and drain off some of the energy you hadn't got any more even if you'd ever had it.

This is not to say I don't feel for you a lot, you and Harriet and the kids, lying there. It's a cruel break and I wish you up on your feet because frankly Ed I can't see myself saying the sort of things to a man in a hospital bed, standing over him, that I've been putting on paper here. And perhaps only somebody as mad as I am with a mean streak of bitch would put it on paper even. I pray for your complete recovery. So that we can get together on equal terms after my son is born and talk this thing over calmly and sensibly in a truly adult way. That's what Hans would have wanted.

Your (in spite of everything) friend
Lisa Hart

Lisa hesitated a lot about sending this off but eventually she gave it to Mrs Buck to post with the result that when Aston dropped in on Ed unexpectedly some days later he was shown the letter.

'She's right to be angry,' said Ed. 'I've had Hugh Cornish in to see me and he said if he'd known my real intentions he would never have collaborated. He's being disingenuous, of course. But that's his style.'

'Who's Hugh Cornish?'

'Hugh? He's the chap who got the old paper, mixed the ink and actually did the writing. I concocted the text. You'll have to help me make my peace with Lisa. Does she know you're here now?'

'No, the car had to have its MOT and I was in this direction so I thought I'd drop in. Lisa didn't tell me she'd written to you. I'd have said, well if that's the way you feel, fine. Just write it all out, then take a deep breath and put it in the wastepaper basket.'

'I'm glad she sent it.'

214

'Interesting what she says about witches, isn't it?' Aston really needed glasses for reading but he hated to admit it and would not go to an optician. So he held the letter to the light, about nine inches from his face, and screwed up his eyes. 'Quite true, you know. African witches believe they can really rough somebody up if they get a bit of his hair. I don't mind telling you I saw to it my hair was burned after I'd had it cut. Fingernails and toenails went into a special little box to be disposed of later. Now I can quite see this faking and planting an old letter would be a more European form of witchcraft. Is that the way you'd see it too?'

'I don't believe in witches and I certainly wouldn't have intended any harm to Lisa. Quite the contrary.'

'Take it from me, old chap. You're a witch and it was witchcraft all right. Whether you intended it or not, it sure was witchcraft.'

'Oh, for Chrissake! Tell her I'll write.'

'I didn't want this to blow up before the baby was born. Lisa's okay, really. Brownlow says she'd better be extra careful now she's on the last lap. Reckons he'll be whipping her into hospital any time after the middle of next week. What about you?'

'I'm due to be tried out in a wheelchair sometime.'

'Knew a chap paralysed from the neck down. Stiff as a board. Come to think of it he could move his feet. Just a bit. His wife ran one of those open MGs and she used to prop him up in the passenger seat like a dummy. But that was from polio. He hadn't broken his back.'

'I haven't broken my back. Crushed vertebrae.'

Aston rubbed his gold earring between thumb and forefinger, thinking hard. He sat there with his face thrust forward the better to display his big moustache and look fierce. 'Apart from Lisa there's nobody else got it in for you?'

'Can't think of anybody.'

'Aw! Come on. Everybody's hated by somebody.'

'No, honest. You think maybe one of the other hunt members has been sticking pins into a wax image of me.'

'No laughing matter. I ask because I don't think Lisa would go as far as that. Somebody might. Somebody might have a jinx on you. Your boss, maybe. There are ways of finding out.'

'A jinx?' A nurse brought a cup of tea and put it down on Ed's bedside table. She asked Aston if he would like one too. He said he'd prefer a scotch and soda and jokes were made about hospital catering. When she had gone Ed said there was something he had always wanted to ask and never quite got round to it. 'That black soldier you had staying with you all those years ago. He was Idi Amin, wasn't he?'

'I'm not prepared to discuss that, Ed. Can't quite focus my mind, you know.'

'I see.'

'You think Amin's got a jinx on me? Is that it? Because you'd be bloody right. Do you know what the latest buzz is? First of all he was trying to book all the rooms in one of the big hotels. Nothing in that, of course. All the hotel rooms in London are booked anyway. Have been for months. Then he was somewhere in the Channel in a submarine. Then he was in Libya with a Boeing 707 standing by. Now your brother-in-law at the FCO has it all worked out the Boeing will be landing at one of those old wartime air strips, the one at Upton Edge, that might be it, and the President and his entourage would make for Wood End, that being a place he knew of old. You must have told Tom.'

The nurse came back with Aston's tea and propped Ed up on some pillows. Ed was struck by Aston's remark he could not focus his mind because that was the way he felt too. The trauma he had been through and was still suffering from seemed to have affected his memory. He could not remember names. During the night he had been kept awake trying to remember the name of the Prime Minister. It was Callaghan but it did not come back to him until morning. He had no recollection of telling Tom about Amin at Wood End but he might have done. Or he might have told Harriet and she could have passed it on.

'It's nonsense though, isn't it? I mean, Amin descending on you without warning.'

'No. He's a good navigator. He's capable of dropping in by parachute.'

Jo had been home from school by the time Aston reached Wood End, had had a meal and been taken off again in the Peugeot by Mrs Buck to see an old movie that was being re-run in Oxford, 2001. It would be the second time Mrs Buck had seen it but, as she'd been baffled, she hoped Jo would be able to explain. Jo had a hunch it would provide hints where her ET signals were coming from. Lisa gave special permission because she felt guilty about Jo having such a boring home life, and in the light of what Jo had just told her she wanted her out of the way in any case. In Mrs Buck's absence, then, Aston had the job of cooking the evening meal. Not that there was much to it. Mrs Buck had prepared the vegetables and put the lamb chops under the grill. He had only to switch the grill on. But first of all he went up to see whether Lisa fancied something else. No, lamb chops were just great.

'Something a bit way-out has happened,' Lisa told him.

'What's that?'

'Jo said the headmistress sent for her and when she got to the office there was Sister Tabitha and a priest. She couldn't remember seeing this priest before but he began talking to her as though they were old friends. Called her Joanna, that sort of thing. Then he told her he was an old friend. He knew her from way back, and he knew you and he knew her mother in Africa. Cut a long story short, he was in Kenya.'

'Father Curtis?'

'He's coming here this evening.'

'Oh, Jesus! That's all I needed.'

Aston had lost touch with Father Curtis years ago. Soon after that disastrous blessing of the house he had left Kenya and, Aston gathered, gone back to Europe, to Rome, for further guidance and instruction, which he was obviously in need of. Aston could see him clearly; a tall, stooping, unnaturally pale man of about thirty, fidgety-fingered, always drumming, tapping, stroking, clasping and unclasping his hands while he talked, often about Lancashire which was his home county, or about sport – cricket in the summer and soccer in the winter when he listened to the commentaries broadcast by the BBC World Service. The thought of meeting him again was intolerable. What did he want? How had he tracked them down? Was it too late to put him off?

'You can't do that,' Lisa said when he told her he was going to ring up the school. 'He'll be harmless.'

'I don't want him here. He's a fool. How did he know where we were anyway?'

'Apparently he'd someway learned we were back and living not far from Oxford so he rang up all the RC schools in the area, just on the off chance, to see whether they'd a Joanna Hart on the books. Anyway that's what he told Jo.'

'Who'd tell him where we were living?'

Lisa shrugged. 'The Catholic church is one big intelligence system. They're even plugged into the other denominations. That's what the ecumenical movement is all about.'

Father Curtis drove up in a very old Morris Minor estate car with what looked like a lot of recording equipment in the back soon after six o'clock. He stood in the sunshine swivelling his head from side to side like a man with tunnel vision; but Aston guessed he was just nervous and stepped out of the house to meet him. Father Curtis was wearing a neat black suit, black shirt front, clerical collar and wide brimmed hat and he just stood there, looking at Aston for sometime, without speaking.

'Mr Hart,' he said at last. Aston had forgotten the squeaky voice. 'It has been so many years and your little girl tells me you have married again. That's good. For a long time now I've been under a compulsion to make contact with you. To be honest, part of me is frightened but I'm pushed by something quite strong. Forgive me, but may I shake your hand?'

'You look just the same, Father. Won't you come in? I won't ask you to meet my wife. She has to take things easy. She's in bed.'

'Nothing serious, I hope.' He walked with a limp.

Aston explained. He led the way into the sitting room where he at once proposed a drink which Father Curtis refused. 'What frightens you, Father?'

'The way I must inevitably bring back evil memories. I was so inadequate. So hopeless. You must have seen all that.' There was nothing the matter with the man's eyes, Aston decided. He really was nervous. 'For years I dreamed about Shirley. Then the dreams stopped. But while they lasted I was like some poor revenant pacing the scene of some crime, eternally wringing his hands. Mine was a great spiritual crisis. I was tested and found wanting.'

'But the dreams stopped?'

'Yes, and at roughly the same time this yearning began to grow up just to see you and ask you how you are and how Joanna is. It's wonderful news you're married again. And it's even more wonderful you're to have another child.'

'Do you keep in touch? I mean, with people in Kenya.'

'Christmas cards. That sort of thing. Nothing more, not for years. Then the certainty hardened inside me that I must go back there. I've been in training. I joined one of the missionary orders, the White Fathers, and I'm going back, not to Kenya. I'm being sent to Uganda.'

'Quite an assignment.'

'With great joy, I'm going.'

A bell tinkled in the distance and Aston said, 'Excuse me, Father, that's my wife ringing for something. I'll just pop up and see what she wants.' Some minutes later he returned. 'She wants to see you.'

'But you'd rather she didn't?'

Aston was taken aback by this sensitivity. 'Frankly, yes. She's in a, well, delicate state.'

Father Curtis was sitting with his left leg straight out before him. 'As it happens I find it difficult to climb stairs. Bad rheumatism in the knee. Another good reason for getting out of England. So would you make my apologies?'

'You've come to ask me about Uganda?'

'No, not really. I'm well briefed. I know what I'm in for. As I hope I've conveyed, in my life I have found a sense of direction and that is why I go with such joy. But I wanted to see you and Joanna first.'

'You don't owe us anything, Father.'

'No? Where is Joanna, by the way?'

'Gone to a movie.' The bell tinkled in the distance once more and Aston went into the hall to shout, 'Father Curtis can't manage the stairs. He's got a gammy leg.'

Father Curtis then asked whether Aston thought President Amin would be coming to London for the Commonwealth Conference. Not, he implied, that it mattered much one way or the other.

Aston said he didn't know. He hoped not. 'One theory is that he'll be coming here.'

'Here? To this house? Why?'

'Old connections. He still sends me birthday cards. And there's an old airfield practically within walking distance where his plane could put down.'

219

'You're not serious?'

'Stranger things have happened.'

Father Curtis thought about this. 'Like you, I hope he doesn't come.' Then gathering himself, pushing his shoulders back, sitting up straighter and revolving his broad-brimmed black hat on his knees, pushing it this way, then that way, tapping it, drumming his fingernails against the crown, he began talking about the blessing of the house near Limuru once more.

'I was too young and wet behind the ears. I've never felt so inadequate and desolated. I felt stripped. No manly qualities, still less the priestly qualities. Worse, until that moment, in spite of all the instruction and training, I'd only toyed with the idea of evil. I knew it was there but it didn't strike me to the heart. I was naive. Do you know what I'm trying to say?'

'No I don't. Not really.'

'From that moment on I was struck to the heart by the reality of the Devil and the knowledge he can't be resisted without God's help. I knew at last what Our Lord meant when he said we should ask our Father in heaven to deliver us from evil. That is so crucial. And I had not known this, not profoundly, before. I knew in knowledge but not in experience. I wanted to tell you this.'

'Why?'

'To assure you that your dear wife is a blessed soul in heaven. Much fasting and praying have brought me this assurance which I now pass on to you. God is most merciful.'

Aston wished Father Curtis had taken a drink because this was the moment when he would have offered to freshen his glass. It needed a ritual because he could not find words of his own.

'Another thing, Mr Hart. I wanted to see that Joanna was being brought up as a good Catholic. Not that I had any doubt. Well, I'll be saying goodbye now. First of all to Paris.'

'Paris?'

'It's a French order, the White Fathers, but they take in the benighted English too.' Father Curtis had an unexpectedly loud laugh. 'My apologies to the lady wife upstairs for disturbing you. I wish you and her all happiness in your coming child. Is Mrs Hart a Catholic? No, no, no, well, of course I understand all that. Joanna will be so full of joy too, having a little brother or sister.'

When Father Curtis had gone Aston went up to find Lisa was cross not to have seen him.

'I'm superstitious about that man coming anywhere near a wife of mine. He's going back as a missionary, to stir up trouble, no doubt. He seems to know what he wants. That balls-up of his seems to have weighed on his conscience.'

'Is that what he came to say?'

'Almost as though he thought I might be worried about him and he'd put in an appearance to show he was okay and that frightful business marked some stage in his spiritual develop-ment. I thought he was smug. If you're a priest you've got to think like that. It's not the way I think. He wanted to check on Jo, too. That she was having a Catholic education.'

'You can be very hard, Aston.'

He kissed her on the mouth. 'That's one of the nicest things you've said to me. Keep it up. Truth is, though, I'm not hard enough.'

'I like you hard,' Lisa said.

'One other thing he wanted to tell me. Shirley was okay. She's in Heaven.'

13

Lisa dreamed that her labour pains had started and she was being driven to hospital in the Peugeot by William Shakespeare himself dressed as a priest, in black biretta and soutane, with a big wooden cross on his stomach. Where Aston was she did not know. William Shakespeare kept reassuring her that they would get to the hospital in time and when they did she would have a baby boy who would grow up to write plays every bit as good as his own. Lisa said no, this was not possible. It wasn't that the boy would be short on what it took; the times were different, nobody believed anything really mattered any more, it was absurd to think that even her little boy could pull anything off – anything that would compare with the achievements of the Renaissance. The language wasn't there, for one thing. And there was no sense of wonder. No vision. The unborn baby kicked her awake and she lay there listening to the bird song thinking what a fool she was. Of course the boy would be able to do anything. Where was Aston?

He was having to spend more time in London, away for three or four nights at a time. He did not like Lisa being there just with Mrs Buck and Jo. He wanted them all to go over and stay with the Parslers. They had plenty of room, Harriet was more than willing. With Ed still in hospital it would be company for her too; but Lisa would not hear of it. This was her home and she was standing her ground until either Aston or Mrs Buck drove her to the maternity ward. Aston seemed to believe more and more there was something in the idea Amin might unexpectedly descend on the house. Lisa understood why he had become jumpy. She knew perfectly well that, although Aston didn't talk much about it, he had seen a lot of Amin at one time but that was years ago. Except for those silly unwanted presents and birthday cards there was no contact between the two men. If there was a relationship it was one way, with Aston on the receiving end, so if Amin did turn up that would figure. But honest, she didn't think he would. He'd be exposing himself to rough handling and she guessed he was strong on dignity, getting the right red carpet treatment and the right number of guns saluting. No, she did not think he would come but if he did it was bound to be at night and she'd dial 999 at the first shout or knock in the dark. Back in the States there was a time when she had a handgun. No longer. She wondered what the legal position in Britain was if a householder shot a visiting head of state who was trying to force entry.

She had not been pregnant before and wondered whether having crazy thoughts like this were usual. When Prime Minister Callaghan said in the House that he would not take it as an affront if President Amin decided to stay away from the Commonwealth Conference it even went through her head this was not the firm refusal of entry you might have expected. So there was a possibility Aston was being set up. Out of regard for world opinion difficulties, but no actual barriers, were being put in the way of Amin's visit. The real intention, with Aston as fall guy, was to let him in so that in Amin's absence from Uganda a coup could be organized back there. After all, that was precisely how Amin had taken over from Obote at the last Commonwealth Conference, and didn't everyone want to get rid of Amin? Weeks before Prime Minister Callaghan was reported as saying, 'I don't think we want to state our position so clearly that Amin will know what our response will be. I think he should be kept wondering.' Why all this speaking with forked tongue? Was Aston jumpy because he suspected he was the goat, tethered and bleating in the forest clearing, just put there to draw the killer tiger? No, that really was crazy, she thought in a confused sort of way. There were no tigers in Africa.

The end of May came and went and, in spite of the dream, there were no labour pains. Mrs Buck said it had been just the same with her first born. Philip had been very reluctant to come into the world and even now he hadn't come to terms with it, staying in bed in the morning and expecting to be waited on. God help his wife when he had one. But who'd have him? Her husband had to take her out for a bumpy ride in the car before Philip could be persuaded to emerge though, thank God, there'd been none of that bloated feeling the second or third time. The midwife had said she was just made for childbearing and Margaret and Jacqueline had just come out plop! Babies like that grew up to be the best wives. Her own mother had said she was born so easy and natural she was scarcely aware of it. She just looked down and there was the little baby and the blood and the cord.

'Me!' said Mrs Buck. 'It's worth remembering sometimes the mess you was born in. No good 'aving fancy ideas. Life is muck. Ask the farmer. But I don't know why you're baby-bound, missis, when the worry has been just the opposite. If you ask me a kid who threatened he was going to be a miscarriage, then changed his mind and said he was staying on, that kid is going to be a problem. Wilful and obstinate like, well, like one of these union shop stewards. Philip works over at Cowley, so I know about them. When he's working, that is. Why don't you get Mr Hart to give *you* a bumpy ride in the car?'

One day Brownlow dropped in after surgery, examined her and said, 'If there's no sign of movement by, say Friday, I think the best plan would be to put you into the maternity unit and make preparations for inducing.'

'You mean stimulating the birth?'

'Yes, inducing.'

'No, I'm not having that.'

'It's common form. You don't want any trouble.'

'The birth has to be natural. I don't mind suffering. Say, I even think I ought to suffer. Whatever good ever came without suffering?'

Brownlow could have talked her out of it. But he did not know she had no intention of leaving Wood End until she was sure about Amin. This was her territory and she was not going to have it invaded. The chances were that Aston would be away in London and Lisa was determined to see to it neither Mrs Buck nor Jo were prevailed on to unlock the door. The conference was due to open on the seventh, which was a Tuesday, and Lisa calculated that if Amin had not turned up by the eighth then it would mean he was not coming. Great! She had exorcized the demon! Aston would certainly be in London on that date. Mrs Buck could drive her into hospital and after the eighth Lisa would make the trip with her mind at rest. She believed Amin was capable of anything. He was enormously strong, could smash a window or door. With a few cronies he would hole up in the place, take Mrs Buck and Jo hostage and bargain with the police on how he was to be escorted to Lancaster House. Lisa saw all this happening, and vividly, but she did not see herself being taken hostage. She'd cope if he came before the seventh. She would impose her will. She would scream at him from a window while Jo telephoned 999.

In years to come she would tell the story. 'When Will was about to be born it was like wagons in a circle with the Indians whooping away outside and shooting fire arrows. The difference was the frontiersmen had guns and I didn't have a gun. So it was that much more scary. I was in this strong point, and about to give birth. Does that make you feel vulnerable? She was Lisa! It sure does. But it was basic and that's what I liked about it. I was tested on basics. And the men out there were not Indians, they were black Africans. So I threw boiling water and did they yell! We hadn't the facilities for providing molten lead. Or boiling oil.' She was a heroine and Will's birth would be heroic. 'Well, a mother defends her young, doesn't she? And her home? The castle under siege, wagons in a circle, enemies without who threaten the homeland, that's the archetypal situation, isn't it? My father would have seen it that way and I felt he was right there with me when I was penned in that house. My papa was a realist after all, I guess, and I really experienced his presence. Don't you feel real civilized culture has its back to the wall? And you've got to fight for it.'

Brownlow came in on the Friday and said he wanted Lisa to go into hospital immediately. Lisa said no sir, not until she was sure Amin stayed away. This was new to Brownlow. Previously Lisa had taken the line she was against inducing the birth because it was not natural. When she gave this other reason he was incredulous.

'Don't you understand the baby might die?'

'No, he won't die. I have a perfect understanding with my child. We're so happy. No problem. I have no fears whatsoever.'

Lisa refused to give him a telephone number where he could reach Aston so, on his way out, Brownlow picked up the little indexed book by the telephone where Lisa had registered the numbers she needed most. He found two numbers for Aston, an office number and another that Brownlow assumed was his hotel. Looking up, he saw that Mrs Buck was observing him.

'If Mrs Hart doesn't go into hospital this weekend I won't be answerable for the consequences,' he said and made a note of Aston's two numbers in his diary. The upshot was that Aston was on the telephone to Lisa later that evening.

After listening to what he had to say, which was largely a repetition of the warnings Brownlow had given him, Lisa said, 'Can you give me your word you don't think Amin will be coming?' She could hear his hesitation. 'Don't lie to me Aston, I'm all screwed up tight.'

'Even if he did come what the hell good do you think you'd do? You've got yourself into a state and it's not helping. Christ, relax can't you? You'd be much better out of the way. I mean, apart from the fact you ought to be in the hospital having our baby.'

Lisa paused a long time. 'I'm not going, Aston. I'm not having that man in this house.'

'I'm frightened, Lisa. For God's sake, be reasonable. Brownlow said the baby might die.'

'He's just panicking. I can assure you, Aston, I am in control.'

Lisa now saw herself under a threat she could only meet by remaining perfectly calm and perfectly resolute. She would outface anyone. When the man of the house was away it was the duty of the women to take over. Mrs Buck was told to check the front and back doors were locked at all times and that the windows were secured.

'There's a police car down the road,' Mrs Buck told her. 'In that turning before you gets to Spittles's orchard. Don' like the look on un.'

'Say, that's fine. So we're not alone, Mrs Buck.'

Mrs Buck said the idea Amin might arrive was just so much rubbish. It didn't stand to reason, that big, shiny black man would be putting a noose round his own neck and he was too fly for that. 'Take it from me, missus, 'e'd be picked up like a drunk. Who by? The police. They pick up six drunks in a week.'

Aston came home on the Sunday afternoon, having told Tom Hubbard that he would be returning to London the same evening. After a talk with Lisa in which she was as firm as ever in her refusal to budge, Aston went over to see Brownlow and discuss the possibility of removing her to hospital by force. Brownlow was against it. If something went wrong there would be hell to pay. He wasn't even sure it was legal. If a woman refused to go into hospital he reckoned you could only get a committal notice from a Medical Officer of Health if Lisa was held to be insane and clearly she was not. She was just obstinate as two mules. In any case he reckoned they still had up to forty-eight hours before there was a real crisis. Then if she still wouldn't go he would require her to sign a statement that her refusal was considered and all the consequences were on her own head.

'But the baby will get enormous.'

'No, a baby stops growing after forty-two weeks.'

'What's the worst that could happen?'

'We haven't got to that stage, not quite. There are three things. The baby might lose the blood supply and just die. Or there may be membrane rupture with your wife losing a lot of fluid. Then the real danger is septicaemia. And – '

'Okay. I understand. Well, I'm staying. I'll ring up the office and say I'm not going in. Sod the conference. Matter of life and death. They can do without me. Lisa's going into hospital. My problem is persuading her I can cope with Amin alone. You ever known a woman like this? Is it the way pregnant women get?'

'No, I've never had another case like it. When women go off their rockers it's usually afterwards.'

'I'll go straight back and tell her I'm staying. So you'll fix it with the hospital?'

'Give me a ring when you've had a talk with her.'

To Aston's surprise Lisa took a poor view of his deciding not to go back to the office. A man who let domestic problems get in the way of work was a jerk. He'd been paid money to do a job. And, for hell's sake, she didn't want anybody saying her husband had taken money for a job and then not delivered the goods.

'I'll be really sore, Aston, if you don't go back to town tonight.'

'I'm staying,' he said. 'I can be as pig-headed as you.'

'Sow-headed.'

'Okay, sow. So I love a sow. I really do.'

Come the Monday, and Lisa still would not budge, a woman Aston did not recognize drove up in a toffee-brown Mini. She had frizzed out auburn hair, blue eyeshade and red fingernails. She said, 'Hello, Aston,' having climbed out and revealed that she was wearing a long white raincoat, 'We're off to Durban on Thursday and this'll be my last chance to see you all. How's Lisa?'

Aston would never have guessed but for the mention of Durban. He was amazed at Olwen. He had thought it through. Durban – South Africa – that doctor – his wife.

'She ought to be giving birth but she won't go into hospital.'

'Yup! I thought it was due.'

'Brownlow's worried. Looks like pregnancy has made her crazy but Brownlow says if the birth isn't induced there'll be trouble. The baby could die. Lisa thinks her presence is required here in case Amin comes.'

'Amin?'

'The latest is he's already in the country lying doggo. If that's right there's just a chance he'll make for here. That man's capable of anything. Lisa just thinks she can keep him out by just being here and putting out rays.'

'Rays?'

'Laying down a field of psychic energy. That's what she calls it. Think you could talk to her? I mean about going in and getting this birth over. If she's not ready to go by tomorrow Brownlow and I are all set up to take her.'

Olwen considered this while Aston studied her. She had lost a couple of stone too and her face, when looked at more closely, was a bit haggard and drawn. It was worldly-wise, adventurous and sexy like one of those Kenya wives in the upper wealth bracket whose hobby was drink and adultery. As Aston remembered him her husband was a supercilious bastard but maybe he had just been on the defensive all the time because of the way his wife was running around.

'She'll go, Aston. Where is she? I'll talk to her.'

Lisa, whose moods changed from gutsy confidence through boredom to flickerings of fear, was glad to see Olwen, once she had established who it was, walking into her bedroom unannounced.

'Well, what's this about fields of energy?' Olwen asked after they had exchanged the usual pleasantries.

'I really do feel I can radiate.'

'If what Aston tells me is right it isn't radiating anything you ought to be thinking about. It's your baby. Don't you want it?'

'What are you saying?'

'The way you're behaving anybody would think you didn't mind if it was stillborn.'

'No way is he going to be anything but okay. I'm really on course. You know what? For the first time in my life I feel on course. I'm in charge and to hell with everybody. This is one thing women can take decisions about. I know where my duty lies. You know about Joan of Arc, I guess. Well, I don't have voices but I do feel borne up by something really big. Harriet Parsler was in here the other day and I told her I was really plugged in. You've heard about Ed. Isn't it terrible?'

'Makes me all the more pleased Jerry and I are off to Durban.'

'How come?'

'You didn't know Jerry and Harriet were having it off? Blown over now. But with her husband laid up I can see Harriet looking round for another man to gobble up and Jerry must be high on her list. She's getting on, isn't she? Suppose you've got to admire her energy.'

'You mean your husband and Harriet had an affair? You're kidding?'

'Why should I want to kid anyone about a thing like that?'

'Oh!' said Lisa, 'Oh! Oh! Poor Ed.'

But was it really poor Ed? Olwen's news was totally unexpected but once it had sunk in Lisa experienced a thrill of excitement. Was this her doing? However innocent and unsexy Ed had been in setting her up as his muse was there any chance Harriet had been jealous and found what consolation she could in Olwen's husband? If so that was wicked!

'You don't think Ed sort of neglected her?'

'No, I do not. Harriet grabbed Jerry like she grabbed a good many other men, I guess. Then she drops them. That's the way she is.'

The thought of Ed putting up with Harriet sleeping around continued to thrill Lisa, so much so she forgot she was pregnant

229

with a birth overdue, forgot she was laying down a field of psychic energy to keep Amin out, and lay back on her pillow with eyes closed in a gentle swoon of excitement. She had a vivid picture of that tall, gingery South African and Harriet making love while Edwin stood in the background, smiling to himself, and of course suffering like hell.

'Poor Edwin! He must love her a lot to take that kind of caning. He's a saint. I'm a saint too.'

'You a saint?'

'Didn't I tell you I was plugged in like Joan of Arc? Gee! I'm a saint so it gives me real pleasure to think just why Ed's a saint as well. It's all I needed. He's had Harriet cheating on him and, hey, wouldn't I just have loved to see the action? What's the word. *Voyeur*. See the action and think he's putting it into you. Ed, you've been screwed too. It's all very well slipping that mask on but there's all hell going on underneath and, boy, am I glad?'

Olwen was amazed at this outburst. 'What's he ever done to you?'

'Made a fool of me. At least, he tried to. But I wasn't fooled. I was okay. But this news you've given me, Olwen, that's fantastic. It's set me off. You know that? It's real arousing. Aw! Christ! It's starting!'

Lisa's son was born about six hours later and she was a long time about it. Finally the gynaecologist used forceps and ever after Willy's head was not quite symmetrical, a sort of depression on one side which he became acutely conscious of. One reason why in later life he wore his hair so long. Aston was present at the birth. When Willy appeared he had the most extraordinary stern expression on his red, sweating face – big set lips and eyes like elderberries, looking straight ahead. All the way to the hospital Lisa had made cracks. She had laid off liquor for the pregnancy and my! wasn't she just looking forward to her first bourbon! Olwen sat in the back seat of the car with her while Aston drove. Actually, she gave up most of the seat to Lisa, so that the pregnant woman could lie there with her knees up and a cushion under the small of her back. Olwen had taken the Midwifery Diploma as part of her training and had helped to bring lots of babies into the world, so Lisa had no cause to worry, even if she gave birth in the back of that car. Olwen could cope. Childbirth was just about the most marvellous thing in life. To see the raw little man-or-woman-ikin take a first look at the world. To see the new life held up like a skinned rabbit, and the breath going into him for the first time. It was God breathing life into Adam, the clay sucking and yelling. To be a mother, that was real fulfilment.

'You got kids of your own?' Lisa asked.

'No such luck.'

'And you a midwife! Say, that's hard.'

If there was one subject Lisa kept coming back to it was Ed.

'You don't mind me telling Aston, do you, Olwen? I still can't believe it. Did you know Harriet had an affair with Olwen's husband? What do you know? Sort of exciting and cruel. But that's why it's exciting, it's so cruel.'

'Stop it,' said Aston.

'Eh?'

'Stop it, sweetie. You don't know what you're saying.'

Lisa never had any doubt it would be a boy. She looked deep into its eyes as she gave suck, looking into him and through him into a regress of generations, right back to the sister of the Master. She was finally where she had always wanted to be, into cultural history in a way that made sense to her. If only she'd been Jewish she would have been a link in the great chain of cultural being as of right. But she wasn't Jewish and she'd had to forge this link for herself. It was like being accepted into some great and ancient household and no woman had ever been so happy. Oh what a brave new world Willy Hans Hart had entered!

Then she thought again of Ed. Maybe she'd call him. She had a phone at her bedside and no doubt he had too. She wanted to call him while Willy was crying, so that Ed could hear for himself what, in a small way, he had been responsible for. Had it not been for Ed she would never have met Aston. So, Ed was another sort of link. She felt so *good*. She had majored with stars in the great examination of life. And she would have other children. There would be no end to her triumph!

Lisa and Aston watched the Silver Jubilee on TV. Willy was away in the ward with the other newly born while their parents watched the pageantry. First of all the coaches and the mounted Lifeguards clattering down the Mall with the flags fluttering and the trees dimpling and waving their early summer green in the breezy sun.

'I go for all this,' Lisa said. 'It just makes everybody happy. He won't come now, will he?'

'Who? Amin? Out of the question. If he'd meant to come he'd have wanted to gatecrash. He'd be in full fig out there somewhere. No, I guess he never meant to come.'

'You're wrong there, Aston. He was dead set on coming but I headed him off. My psychic field was too strong for him. The way I feel now I've just cleaned the whole place up. And laid the spirits. You've got to admit it, Aston, you feel sort of purified, don't you. Be honest!'

'Never felt better!'

'See what I mean?'

They watched the service in St Paul's Cathedral. When the congregation sang 'All people that on Earth do dwell' Lisa joined in, but the difference was that she sang the German words.

'That's a real victory hymn,' Lisa said. 'Those folk think they're celebrating the Queen's Jubilee. I don't see it that way. They're celebrating Willy. They don't know it. But one day everyone will know it, because the way I see it, this is his day.'

Some time later Ed was discharged from Stoke Mandeville in a wheelchair and Harriet threw a welcome home party. He was so chirpy, she told everyone, you really must come, and most of them did. Except for the Clutsams everybody turned up. There was a lot of cloud about but the sun kept breaking through and the Revd Paul Brough stalked about the garden in his rusty black, rather tight trousers and a flapping white cotton jacket. Hugh Cornish had just come back from a holiday in Greece and his large, fluffy eyebrows stood out in snowy contrast to his red face. Tom and his wife, Meg, drove over from Great Missenden. When he and Aston came face to face it was for the first time since Aston had ditched his Lancaster House job and Tom said, 'You're still around, then?'

'Come off it! If it hadn't been for me Amin would have been all over the Silver Jubilee and the Commonwealth Conference. I spent the whole of that weekend on the telephone to him just talking him out of it. You don't believe me?'

'No.'

'He didn't come. That must prove something.'

Ed was in one of those wheelchairs the passenger could propel by pushing on two rather smaller wheels but he found it difficult to get up slopes and Tom went over to help. Ed had a plaid blanket over his legs because, as he explained, they seemed to be so cold all the time. But, as Harriet had said, he was chirpy. He had grown a rather splendid moustache, silky brown, drooping at both ends, so that he looked as though he had been eating a choc ice in a messy sort of way. Against his normally chalky, puffy face, this moustache was now his most incisive feature, much darker than his hair which was silvering and wispy. Lisa, who had been watching him for some time with Willy fast asleep in a carrycot at her feet thought how ever since she had met him all those years ago, twenty or more, she had considered him an old man. In the intervening years his appearance had not changed much. But he was always old. Now he didn't look so old. If she were seeing him for the first time she would think he was one of those men who looked young for their age. Might have been in his mid-forties. The very fact she could think of him in this way must mean she was getting old too.

He sat, squinting into the sun talking to Lisa. He had admired Willy and said how like Aston he was; the same sort of face, rectangular at the top and then this chin like a wedge.

'Have you forgiven me, Lisa?'

'If it makes you feel good I'll say, yes, I forgive you. No hard feelings at all. But I'm not a sucker, Ed. You're not forcing me to say I'm a sucker.'

Ed turned his chair at right angles to see her more clearly. 'That's the last thing. To me you'll always seem good in some superhuman way. And I've got poems to prove it.'

'You'll have more time for that sort of thing now you're retiring.'

'Who said I was retiring? I'm just on sick leave. But I guess you're right. Harriet keeps saying what with the technology nowadays I could work at home just as well as I do in the office but who are we kidding? So, yes, I've got to face up to it. Retiring.

233

You know what, though? It doesn't mean more writing. I've got so used to writing in the margin of my job. When it goes it removes that sort of pressure. It may turn out I need it.'

Harriet came over and admired the baby who was now awake and squalling. 'Don't you think Ed's come on marvellously? Slow, of course. But I'm determined to get him on his feet again. Aren't we, Ed?' Harriet drifted off, to get out of earshot of Willy, Lisa thought. Well, she had her duties as a hostess. But for a moment Lisa was miffed and felt an almost overpowering urge to talk to Ed about Harriet. Was it true what Olwen had told her? But she repressed it.

'Lisa, you must be very happy, my dear.'

'Yes.' And the urge to talk about Harriet was transformed into the need to show Ed she was not only not a sucker but she was a white witch who could exorcize hostile spirits. She had stood between Aston and the possibility of further supernatural persecution. She had protected Jo too. President Amin had been a black circling presence who had been driven away by her enchantments. She had succeeded where that Father Curtis had failed.

All she said was, 'Sure I'm very happy. Everything's just going for me. Actually I feel so much electricity running through me I've got this idea that if I told you to get out of that chair and walk you'd be able to do it.'

'Go ahead.'

'Okay. Get out of that chair and walk, Ed.'

Ed threw back the blanket and tried to move his legs. He grunted but nothing happened. He lay back with his eyes closed.

'For a moment I thought it was going to work, Lisa. If anyone could have worked that miracle for me it would have been you.'

'Don't give up. You can't hit the bull's-eye first shot. We've got to stick at it.'

Lisa tried again and again in the weeks and months that followed. She was emitting so much nervous energy it rather annoyed her that Ed didn't respond more dramatically. Harriet was enthusiastic about Lisa's efforts.

'He so believed in you. But wouldn't it be even more effective if we got the Rector in too?'

'What would he do?'

234

'Pray, I suppose, and lay on hands or whatever they do in faith healing.'

Ed made regular trips for physiotherapy back to Stoke Mandeville. Whether it was due to the hospital treatment or to Lisa's powers no one seemed to know with any certainty. But by Christmas Ed was moving his knees up and down.

Lisa screamed when she saw the movement. 'Look at that! About time too. I was beginning to feel drained.'

Aston was so delighted with his son that he came to accept that if Lisa could produce such a child she could do anything and, yes, he admitted under pressure from her, even to making Wood End a lucky, happy, house. No more inexplicable fires. No cold blasts of air. No shattered glass. No devils to exorcize.

On the day Ed was able to stand on his own two legs, supported by Harriet on one side and by Tom on the other he telephoned Lisa with the news.

'I feel like Lazarus, just a bit,' he said. To his surprise he had to remind Lisa who Lazarus was and this caused him to go on. 'If my father had been alive he'd have wanted me in the saddle again. Strapped on, if need be.'

'What's your father got to do with it?'

'A great guy. Still miss him. After he died, I looked at him. Something I'll never forget. Puts everything in perspective. Death.'

Lisa had Willy in a pushchair and was about to take him out into the sunshine so she did not want to chat for long.

'How morbid can you get? I think it's here and now, and the excitement of it all, that puts bad things into perspective. Think positively, Ed. Life is life is life.'

A silence so long she thought he might have gone away.

'You can say that, Lisa. And that is why I turn to you. As a sunflower turns.'

'I guess,' said Lisa, 'we're all crazy in our own different ways. And that's only half of it. There's something else out there.'

'Such as?'

'Spirits. Some of them bad. But all leaning in a great wind. Some great wind. That's what I can feel, that wind.'